"Your brother w...
and find out who's b...
Gideon...

Ivy could figure that out for h... ... she knew her brother wanted to protect her, whether she liked the idea or not. "I'm not being threatened. Just my animals."

"Even so, I'll be stayin', ma'am." He took a step toward her, his features stony, forbidding in the amber light.

Ivy had done just fine on her own since Tom's death, and she didn't need a man around. She licked her lips, ignoring the way her visitor's gaze went to her mouth. "Nothing has happened since I sent the wire."

"But you're spooked. You thought I was here to harm you."

"Maybe I overreacted."

"You said your horse was dead, ma'am."

"Yes."

"That's a message of some kind."

She agreed, but the thought of him staying rattled her.

"It can't hurt to have another person here," he said.

While that was true, he wasn't just another person. The idea of his being so close made her shiver, and if she were honest, part of that was due to excitement, not dread.

* * *

The Cowboy's Reluctant Bride
Harlequin® Historical #1175—March 2014

Author Note

Gideon Black and Ivy Jennings Powell were first introduced in my short story "Once Upon a Frontier Christmas" (part of the *All a Cowboy Wants for Christmas* anthology). From the moment Ivy held Gideon at gunpoint in her brother's barn, sparks flew between them.

After a marriage gone bad, Ivy has sworn never to trust another man. Gideon has his own misgivings about females, stemming from the time he served in prison as the result of a woman's lies. When a series of escalating threats spooks Ivy into asking for help from her convalescing brother, he sends Gideon.

Now this distrusting pair will have to rely on each other in order to determine who is trying to harm Ivy. But as the danger grows so do their feelings, and their relationship becomes something neither expects. Something neither of them wants.

One of the things I love most about writing historical romance is my research into the past, but sometimes getting even a kernel of information about a subject can be like pulling teeth. This was the case when I tried to find out specifically the date screened doors came into use. After much digging I found information that said wire screening was available in the U.S. in the 1870s. There was no specific year given, so I took the liberty of having screened doors at my heroine's house.

I hope you enjoy Gideon and Ivy's story!

Happy trails.

THE COWBOY'S
RELUCTANT BRIDE

—

DEBRA COWAN

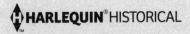

Recycling programs
for this product may
not exist in your area.

ISBN-13: 978-0-373-29775-7

THE COWBOY'S RELUCTANT BRIDE

Copyright © 2014 by Debra S. Cowan

Printed in U.S.A.

In memory of my grandmother, Lottie Warren,
who passed on her love of reading to me.

DEBRA COWAN

Like many writers, DEBRA COWAN made up stories
in her head as a child. Her BA in English was obtained with the intention of following family tradition
and becoming a schoolteacher, but after she wrote
her first novel, there was no looking back. An avid
history buff, Debra writes both historical and contem-
porary romances. Born in the foothills of the Kiamichi
Mountains, Debra still lives in her native Oklahoma
with her husband.

Debra loves to hear from readers. You can contact
her via her website at www.debracowan.net.

Chapter One

Indian Territory, 1873

The next person who set foot on her property would meet the bad end of a bullet. Tightening her grip on the pistol, Ivy Jennings Powell paced from one side of her large front room to the other. She had been waiting, watching since she'd found one of her horses dead three days ago.

Lightning cracked the March air like a whip. Thunder rumbled. Outside her snug frame home that served as a stage stop, the storm howled.

When lightning struck again, it illuminated the massive oaks and pines swaying in the wind. After a short drumroll of thunder, the weather calmed somewhat. A steady rain drove against her roof and the rush of the wind quieted, though she could still hear the lashing of trees. A thud sounded on her front porch and her gaze shot to the window, its isinglass shade pulled down. She tried to identify the noise. An animal?

If so, it wasn't one of hers. They were all shut up tight in the barn or the chicken coop. From the center of the long table against the opposite wall, a lamp spread soft amber light through the room.

Since the death of her husband a year and a half ago, Ivy had been alone in this southeastern corner of Indian Territory. She and the neighbors scattered miles apart lived just over the border from Texas and Arkansas.

A movement at the window had her going still in the middle of the room. Was that indistinct shape the silhouette of a man? After the past three and a half months, Ivy half expected it. She had wired her brother, Smith, about her troubles, but he hadn't replied yet, and she didn't think he would arrive unannounced. His home, Mimosa Springs, was a two-day ride west.

Today's stagecoach and its passengers had come and gone. The Choctaw people who lived around her were a peaceful lot, and there had never been any trouble between them and whites.

The doorknob rattled, and Ivy's mouth went dry. Even so, she marched to the locked door and yelled, "Who's there?"

A muffled masculine voice answered. With the crashing of the storm, Ivy couldn't understand a word.

Thumbing down the hammer on her revolver, she unlatched the door. Before she could swing it open, the wind nearly jerked it out of her hand. She aimed her gun at the visitor, barely aware of the door slamming against the wall.

A giant of a man stood there, hands in the air. In the wind-whipped shadows, she could see only the impression of a hard jaw and glittering eyes beneath the hat pulled low on his head.

Lightning slashed across the sky of churning gunmetal clouds, illuminating a scar on the man's neck.

"Are you going to pull a gun on me every time we meet up?"

Ivy tensed. She knew that voice. It was deep and gravelly and put a flutter in her stomach. Just like it had the first time she'd seen him in her brother's barn three months ago. That meeting had been at gunpoint, too.

The man towered over her, water dribbling from the brim of his hat onto the porch. The clouds moved, and she peered through the shadows. "Gideon Black?"

"Yes, ma'am." He slowly lowered his hands.

"What are you doing here?"

"Smith sent me." He had done prison time with Ivy's brother. And after his release, he had accepted Smith's offer of work and arrived at the Diamond J just before Christmas. Ivy had met him when she returned home after learning her presumed-dead brother was alive and back in Mimosa Springs.

Gideon Black had sparked an unwelcome response in her back then. He still did.

The rain ebbed to a steady shower, though the wind still tangled her skirts around her legs. He had to be soaked to the bone. Releasing the hammer, she stepped back so he could enter. "Come inside."

"Miz Powell, I've been riding for two days and I ain't—" He stopped, then started again. "I haven't washed up."

"I'd say you just had a pretty good washing," she said wryly, pushing some loose strands of hair out of her face. "I'll get some toweling."

She was halfway across the front room before she realized Gideon Black hadn't followed her inside. She turned, noticing that his frame took up the entire door-way. Hat in hand, he frowned down at his mud-caked boots with a helpless look on his face. Was he worried about making a mess?

"Mr. Black, it's all right."

His gaze flicked over her. For a brief moment, his expression was…hungry. Then his features were unreadable.

She gave an encouraging smile. "Come in. The mud will dry, and when it does, I'll sweep it up."

"Yes, ma'am." He finally stepped inside.

She went to the spare room reserved for stage passengers to rest or wash up. Why hadn't Smith come? Or their father? At Christmas, her brother had demanded that Ivy notify him if the anonymous poems and drawings she'd been receiving became suspicious or more frequent. They had. They had also turned threatening. At least to her way of thinking. Other things had happened, too. One of the horses had been killed, and her dog was missing.

From the wardrobe, she grabbed several towels, returning to find that Gideon had removed his poncho. He leaned against the door frame, taking off his boots. He put them upside down on the boot tree, just inside the door.

Something about this big man in his stocking feet put a funny ache in her chest.

He shook the rain off his hat then backed inside and shut the door. His shoulders were as wide as a wagon brace. He hung his hat on a peg near the door.

Ivy's gaze trailed over him. Short dark hair sleeked against his head, a few strands curling against his bronzed nape. His shirt was damp and the fabric clung to his muscular back and arms, revealing clearly defined shoulders and biceps. Buff-colored trousers molded a tight backside and powerful thighs. The pants were mostly dry, probably coated with tallow for weather like this.

He turned to face her, and her gaze snapped to his and held. There was a heat in his blue eyes that burned right through her.

Then his attention shifted, moving down her body.

She tensed. What was he looking at?

"Miz Powell, do you think you could put that Colt down?"

"Oh. Yes." She wished he wouldn't call her by her married name. She slid the gun into her skirt pocket.

She handed over two towels because of his size. He stayed near the door, rubbing his hair and face with the cloth. Biceps knotted at the motion, hinting at a raw, leashed power. She'd forgotten just how big he was.

With her own towel, she patted at her damp hair. She'd forgotten about his scars, too. The whisker stubble couldn't hide the long, thin mark that ran along his left jawline or the thicker one that appeared to completely circle his strong, corded neck. She wondered if he had others.

When they had first met, she had noticed the scars right off, but they weren't what held her attention. It was his eyes. A clear piercing blue. And hard. He had a hard mouth, too. The man appeared to be hard all over. A flush warmed her cheeks.

The storm settled into a steady rain, pinging against the side windows. The damp heat of their bodies filled the room. She caught a heady draft of man and leather. Gideon's broad chest rose and fell in a regular rhythm, but Ivy's pulse was still haywire.

Through his near-transparent shirt, she could see the dark hair on his chest, the way it veed down the center of his abdomen. Suddenly, she was aware of her breathing. And his. It was unnerving. Unwelcome.

She frowned as he reached into his back pocket and took out a square of leather.

He opened the pouch and withdrew a piece of paper, holding it out to her. "From your brother."

She took it, trying to ignore the jolt that traveled up her arm when their fingers brushed. A muscle flexed hard in his jaw.

The paper was dry, and she realized the pouch was deer hide. She quickly scanned the note. "This is the wire I sent to Smith after finding my horse dead."

"Yes. I brought it so you'd know he really sent me."

The thought that he would lie had never crossed her mind, but it should have. Ivy knew better than anyone that people lied.

Her heart rate finally leveled out. "So my brother isn't coming."

"No, ma'am." Gideon frowned. "Didn't he say so when he wired you back?"

"I haven't gotten anything from him."

"He sent you a telegram. I was there when he did."

The missing telegram was just the latest in a sequence of odd happenings. In the past three months, a telegraph office, a hotel and a lumber mill had opened in her growing town. "I'll check with the telegraph office the next time I'm in Paladin or ask the stage driver when he returns. He might know what happened to it."

Refolding the paper, she handed it back to Gideon, mindful not to touch him this time.

He seemed to move just as carefully. "When Smith found out about the horse, he wanted to come, but he couldn't."

"Because of spring calving?"

"Partly." Gideon returned the message to his leather pouch and slid it into his back pocket. "And he just had surgery on his leg. He isn't getting around too well yet."

"Surgery?"

"Doc Miller reset his leg. He straightened it out some."

While in prison, Smith's leg had been badly broken in several places. Ivy was glad to hear her brother might be getting some relief from the pain he endured daily. She understood about her brother, but it wasn't like Emmett Jennings to stay behind. "What about my father?"

"He wanted to come."

Alarm flickered. "He's not ill?"

"No, ma'am, but he is getting up in years. Smith feels your pa's reflexes aren't what they used to be. His hearing is going, too."

From her trip home at Christmas, Ivy knew that to be true.

The large man in front of her shifted from one foot to the other. "Smith doesn't feel either of them are able-bodied enough to protect you."

Judging by the deepness of Gideon's chest and the ridges of muscle that corded his abdomen, her visitor looked able-bodied enough for all kinds of things. She wondered if his arms were as steely and strong as they looked.

Irritated at herself for noticing so much about him, she cleared her throat.

"Knowing my brother, I don't imagine he sent you all this way just to tell me something he could've put in a wire."

"No, ma'am. He wants me to stay and find out who's behind your trouble."

She could figure that out for herself, but she knew her brother wanted to protect her, whether she liked the idea or not. "I'm not being threatened. Just my animals."

"Even so, I'll be stayin', ma'am." He took a step toward her, his features stony, forbidding in the amber light. "Till your brother says different."

Ivy had done just fine on her own since Tom's death, and she didn't need a man around. She'd only sent word to Smith about this latest incident because she had promised she would.

She licked her lips, ignoring the way her visitor's gaze went to her mouth. "Nothing has happened since I sent the wire."

"But you're spooked."

"Not really."

His eyes narrowed. "You thought I was here to harm you."

"Maybe I overreacted."

"You said your horse was dead, ma'am."

"Yes."

"That's a message of some kind."

She agreed, but the thought of him staying rattled her.

"It can't hurt to have another person here," he said.

While that was true, he wasn't just another person. The idea of his being so close made her shiver, and if she were honest, part of that was due to excitement, not dread.

She needed some space from him right now.

"You'd probably like to change out of that wet shirt. And I'm sure you'd like to get some rest."

He studied her as if trying to determine if she were attempting to get rid of him. Which she was.

He nodded. "In the morning, you can tell me every-thing that's happened."

She could protest, or she could graciously accept the protection her brother had sent. "All right. You can stay in one of the guest rooms."

"The barn will be better. That way, I'll be in a good position to see or hear anything suspicious."

She hoped relief didn't show on her face. "There's a bunk out there, and the roof is sound. Let me get you some bedding."

A few moments later, she returned with a sheet and quilt. It was likely cool outside now. He could use whichever covering he wanted.

As badly as Ivy wanted him to go on, her mother had drummed manners into her. "Have you eaten supper?"

"Your ma sent plenty of food along with me."

"That's good. Breakfast will be at six, dinner at noon and supper at six."

"Are you expecting the stage?"

"It came today. It won't be back for a few days."

He nodded, then after an awkward pause, turned for the door. "Good night, Miz Powell—"

"Please!" she burst out. "Just…call me Ivy."

"All right," he said slowly, a curious look on his face.

Well, he could wonder all he liked. "Thank you."

Who knew how long he would stay? The man was clearly doggedly loyal to Smith.

Gideon stopped to tug on his boots.

She opened the door, glad to see the rain had let up a bit. "I know you saved Smith's life and I know he's grate-ful, as am I. But why do you feel you owe him so much?"

"He gave me a chance." Boots on, he straightened, his voice raspy. "A lot of folks wouldn't."

"Still, he's asking a lot of you. A two-day ride for an unknown length of time." She gave a light laugh. "You're going to be very busy helping your friends if you have a lot of them."

"I don't."

The hollowness in his blue eyes told her he wasn't being flippant. She felt a sharp tug on her heart.

He paused in the doorway, looking down at her with an inscrutable expression. "I won't cause you any extra work and I'll help around here with whatever you need, but I ain't—" He broke off, looking self-conscious. "I'm not leaving, either."

"As long as you're here, no liquor. I don't hold with drinking."

"That won't be a problem, Miz Pow— Ma'am."

She barely had time to nod before he put his hat on his head then jogged toward the barn. She stared through the haze of rain until he opened the door and drew his big black horse inside. Lifting a hand toward her, he shut them both inside.

Ivy closed the door, her chest tight, her nerves tingling.

Her visitor wasn't bent on harming her or her animals, but he made her feel things she hadn't wanted to ever feel again. Man-woman things.

She would figure out who was causing problems on her farm. The sooner she did, the sooner she could send Gideon Black packing.

She didn't want him here. Not that it seemed to matter much to his brain.

Gideon couldn't get the woman out of his head. Just like the first time he'd met Ivy Powell, the sight of her last night had put a hitch in his breathing. And again this morning.

She was the most beautiful woman he'd ever seen. Her features were strong yet undeniably feminine. A stubborn jaw set off by a pair of plump pink lips, delicate winged eyebrows over shrewd midnight eyes. Lush breasts, gently flared hips.

He'd woken up hard and hurting, and he didn't want to spend another night like that. Hell, he didn't want to spend another night here period, but he had promised to find out what, if anything, was going on. The sooner he did that, the sooner he could get back to the Diamond J.

No thunderclouds in sight today. It was bright and sunny. After a breakfast of ham and the best biscuits he'd ever had, Gideon helped Ivy with the chores—milking the cows, gathering the eggs, checking the shoes on her herd of horses.

Now he stood beside her in what had been her husband's office. The room with its front-facing window easily accommodated a standing desk and leather chair as well as a waist-high cabinet holding a lamp.

The back of the desk was raised with a set of pigeonholes across its top for filing. The lower part of the desk had drawers down both sides and one in the middle, which Ivy opened.

Her pale blue skirts brushed against his leg. Sunlight streamed in from the window behind them, gilding her raven-dark hair. Again, she wore a single braid, which revealed her elegant neck. And there was no escaping her soft magnolia scent, potent enough to knot his gut. Her skin was as fine-grained as satin. Gideon bet it felt like satin, too. Her lashes and eyes were as dark as her hair, setting off her refined features. And her mouth…

Beside him, she shifted, jerking his attention to the paper in her hand.

"Here's the last one." She handed him a drawing similar to several she'd already shown him.

Blood humming, he took the paper. This illustration of her house and farm was even more detailed than the others. The first sketches left on her porch had shown the property from the front in broad charcoal strokes—the trees around the sprawling white frame house, the edge of a long chicken coop that ran parallel to the east side of the structure, the corral and barn on the west side.

In each successive drawing, the view moved closer to the house. The likeness grew more detailed. The etchings had progressed from pleasing to almost… obsessive.

In this latest one, Ivy's bedroom was shown in stark detail from the large bed near the window to the half-open wardrobe that revealed a few dresses down to the star pattern of the quilt on her bed.

"Is this an accurate picture of your bedroom?"

"Yes, right down to the quilt," she answered tersely.

Gideon wondered how long the "artist" had been at her window. Had Ivy been in her room at the time? Anger flared that someone had gotten so close to her private space.

Beside him, she drew in a shaky breath. "What do you think?"

Her bedroom was located on the west side of the house, which gave Gideon pause. Why the change from the front view? "Do you know anyone who draws this well?"

"No." She looked surprised. "It never crossed my

mind to wonder. Do you think someone I know is doing this?"

"Could be." The worried expression on her face bothered him, but there was no help for it. "What else has happened?"

"My chickens are disappearing."

"That could be due to coyotes or wolves."

"Yes, but if an animal were responsible, I think I would've found at least a feather or some blood in the henhouse. There's been nothing."

"You think a person took your birds?"

"It's possible." Her mouth tightened. "I wish I knew what this person wanted."

Gideon turned around to look out the window across the grass of her yard to the red mud and puddles of the road beyond. "Have you thought about getting a dog?"

"I had one. Tug." Ivy eased up beside him, bringing that damn scent with her, causing his nerves to twang. "He disappeared a couple of days ago."

Needing to escape the barely there touch of her body against his, he stepped toward the door. "Let's walk."

He waited for her to precede him, then followed her through the front room and outside. They moved down the porch steps, angled toward the barn. Her braid hung to the middle of her back, drawing his eye to her small frame, the sharp tuck of her waist before her hips flared slightly.

Coming up beside her, he took in the corral and barn. The fence that ran around the property could use a fresh coat of whitewash, but everything was in good shape.

Gideon moved toward the back of the barn, shortening his stride so Ivy could keep up. "Is it possible your dog ran off?"

"I don't think so. Tug roams during the day, but always returns at night."

"Maybe he found a lady friend."

"Maybe, but even if so, something else has happened or he would've come back."

White clouds floated against a pale blue sky. As they reached the barn, red mud squished around Gideon's boots. Ivy picked up her skirts and tiptoed through the muck. A bit of petticoat flashed beneath the hem of her practical blue day dress.

Shifting his gaze from her, he studied the fence that ran from the side of the house and around back to encompass the outbuildings. He spotted a couple of rotten wood slats, but no other signs of disrepair.

Beyond the back fence, several Holsteins milled about, grazing on alfalfa. Gideon had already seen the black-and-white-spotted animals this morning.

He and Ivy stepped through the back door of the barn and moved inside. The door at the other end was also open, and a fresh breeze blew through the sturdy watertight structure. Oats and bits of hay scattered across the dirt floor. The odors of animal flesh and earth hung on the air.

Gideon had been here earlier checking the horses' shoes. "Where's the horse you found?"

"I towed him to a gully using another horse."

"Could you show me?"

She led him past the house and through the back gate around the cows. Alfalfa blanketed the field in green as far as he could see. As they walked down a slight hill, he spied the glitter of a fast-running creek cutting through a grove of pecan trees. Beyond was a line of thick timber, just like the woods in front of Ivy's house that ran along the road that was part of the old military trace between Fort Towson and Fort Jesup in Louisiana.

Someday, he was going to have a place like this.

Realizing he'd quickened his pace, Gideon slowed, waiting for Ivy. She reached him, breathing hard, her cheeks flushed. He had a sudden image of other things that might make her breathe hard against him.

Inhaling her scent mixed with spring air, his gaze involuntarily went to her mouth. He wanted to know how she tasted and… He bit back a curse.

He hadn't had a woman since he'd gotten out of prison. A visit was long overdue.

He didn't understand this fascination with Ivy, this infernal awareness. Yes, she was beautiful, but his experience with another one like her had cost him five years of his life. Then, as now, he'd been trying to protect a woman, and it had left marks.

Deep, soul-scarring marks. He had no intention of getting more.

He glanced away from the rapid flutter of her pulse in the hollow of her throat. Reminding himself that he was there for her brother, he asked, "Do you own this land?"

"Yes."

Gideon knew Tom Powell had died about a year and a half ago. "What about your late husband?"

"What about him?" She cut him a sharp look.

"Smith said he was killed when he was thrown from a wagon."

She nodded, lips pressed tightly together. "I don't see what that has to do with anything."

"How do you get along with his family?"

"Fine, though I rarely see them. Tom's grandmother is his only living relative. She's in Chicago. Why?"

"Just trying to figure out if anyone would want your business."

She shook her head. "She has no interest in that or in living here."

"I'm also trying to decide if anyone has a grudge against you."

"I don't think so."

"What about suitors?"

She stopped, staring blankly at him for a moment. Then a look of horror crossed her features. "No one is courting me! No one is even interested."

Gideon found that hard to believe. "Did your husband leave any debts unsettled?"

"No." She shifted her gaze to the pasture.

Several yards away, Gideon saw a gully, its red mud walls carved out of the pasture's earth. Overhead, ravens circled with a raucous call.

Beside him, Ivy muttered something under her breath, wrestling with her blue skirts now damp from the wet grass.

Gideon slowed. "How does your arrangement with the stage line work?"

"The mayor of Paladin has a contract with them, and he sublets the farm from me to use as a stage stop. He pays me a monthly stipend for the food I provide the passengers and for the horses I board for the stage line."

"Does the stage change teams every time it stops?"

"Usually, not always."

"How many of those horses in your corral belong to them?"

"Ten. The other three are mine."

Her answers were short, brisk. Because she didn't like that he was asking questions? Or because she could sense how she affected him?

Beneath the scents of grass and earth, he caught her musky floral fragrance, and it pulled his muscles taut. He put a little space between them. "Do you have any passengers who come through regularly?"

"A couple."

"Have any of them ever made threats? Been unhappy with anything?"

"No."

She lived out here alone. She'd received the poems and drawings. Her dog was gone, some of her chickens had disappeared and she'd found a dead horse, which he had yet to see. All those things had spooked her enough to prompt the wire to her brother.

They reached the edge of the gully, which looked to be six to seven feet deep. A sour, overwhelming stench reached them, and Gideon pulled his bandanna over his nose, noticing that Ivy pressed a handkerchief over hers.

The horse lay at the bottom in several inches of muddy water. The animal was stiff, its brownish-red hide chewed from neck to rump. The black tips on its ears, mane and tail identified it as a bay.

Beside him, Ivy made a soft, distressed noise, but when he glanced over, she was composed, calm, albeit pale.

"Wait here," he said. "I want to take a closer look."

She nodded, staying where she was as he carefully maneuvered his way down the slippery mud walls. Birds and other varmints had picked away at the horse's flesh.

Gideon could see now that the bay was a gelding. There were no broken legs, no broken bones anywhere that he could find. After thoroughly examining the animal, he returned to study its chest. The long gash from the base of the bay's neck to the top of his chest looked to have been caused by a knife. A large knife.

He made his way back up the slick slope, struggling to keep his footing a few times. Finally, he stood beside her, the knees of his trousers covered with red mud. He took off his hat and drew his arm across his sweat-dampened forehead.

Feeling her gaze on him, he glanced over.

She shifted her attention to the dead horse. "Who could do something like this? And why?"

"I don't know."

She exhaled heavily, clearly vexed.

"What will happen when the stage line finds out about their dead animal?" he asked.

"I don't know. It's possible they won't trust me with other animals or even their business."

"There was nothing in the contract about things like this?"

"My husband signed it, and I've never read the whole thing," she said tiredly. "It's somewhere in his desk. I'll look for it when we return to the house."

He nodded. "And your missing chickens? Does that significantly affect the meals you offer?"

"Yes."

Staring at the horse, he thumbed his hat back. "Considering the chickens and the bay, this could be directed at your business. It makes you look bad to the stage line and to the mayor who subcontracted you."

"What about Tug? And the drawings, the poems? Those seem personal, not business."

True. "You say no one has a grudge against you. Maybe you have something they want."

"Like what?"

He shrugged. "Your contract with the stage line?"

"No one else around here spoke up when the mayor asked who was interested in contracting with him for the job."

"Maybe someone wants your land?"

"That makes no sense. I've worked hard to make this a nice place, but it isn't sitting on top of a gold mine. And no one's approached me about buying."

Something was going on. Gideon just wasn't sure how threatening it was. Except for the drawing of her bedroom. That weighed on him.

Turning in a slow circle, he examined every angle from the house. Only the barn roof could be seen from here. His gaze slowly swept the line of fence, the lush alfalfa rippling across the pasture. He paused at the thick line of trees running along the back of her place.

After a moment, he realized what bothered him. "I'd like to take a look at the woods in front of your house."

"All right."

Retracing their steps, they reached her house several minutes later then cut across the wet yard and out the gate to the road.

She hurried along beside him, her cheeks flushed. "Why are you interested in the woods?"

"None of those drawings showed the rear view of your property."

Realization flashed across her face. "Except for the one of my bedroom, they were all from the woods bordering the road."

"Yes, and there might be some sign that someone's been lying in wait."

"You mean spying on me then vandalizing my place?"

He nodded.

"They're watching me?" She sounded more angry than alarmed.

He sneaked a look at her indignant features. If someone were hanging around, heaven help them. The woman had already held him at gunpoint twice for no other reason than just showing up.

They crossed the muddy road onto the soggy grass and reached the edge of the south woods.

"Has the railroad ever talked about coming through here?" he asked.

"Oh, they've been talking about it for years, but it hasn't happened. Besides, if there were plans for a railroad, everybody would be chattering about it."

She had a point.

As he reached the edge of the trees, she caught up to him.

"Do you really think you'll find anything in there?"

"I don't know." He was checking anyway. He'd promised Smith.

"The rain will have washed away any footprints," Ivy said.

"True, but there might be other signs that someone has been around."

"Like what?"

"The remains of a fire, maybe, or a shelter or something."

"Oh."

"I'll be right back."

"I'm coming, too."

When he hesitated, she said, "Two pairs of eyes are better than one."

"Okay." He led the way into the dark denseness. Thick branches still dripped with rain, and wet pine needles slid beneath his feet.

After several minutes of walking through the damp air, Gideon had found no sign of anything except rain. He wanted to find the spot that would give him the view shown in those drawings.

Looking over his shoulder, he could see daylight through the wall of trees at his back. "What's beyond here?"

"More pasture."

He watched as she began walking into the wooded area that faced her house. Ahead of her, between the trees and bushes, he saw a wedge of light.

He followed. At times he would see her white frame home, then it would vanish as if the branches closed up. A trick of the shadows, he realized.

As he came within a foot of Ivy, he could clearly see her house through two stubby pines. Without warning, she stopped cold. To keep from running her over, he clamped his hands on her waist. She jumped, unbalancing them both for a second. He steadied them then released her.

"Look," she breathed, pointing at something in front of her.

He dragged his attention from the taut curve of her waist and followed her gaze to the patch of ground she indicated.

Sunlight filtered through the thickness of the trees,

falling on a blackened pile of sticks. Gideon stepped around her and knelt over the remains of a campfire.

"Someone's been here." He touched the soggy wood. Because of all the rain, he couldn't tell how recently.

"Do you think they'll come back?" She moved closer, her skirts brushing his arm.

He stood. "If it's the person causing trouble, yes."

She wrapped her arms around herself, looking at the forest surrounding them. "Do you think someone is here right now?" she asked in a low voice.

He glanced down, seeing a flare of alarm in her eyes. She hid it well, but she was worried. He wanted to reassure her, which made him snort. He was hardly made for that.

Still, he tried. "It's so quiet that I think we would hear if anyone else was nearby, and I haven't heard anything."

She nodded, but her gaze darted around.

He focused again on the slant of light through the trees and stepped to the left, completely concealed behind a thick pine. From here, he could see Ivy's house clearly. Everything, including the barn, the corral, the road leading to her home. Just like the drawings.

It was a perfect spot to observe the farm and matched the view of the illustrations.

Nerves taut with the same instinct that had kept him alive in prison, Gideon studied the ground then bent to pick up a broken pine branch. With his boot, he cleared a spot on the soft ground then laid the branch next to the tree where they stood.

"What are you doing?"

"If someone does come back, they'll likely build a fire here again." He anchored the wood on either end with small rocks. "Not only because it's a perfect place to watch your house, but also because I doubt they'll risk marking another spot."

He checked the other side of the tree, pleased to discover the Powell farm wasn't visible from there. "When they get in place, they'll break the twig."

"That's smart," she murmured, "but an animal could break it."

"Yeah, but if a person does it, there will be some other sign of that. A boot print, marks on the tree maybe."

"That means you're going to have to check here every day."

"Right."

"We can take turns."

"I'll do it."

"I can help."

"Miss Ivy, your brother sent me here to do this job."

"I'm helping," she said baldly.

She might look softer than velvet and be a whole lot prettier than Smith, but she probably had every bit as much grit as her brother. And she might need it.

The dead horse and the campfire remains proved someone had been here. To frighten Ivy? Or for something worse?

Gideon had to find out. Which meant he wasn't going anywhere, no matter how badly Ivy might want him to.

Chapter Two

Gideon Black's face had gone from blank to grim upon seeing the remains of that campfire.

By the time they sat down to lunch, Ivy was impressed with the man, though she didn't want to be. For whatever reason, she hadn't thought to look in the woods for signs of the person causing her trouble.

Maybe because she was so tired. She'd barely slept last night for replaying the night of Tom's death over and over. She'd managed to stop the memory, but not the guilt. As a result, she had slept poorly, and she couldn't blame that on her guest.

Gideon gestured to the platter of ham and corn bread. "This is good."

"Thank you." Sitting across from him, her skin felt prickly.

And hot.

The man was the size of a mountain. He dominated the space, making even the table that could seat ten people look small. His face, rugged and strong, was weathered by the sun and life. Grooves cut on either side of his mouth hinted that he must've smiled a lot at one time. She'd seen no evidence of it.

Using the cloth napkin she'd laid next to his plate, he wiped his lips then took a sip of coffee. "When does your contract with the mayor end?"

So he was still trying to figure out why someone might want to cause trouble for her. "In a year."

"Is there anyone who might want that?"

"Not to my knowledge." She sighed. "The mayor will have to be told about the horse. I'll need to drive into Paladin."

"I'll go with you."

The thought of riding all that way in the wagon with him made her skittish. "It's not necessary."

"Still, I'll go."

Her own food sat untouched as he forked open another piece of corn bread and spread it with honey. Why had Gideon been in prison? Maybe it had been due to a mistake like her brother being wrongly identified as a train robber. A clerical error had incorrectly listed him as dead rather than as one of the prisoners transported to Leavenworth.

"Mr. Black?"

"Gideon."

"Gideon. How long were you in prison?"

His head came up, those blue eyes burning into her. Wariness etched his features. "Five years."

"Why were you there?"

He laid down his fork. A long moment passed. "For murder."

She drew in a sharp breath. There was no need to ask if he was serious. His eyes hardened, squelching a brief flare of remorse and anger.

"And were you guilty?"

"Yes." He watched her carefully, as if expecting her to order him to leave.

She wasn't afraid of him. If Smith thought Gideon was dangerous, he never would've sent him.

Just as he took another sip of coffee, she asked, "Who did you kill?"

He shook his head.

"I think I have a right to know, Mr. Black. You're living here."

Looking pained and irritated at the same time, he set his cup down. "A rancher's son."

"Did you kill him in self-defense?"

"No." His jaw tightened as he held her gaze, his entire frame rigid with tension.

She wanted to press him for more, but the raw bleakness in his face reached right into her chest and squeezed. She couldn't do it. "Thank you for telling me."

He said nothing, just resumed eating.

For a moment, the only sounds were the scrape of forks on the plates, the occasional call of a bird. The man clearly didn't want to discuss himself. That was fine. She had other questions.

"Smith won't talk much about his time in prison."

Resignation chased across Gideon's face, and he again set aside his utensils. His voice was flat. "He doesn't want you to know."

Because it had been horrible. Ivy's throat tightened. Her brother was home. That was what mattered. Their parents and his wife, Caroline, were helping him heal. Who was helping Gideon Black? Did a murderer deserve help? Smith thought so. "Do you have any family?"

"No, ma'am."

"No one at all?"

"No."

His tone was polite, yet she could sense his agitation. "How did you and Smith become friends?"

After a longing glance at his food, he said, "There was a, um, misunderstanding between him and some other inmates. I helped straighten it out."

His words were so careful, so deliberate that she knew he wasn't telling her everything.

"Was that when you saved his life?"

"Yes." His muscles were drawn taut beneath his buff-colored work shirt, his shoulders straining at the fabric.

"Was that when his leg was broken?"

The jerky nod and coiled energy in his body warned her off, but she couldn't help another question. "Is that how you got those scars?"

His face completely closed up. She'd never seen anything like it. His features turned to granite, blue eyes blazing, his mouth white with restraint. Angry color slashed across his sharp cheekbones.

He rose, his massive frame blocking out the sun. "Would you like me to take my meals somewhere else, Miss Ivy?"

"No." She stood, too. Would he really go? Absolutely, she realized. There was no bluff on his face. "Please, finish your meal."

He stared at her for a long moment, then started to sit. The sound of an approaching horse had them both turning toward the open screened door. A couple of chickens squawked and hustled out of the way of a brown mare, its hooves flinging red mud as it trotted toward the house.

She held back a groan. "I wonder what he wants."

Gideon strapped on the gun belt he'd shed for their meal. Plucking his hat from the peg beside the door, he looked at her over his shoulder. "You know him?"

"Yes. It's Conrad, the stagecoach driver. Neal Conrad, but he goes by his last name."

"Didn't you say he was just here yesterday?"

"Yes. I can't imagine what he wants."

She stepped onto the porch, and her guest followed. An enticing mix of man and leather floated to her. She could feel the powerful width of Gideon's chest at her back. While she appreciated the gesture, Conrad was an annoyance, not a threat.

The stage driver, a man with sharp features and flowing blond hair, jumped off his horse and whipped the reins around the hitching post. "I came as soon as I could."

Giving Gideon a narrow-eyed look, Conrad reached her in two strides, arms outstretched.

She stepped back, managing to avoid contact. He was always touching her, and she didn't like it.

His blue-checked shirt and dark trousers were clean. His eyes were deep brown, his features as perfect as a drawing and he possessed about as much substance as a piece of paper. He was trim and well built, a handsome man. And he knew it.

"What brings you out two days in a row, Conrad?" Ivy asked evenly.

"I came to check on you. See how you fared in the storm."

"Just fine."

He turned his attention to Gideon, his eyes hardening when he saw how close the other man stood to her.

"Who are you?" he asked sharply.

Ivy barely stopped herself from snapping that it was none of his business. Before Gideon could answer, she did. "Conrad, this is Gideon Black, a family friend."

"Are you staying here or just passing through?"

As if that were any of his concern. Ivy fought the urge to order the stage driver off her property, but that wouldn't be smart, businesswise. "He's my guest, Conrad. He brought a message from my brother."

The man scrutinized Gideon before his gaze swung to Ivy. "Is everything all right?"

"Yes. Gideon and I are just having a visit."

The subject of the conversation had yet to say a word, but Ivy didn't miss the shrewd glint in his eyes as he sized up the other man. She also didn't miss the way he kept one hand on the butt of the revolver in his holster.

"I drive the stage," Conrad announced unnecessarily.

"So Miss Ivy said." Gideon folded his arms over that broad chest. With a scowl on his compelling features, he looked as approachable as a rattlesnake.

Seeming to dismiss Gideon, Conrad turned to her with a smile and took her elbow, towing her inside.

As he always did, he walked into her house without an invitation. Gideon followed them over the threshold, disapproval pulsing from him.

When Ivy pulled away, Conrad paused at the dining table, his smile still in place. "You were probably frightened last night. That storm really kicked up a fuss."

"I wasn't frightened," she said stiffly.

"Maybe you've got some of that delicious coffee?"

Conrad's gaze fell to the two plates on the table. The two cups. Mouth tight, he sat in the chair next to hers.

She didn't like it, but she didn't need to upset the man who recommended her stage stop and was responsible for bringing passengers here.

Gideon remained at the door like a sentry. Tension arced in the room, and she thought she could physically feel him willing the stage driver to leave.

Conrad drummed his fingers on the table.

She took another tin cup from the cabinet that held the tin plates and mugs reserved for the passengers. Going to the stove, she wrapped the hem of her apron around the hot handle of the coffeepot.

As she poured, he said, "It would've been better if you'd been in town last night, not out here all alone."

"I was fine." Her words were short as she handed him the cup. She glanced at Gideon, noticing that his face hadn't changed one bit. It still looked carved out of stone. Forbidding. Conrad was either blind or not intimidated.

"You know how I feel about you being out here all by your lonesome," he said.

Yes, and she didn't give two figs about it. It took effort to keep her voice level. "I appreciate your concern, but I can't leave my home."

"You shouldn't be running this place by yourself." He sipped at the steamy brew. "You shouldn't be running it at all."

"Conrad," she said sweetly, her eyes narrowing. "I've been running it since Tom passed, and I intend to keep doing so."

"Now, now, don't get your back up." He clumsily

placed his cup on the table, liquid sloshing out as he stood and moved toward her.

Gideon took a step in her direction. Only one.

It was enough to stop the other man. Conrad blinked then turned to Ivy. "I'm only thinking of you. You need a man around here to help you."

She certainly did not.

"She has one," Gideon said.

Surprised, Ivy shot him a look.

The stage driver's lip curled. "I meant someone she can depend on regularly."

With the exception of her brother and father, there were no men she would depend on. If she needed a man on the farm, she would hire one.

She walked out to the porch, hoping the stage driver would take the hint. "Everything is fine, Conrad. Thanks for checking on me."

After another slit-eyed look at Gideon, the man gave her a quick hug, moving away before she could remove his arm. He touched her often, never with permission, although he'd never tried more than a hug. Which was good, because Ivy wouldn't hesitate to use the pistol in her skirt pocket.

"Is your stock all right?" Conrad asked. "All accounted for?"

"Yes." She wasn't telling him about the dead mare.

"I'll check the horses. If any of them need shoes, I brought some."

"That's not necessary, Conrad."

"It'll just take a minute."

"Only one of them needed to be shod, and Gideon did it this morning."

"That's really not your—" He broke off, glowering

at Gideon before giving Ivy a sideways look. "That's nice, but I usually take care of that for you."

"And I appreciate it, even though I can take care of it on my own," she said sharply. She was sick to death of Conrad acting as if she were helpless. At least Gideon hadn't acted that way. Yet.

Wanting to hurry the stage driver along, she moved down the steps to his horse. "I'll see you on your next stage run."

"Yes, all right." Coming to stand beside his mount, he looked over her head at Gideon, but spoke to her. "I'll see you soon."

She made a noncommittal noise as he mounted up and finally rode off.

Ivy exhaled, glad to be rid of him.

"Is he always like that?" Gideon asked in a low voice.

"Yes." She turned, in no mood for him to start any of that silly man-take-care-of-woman business. "And I can handle him just fine."

"You sure can. He must not know about that pistol in your skirt pocket. Why do you put up with the way he treats you?"

"He could discourage passengers from staying for a meal."

"And that would cost you money."

"Yes." She moved past him and back into the house to clean up the dishes. Gideon followed, but stopped in the doorway. Sunlight haloed his giant frame.

"Besides, he leaves a lot quicker if he thinks he's getting what he wants."

A half smile tugged at Gideon's mouth, and it made her smile in return.

She carried the plates and cups across the room and past the stove.

"You say he was here yesterday?" Gideon asked.

"Yes."

"Before that, when was his most recent visit?"

"Four days ago." She glanced over her shoulder. "Why?"

"That means he was here the day before—"

"The day before I found my horse killed," she breathed, hastily putting the dishes in the dry sink. "Do you think Conrad had something to do with that?"

"Can you remember if he was around just before the other incidents?"

"I can't remember about the chickens, but…he wasn't here the day Tug went missing."

Gideon frowned. "That you know of."

"That's right." Did he take anyone's word for anything? She bet not. Was that because he'd been in prison, or was there more to it? "He could've been in the woods, and I wouldn't have known. He could've come across Tug. If he did something to my dog—"

"Hey, we don't know anything yet. What motive would he have for causing you trouble?"

"To make me decide I need a man around here," she muttered. "That I need *him*. I know it sounds ridiculous."

"How long have you known him?"

"Since Tom and I married, almost ten years." She appreciated that Gideon didn't dismiss her theory.

Her guest looked her over slowly, sparking all her nerve endings. A muscle flexed in his jaw. "Does he always put his hands on you like that?"

"He didn't pay me much mind until Tom died." And

he had certainly never made her feel halfway dizzy the way Gideon just had with only a look. "Do you think he might be behind this?"

"I'm considerin' the possibility. He wants you."

"Well, it isn't mutual," she said hotly. The idea made her shudder.

Gideon turned and stepped off the porch, kneeling near the hitching post.

Ivy followed him outside. "What are you doing?"

"Checking his horse's tracks."

So if he saw them again, he would recognize them, she realized. She should do the same. She moved behind him and to his other side. He wore his hat now, drawing her attention to the nape of his corded neck. Skirts brushing against his shoulder, she bent over to study the hoofprints, too.

"Is there anything distinctive about them?" she asked.

He pointed to the impressions in the mud. "His mount lists to the right. Like she has one front leg shorter than the other."

Too aware of the way his powerful thigh muscles pulled his trousers taut, she forced herself to look at what he was showing her.

When he half turned to study the stage driver's boot prints, she did the same.

"I can't tell anything about them," she said.

"Yeah, they're just scuff marks in the dirt. I plan to keep an eye out for him. If something happens tonight, we'll have some tracks to compare, and maybe we can start to figure out who's doing these things."

She nodded.

His gaze trailed over her almost impersonally, as if

he were checking to make sure she was all right. He tipped his hat. "If you need me, I'll be around the barn doing chores."

Conrad's visit had almost made her forget what had happened at lunch with Gideon. The way she'd ambushed him with all those questions.

"Do you want more coffee?"

"No, thanks."

"All right." She watched him walk away, taking in the broad line of his shoulders. The way they narrowed to his lean hips.

The reason he wasn't coming back inside was probably because she'd opened old wounds with her questions. The information was a curiosity to her, but it was his life, his past. A clearly painful past he didn't want to share.

That was fine. Gideon Black could keep his secrets. And she would keep hers.

Now Ivy knew he'd done murder. Once she'd had time to absorb that he had killed a man, he'd see the familiar revulsion and wariness in her eyes that he saw in everyone's, except Smith's and Smith's parents.

Gideon eased out a breath. He didn't like her stirring up the past, and he wasn't having it. He would never tell her about the man he'd killed or the woman he'd killed for.

He *was* living here, so she might deserve to know a few things, but she had no right to get inside his head. Inside him.

She hadn't liked that he wouldn't answer every question she asked, especially about Smith. Too bad. There was no way he was telling her that he had saved her brother's life after fighting off five men who were beating the hell out of him. He also wasn't giving up to her how Smith had saved him after Gideon had been jumped and strung up by the neck in his own cell. And she wouldn't be learning that he had other scars he'd gotten before going to prison.

Ivy didn't need to know any of that.

He didn't intend to answer any more questions. If she didn't like it, she could send him packing. Or try. He wasn't leaving until he figured out what was going on. Regardless of what Ivy did, he wouldn't let Smith down. And he didn't have to be her friend in order to protect her.

He could do what needed to be done without taking his meals with her, although it would be difficult to walk away from good food after years of prison slop. Still, he'd done harder things.

He'd keep to himself as much as possible. He was used to solitude. It was what he knew and understood. What he wanted.

If Ivy had told Gideon before lunch that a man might be causing trouble on her farm in hopes that she would turn to him in her time of need, Gideon would've thought the idea was far-fetched. But after seeing Conrad with her, Gideon couldn't dismiss the idea, no matter how downright addled it was.

He hadn't cared for the man's manner at all, especially hadn't liked how often he touched Ivy. Because of their business dealings, he understood why she hadn't run the guy off her property at gunpoint, but that didn't mean Gideon wouldn't if he had cause.

After replacing a cheek billet on a bridle then a worn cinch, he strode out of the barn and across the backyard in search of Ivy. When he didn't find her at the garden or the chicken house, he circled around to the front porch.

He knocked on the door. "Miss Ivy?"

"Yes."

Gideon shaded his eyes to see inside, but she wasn't in the front room.

"What is it?"

He opened the door and poked his head in. Still no sign of her. "I thought I'd look for your dog and also see if I could find anything that might help me figure out what happened to your missing chickens."

"I thought I might look again, too."

He turned toward her voice, coming from his left. Her bedroom. "Does Tug have a favorite spot?"

"There's a place on the river that runs through the woods beyond the back pasture." She stepped into the large front room. His pulse jumped. It took his brain a second to register what he saw.

Hell for breakfast.

Ivy was wearing trousers. Ill-fitting and too large, but definitely trousers.

A plain white blouse was tucked into dark pants that were cinched tight at her tiny waist. Though the pants weren't tight, they shadowed the slender line of her thighs, the hint of her calves. Despite her petite frame, she was perfectly proportioned and all woman.

He clamped his jaw tight to keep it from dropping.

She must have noted his astonishment because she stopped in the middle of the room, angling her chin at him. "What? I'm not wearing a blasted skirt to look for my dog. The grass is wet, and that will weigh me down. Besides, we might have to go through some brush."

"Makes sense." He had no problem with her wearing

a garment that showed so much of her shape, though he was glad no other man was around to see her. "I've just never seen a woman in pants."

"Well, now you have."

Oh, yeah. And he liked it. But as much as he enjoyed the front view, he nearly swallowed his teeth when she turned away and he got a look at her backside outlined perfectly in the loosely fitted garment. His mouth went dry.

"Let's go out the back door," she said.

Unable to take his eyes off her, he followed her like a half-wit across the front room and down the hall. His gaze slid over her narrow shoulders, the sleek curve of her waist, and lingered on her hips. The urge to touch had him curling his hands into fists.

How was he supposed to focus on anything when he was faced with that view?

After plucking a wide flat-brimmed hat from a peg on the wall, she settled it on her head as she pushed through the back door. She started for the fence, and Gideon lengthened his stride to catch up to her. They headed toward the river he'd only seen from a distance.

Bright sunlight and a clear sky gave no hint of last night's storm. The ground was springy from the recent rain. The air was fresh and cool, filled with the smells of mud and grass and animals.

He and Ivy called out several times for the dog. Branches and limbs were scattered across the pasture. There was no sign of Tug or the chickens.

They topped a small rise, and Gideon saw the glitter of water through the trees ahead and to the left.

Ivy gestured toward the spot. "This is the Kiamichi River."

"Little River is the one outside Paladin, isn't it? Where the gristmill operates?"

"Yes." Her soft floral scent drifted on the air.

During their few minutes of brisk walking through the damp grass, Gideon found his gaze on her more than he liked. Finally, they reached the river. The bank sloped gently to the water, slightly cloudy from being stirred up by last night's rain. The river bottom was lined with flat rocks of all sizes.

The cattle and horses had kept the alfalfa grazed near the ground. Here and downstream, mature pecan trees and oaks spread wide canopies of shade. Farther upstream, where the channel narrowed, limbs tangled and arced over the water, hanging so low it would be difficult to guide a canoe through without getting smacked in the face.

Ivy pointed to a thick, scarred oak several feet away. "That tree has been here forever. There's a hollow on the other side, and Tug likes to chase squirrels into it."

As they made their way over to it, Ivy called out, "Tug! Here, boy!"

Birds flew out of the trees, and squirrels scurried across the branches.

Gideon's gaze panned the area as they neared the tree. Ivy tromped ahead through ankle-high grass and stopped on the opposite side of the oak.

"Oh, Tug." She braced one hand on the tree, her eyes troubled as they met Gideon's.

He closed the distance between them, then ducked his head to look inside the hollow.

A large dog with dark, matted fur lay curled on its side, rigid and lifeless.

Ivy knelt, touching the animal's stiff body. "This is why he didn't come home."

Her voice quivered, and tears slid down her cheeks.

The pain in her voice lashed at him. She choked out a sob then another. And another. He didn't know what to do. He'd never had a pet so he didn't know how it felt to lose one, but he did know how it felt to be alone. She'd lost her husband and now her dog.

She covered her face with her hands, her shoulders shaking.

Gideon's heart squeezed. Finally, tentatively, he reached out and put a hand on her shoulder.

She flinched, and he quickly drew back.

After a moment, she straightened, wiping her eyes on her shirtsleeve. "I'm sorry."

For crying or for jumping like he'd taken a branding iron to her? "There's no need to apologize."

"You startled me."

Gideon heard a faint whine and looked down at the dog.

Leaning in for a closer look, he saw a pup nestled in the circle of Tug's curled legs. "There's a puppy."

"Oh, my." Still on her knees, Ivy leaned in and carefully picked it up. "It's so tiny."

"Looks like Tug was protecting it." The whelp would fit comfortably in Gideon's palm. Its coat, a mottle of black, brown and gray, was matted.

Ivy looked up, eyes still wet from her tears. "Maybe you were right about him finding a lady friend at some point and this is his pup?"

"Maybe so." Gideon went to his haunches, pointing at the animal. "Or maybe he didn't come home because he was hurt. His right back leg is at an odd angle."

"No. That was broken the night Tom—" She stopped. "That was broken a while back."

What had she been about to say? Maybe that Tug's leg had been broken the night her husband died? Gideon could see how that would be a painful memory.

"Was he in the wagon with your husband and thrown out, too?"

"No," she said tersely.

He could've sworn he saw guilt flash across her delicate features, but he must have read that wrong. Why would she feel guilty about a dog's broken leg?

She didn't seem inclined to give details, and he wondered why not.

The pup whimpered, and its eyes fluttered open, dark and dazed.

"Oh, you poor thing." Ivy gently examined the animal. "It's a female. Do you see any more pups?"

Gideon stood and searched the nearby area. "No. Don't see a mother, either." He returned, noticing the sharp points on the pup's ears. "This baby is half wolf."

Ivy glanced around. "If the mother were alive, she would be taking care of the pup. Something must've happened to her, too. Maybe that's why Tug has the pup."

"Maybe."

Ivy rose, lifting the pup to eye level. "See the black stripe up the middle of her muzzle? Tug has one just like it. I think he sired this pup. She looks like she might not make it."

"If we get some food in her, she might surprise us."

Ivy's gaze shifted to the adult canine. "I want to bury him near the house. I'll bring the wagon down later to get him."

"I can carry him back right now."

"Would you?" The relief and gratitude on her face did something strange to Gideon's insides.

Going down on one knee, he leaned in and gently pulled the dog from the hollow. A few minutes later, he had the big animal in his arms and was walking with Ivy back through the pasture to the house.

"Do you think someone killed him?" she asked quietly.

He figured she had been wondering that since they'd spotted the dog. He had, too. Now that he had the animal in full sunlight, he could see blood on his coat along with the mud. And a knife wound just like the one he'd found on the dead horse.

Anger blazed inside him. "He has a stab wound in his neck."

"It's likely that the same person killed Tug and the horse."

He nodded.

Ivy's throat worked, and a tear rolled down her cheek. "Do you think Tug died trying to protect the pup?"

"It's possible."

"Who would do this to my dog? Why?"

Gideon wanted to know, too. Thanks to the rain, there were no signs of who might've killed the animal.

Ivy glanced over at her lifeless pet, saying wistfully, "Tug was the runt of the litter, but he didn't stay that way, as you can see."

The dog was huge. And heavy. "What breed is he?"

"I don't know. Just a mix."

He could see stark pain in her midnight eyes. "How long did you have him?"

"From the time Tom and I married."

The animal had been with her through her entire marriage. And her husband's death. Now she had another loss to deal with. Gideon didn't know anything about relationships of that duration. Smith was his longest association, and that added up to a sum total of two years.

They stopped at a grouping of mature pecan trees where Ivy said she wanted to bury the dog. When she started to go for a shovel, Gideon stopped her.

"I'll do it." He wasn't letting her dig dirt or bury her animal.

In short order, the dog was resting in the soft ground. Ivy still held the pup, staring down at the fresh grave with a broken look on her face.

Gideon felt as if he were intruding. "I'll feed the pup if you want to take some time here."

"Thank you." She carefully handed over the little female.

"Milk in the pitcher?" he asked.

"Yes."

Grasping the shovel in his free hand, he started past her.

Ivy touched his arm. "Thank you for carrying Tug and for putting him to rest."

"You're welcome." He left her with her pet and her memories.

Once, he glanced back. She sat next to the grave, her head bowed. She looked slight. And alone. Gideon wanted to return to her. *And do what?* he jeered at himself. *Comfort her?*

He needed to watch his step with that. Earlier, he

hadn't been able to turn away from her suffering. He'd first gotten tangled up with Eleanor for the same reason.

He was here to protect Ivy. He couldn't allow himself to be drawn in by her.

Chapter Three

Gideon fed the pup what little milk she could eat, then made a doghouse for her out of an empty apple crate and added a nest of fresh hay. He put her in the box and set her next to his bunk. For the next couple of hours, he was in and out of the barn, keeping an eye on the whelp.

After pumping the horse trough full of fresh water, Gideon stepped back inside the barn to check on the dog. She was awake, dark eyes watching him warily.

He carefully scooped her up, running a finger lightly over her head. She mewled weakly as he turned for the barn door, intent on getting more milk from the house.

"Mr. Black?"

He looked up to see Ivy walking toward him carrying a small chipped porcelain bowl. She still wore those infernal trousers. His gaze slid over her full breasts and nipped-in waist to her slender hips.

Lust punched him square in the gut, and his whole body went hot. With all he could see of her shape, it didn't take much to imagine her naked. She must've read the expression on his face because her step faltered.

Trying to blank his face, he bit the inside of his

cheek. He hoped she wasn't going to wear those britches all the time. The last thing he needed was her coming around looking like…*that*. He wouldn't be worth a plug nickel.

Ivy's gaze skittered from his to the pup. "How's Thunder doing?"

"Thunder?"

"We found her after that storm. The name seems appropriate."

He frowned down at the animal. "She's a girl."

"What would you call her?" Ivy asked lightly. "Princess?"

Was she teasing him? "Pup sounds just fine to me."

"She needs a real name."

"All right." He held the whelp up to eye level. "Thunder's ready for her second feeding."

Ivy gestured to the crockery she held. "I brought milk."

"She doesn't have the strength to lift her head so I had to hand-feed her before." Gideon eased down onto his bunk and offered Ivy a square of red flannel. "I dipped a rag in the milk, and she sucked the liquid out."

Ivy took the soft fabric, then moved between his legs. So close that the heat of her body teased him.

She rolled the cloth into a tube and dunked the end in the milk then held it to the pup's mouth. The animal lay listless, eyes dazed. Ivy rubbed the wet fabric lightly against Thunder's lips, but she didn't suck.

Gideon tried, with the same result. He then stuck the tip of his pinkie finger in the liquid and put it to the pup's mouth. A little tongue swiped against his skin.

"There ya go," he murmured, glad to see the animal was holding her own.

He dipped his finger again and offered it to her. When she licked off the liquid, he continued to feed her slowly. As hard as he tried, he couldn't concentrate fully on the young dog because Ivy was still standing between his legs.

She might be dressed like a man, but she sure didn't look like one. Or smell like one, either. Her skin was dewy from their earlier exertion, and her sweat smelled clean. Beneath that, he caught a hint of magnolia.

Gideon wanted to close his thighs and draw her closer. If he leaned forward slightly, he could put his mouth on her velvety neck. Her delicate ear.

She looked up. "You're really good with the pup. You must've had a pet before."

"No." He had tended wounded animals before— calves, horses, a crow with a broken wing at the prison.

Gideon continued to feed the whelp drop by drop, but he was completely taken by the woman in front of him. She put a hum in his blood by doing nothing more than standing there.

Ever since he had confessed to murder, Gideon had waited for revulsion to darken Ivy's eyes. He searched her face for it now, but she seemed intent only on the dog.

"Earlier, you said you had no family."

And that he'd killed a man. Was that where she was headed?

"When did you lose them? In the war?"

Because the question wasn't what he expected, it took a second for him to answer. The war had taken so many, entire families in some cases, though not from Gideon. "Never had a family."

"You're an orphan?"

He nodded. Her brother was the closest thing to family Gideon had ever had.

"Smith didn't tell me that."

He figured there was a lot Smith hadn't told his sister. As long as Ivy didn't ask about their prison time, Gideon didn't mind answering some questions. Although he wouldn't talk about the man he'd killed, or that he'd done so because of Eleanor's lies.

Ivy was quiet for a moment, her teeth worrying her lower lip. "Where did you grow up?"

"In Kansas." His gaze traced her features, the ivory satin of her skin.

"Did you live with anyone?" At his frown, she clarified. "Did you have a home?"

"When I was ten, a widow lady, Ruby Whitten, took me in, but she passed away after about two years and I was on my own again."

"Then what did you do?"

Though she appeared genuinely interested, the anxiety squeezing his chest didn't ease. If she were going to ask more about his crime, he wished she would get on with it. "I hired on at a ranch."

"How old were you?"

"Twelve, but I looked older."

"You were bigger than other boys your age." Her gaze traced slowly over his shoulders and arms, making his body go tight.

Want tugged low in his belly, and he knew by her sudden flush that she felt it, too. He cleared his throat, wishing she would step out of the circle of his legs. "Yes."

Damn, he wanted to touch her. He refocused his

attention on the small animal in his hand. The poor thing weighed about as much as a baby bird.

"Did you fight in the war?"

"Didn't everyone?" Even seven years gone, the thought made him tired.

"Sure seemed that way." Sadness pulled at her features as she stroked the pup's head. "Did you work at another ranch after the war?"

He nodded. Hiring on with Eleanor's daddy had been the beginning of his journey to hell.

If she was going to ask so many questions, Gideon had some, too. "Did your husband fight?"

She stilled for a heartbeat. If he hadn't been so close, he would've missed her reaction.

"Yes, he did."

"Earlier, you said his family was from Chicago. How did the two of you meet?"

"Before the war, he came to Mimosa Springs looking for land," she said stiffly. "He wanted a place that wasn't settled, so he looked farther east and decided on this area."

When her eyes hardened, Gideon knew it had to do with her past, not his. She stepped back. "Tomorrow, I'll go to town and speak with the mayor about the dead horse."

That had sure been a quick change. Was it still too painful for Ivy to talk about her husband? The frantic tapping of her pulse in the hollow of her throat told Gideon the subject obviously vexed her.

"I'll see you at supper." She turned and walked out the door.

Gideon watched her go, trying to sort out his jumbled thoughts. Whenever she was around, his brain seemed to engage a second too late. He was here to protect her, and that was all. Instead, he had an insane urge to hold her. To comfort her.

Hell. Not getting drawn in by her was going to be more difficult than he'd thought.

Why had she told him anything about Tom? She didn't like talking about her dead husband, ever.

After breakfast the next morning, Ivy and Gideon set off for town. They had left the pup in her crate, inside the house. The wagon bumped along the rutted road now dried out from the rain. The wooden seat creaking, she stared blankly at the grass and trees they passed.

She wanted to believe her guard had been down last night because of Tug, and maybe that was part of it, but she also knew it had to do with Gideon. For those moments in the barn watching him feed the pup, Ivy had been aware of only him.

No man had ever looked at her like that, as if his next breath depended on her. Which explained why she'd had trouble falling asleep. That and the times she'd gone to the window, wondering if more of her animals were in danger, if someone was out there watching her house.

She smoothed her navy-and-white-striped skirts, and settled her navy reticule in her lap.

Maybe Gideon's being here was good. Maybe a man of his size could discourage the low-down snake who was making trouble for her. Though she didn't like the thought of needing a man for any reason, Ivy couldn't deny that he'd been only help so far.

Neither of them spoke much during the drive to Paladin. The scents of grass and dirt and clean air drifted around them. The occasional purple flower dotted the green alfalfa fields that spread as far as the eye could see on either side. Once, a redbird swooped over the wagon road.

She was uncommonly aware of the man beside her. More aware than she'd been of any man since Tom's death. As much as she tried, she couldn't ignore the granite-hard line of his thigh against hers, the leashed power in his massive frame, the large callused hands that worked the reins so easily. Those same work-roughened hands had handled the pup as gently as she would have.

She sneaked a glance at him. He smelled of leather and soap, and she could see a tuft of dark hair in the open V of his homespun work shirt.

Ivy didn't want to notice any of those things about Gideon Black, yet she couldn't seem to help herself. Feeling suddenly hot, she fiddled with the button at the neck of her white bodice. She might be attracted to him, but the first time he showed his true colors—and he eventually would—her interest would fade.

The day was clear and bright, and they arrived in Paladin before noon. Laid out in a quasi-horseshoe shape with the church at its apex, the small town was bustling as people made their way around town or across the wide main street. At the blacksmith's shop attached to the back side of the livery, a hammer rang against metal.

Besides the mercantile, smithy, bank and jail, Paladin now boasted a telegraph office, a gristmill, a hotel and a sawmill. Nearby, both Little River and Kiamichi River provided water for the town and surrounding farms. Tom wouldn't have liked how the town had grown, how many people had moved here. She'd learned the hard way that wide-open space wasn't the only reason he had wanted away from her family.

She and Gideon braked the wagon in front of the livery and walked around the building. Just outside of town and a few yards away was Mayor Jumper's lumber company. Behind the main office, saws whined and boards cracked; sawdust and wood chips shot into the air. Ivy felt more urgency to go to the bank for a loan to restock her horses and poultry, but she preferred to get her conversation with the mayor out of the way first. She didn't look forward to telling Leo about his dead horse.

She and Gideon stepped inside the lumber company's small, neatly kept office. Outfitted with a standing desk as well as a small corner desk and chair along the back wall, the space was spotless. A couple of ledger books were stacked neatly across the top of the taller desk and just behind it squatted a large safe.

Leo Jumper, dressed in his usual three-piece suit, moved out from behind his work area. He stopped in front of her, using a cane with an intricately carved wooden head. There was nothing wrong with his legs; he carried the expensive walking stick to show off his wealth. The sunlight streaming through the windows on either side of the door turned his neatly trimmed hair a fiery-red.

"Mrs. Powell, how are you today?"

"Just fine." Palms clammy, she introduced Gideon.

"Ah, yes, Conrad told me you had a young man."

Ivy bet that wasn't all the stage driver had said. She didn't bother correcting Leo.

The mayor extended his free hand to Gideon. "Nice to meet you, sir."

She noticed that her guest's hand nearly swallowed

the older man's. Curiosity burned in Jumper's whiskey-colored eyes as they went from her to the rugged cowboy, but Ivy had no intention of inviting questions.

"What can I do for you, Mrs. Powell?"

"I have some bad news." Tension stretched across her shoulders as she explained about finding the dead mare.

His mouth tightened, his gaze narrowing. "Killed with a knife?"

"Yes."

"Who would do such a thing?"

"That's what I'm trying to find out."

"Was the horse roaming?" Jumper's tone was accusatory. "Wasn't it in the corral?"

"She was turned out to pasture with the others."

"This is going to cost me money, Mrs. Powell."

"Yes, sir." As it would her. She was counting on the bank loan to help her get by. "And I'm sorry about that."

Before she could ask if he planned to nullify their contract, the mayor said, "I won't be boarding more animals at your place. I think the stage line will agree with me."

Well, that answered that. "What would you like to do with the other horses?"

"Until I can move them, you should take better care and put them up at night. At least the ones that belong to the stage line."

"I will," she said stiffly, inwardly cursing whoever had harmed the bay and Tug.

Beside her, Gideon stared unblinking at the other man. Though Ivy didn't feel threatened by the mayor, she was glad she wasn't facing him alone.

"I'm on my way out of town so it will be a few days before I can arrange to move the others," Leo said.

"Very well. I've read the contract and know the loss of the animal voids it, but I can offer the use of my horses, free of charge, until I'm able to replace the one that was killed. That way, the stage can continue to run."

Jumper pursed his lips, irritation making his freckled features even more ruddy. "Very well. After I return from my trip, we'll finish this business."

She nodded, unable to speak around the lump in her throat. The loss of income would severely hamper her ability to operate the stage stand, but a bank loan would help a great deal.

The older man exhaled loudly. "I'll stop on my way out and report this to Sheriff Farrell."

"I'm planning to do that, too," Ivy said.

"No sense in both of us going." His gaze narrowed. "Tell Farrell I'll stop by when I return."

"I will. And again, I'm sorry, Mayor."

He nodded, pulling out a gold pocket watch and checking the time.

Ivy took the hint and left with Gideon. As they made their way back into town, she blew out a breath. "I'm glad that's over."

"Did it go the way you expected?"

"Unfortunately, yes." Irritation flared at the mayor's condescending attitude. "I don't expect special treatment, but this is the first problem to arise in the five years since the contract began. You'd think he might take that into account."

"Not big on second chances, is he?" Gideon's voice hardened.

"No, although I guess he can afford to be less than forgiving."

At Gideon's questioning look, she explained. "Besides the lumber company, he owns a stake in a couple of other businesses and the bank. I need to stop there, too."

"Since your contract with the mayor is likely ended, could you strike a deal with the stage company on your own?"

"Yes, I could." Smiling, she stopped abruptly in front of the livery's open doorway. "I should've thought of it myself. Thank you, Mr. Black."

"You're welcome," he murmured.

They continued walking and Ivy halted at the next building, a pine structure with two wide steps leading up to its landing. A sign over the door read Jail, Paladin, Indian Territory.

"I need to have a word with Sheriff Farrell."

"I'll wait for you out here. No hurry."

Ah, yes, he probably had an aversion to cell bars. As she turned to go in, he said, "Miss Ivy?"

The low, deep way he spoke her name sent a shiver through her. Intent on trying to dismiss the sensation, she almost didn't hear his question.

"Is the sheriff someone you trust?"

"Yes, why?" She shifted to face him. Even though she stood on the second step, she still had to tilt her head back a bit to meet his gaze.

He rested a hand on the wooden stair railing. "If you haven't told him everything that's going on at your farm, you should. Especially now that two of your animals have been killed."

She agreed. "Josh knows some of it, and I'll tell him the rest. Did you check the woods this morning?"

"Yes. The branch was unbroken. Didn't look as if it had been touched at all."

"Good." She opened the door. "I'll only be a moment."

She returned shortly. "Josh is out at a nearby ranch handling a dispute. I left a message for him to come out to the farm if I don't stop back by today."

Deputy McCain, who was watching the jail in the sheriff's absence, had asked about Ivy's "young man." Conrad could never be accused of keeping his mouth shut.

Pausing on the bottom step, she glanced across the street at the bank. "I was planning to see Mr. Rowland at the bank next, but I think I'll send a wire to the stage line manager in Boggy Depot first. Butterfield Overland no longer uses our line for their mail, but Territorial Stage Company keeps a regular schedule for passengers. There are quite a few stage stops just like mine across the Choctaw lands. Maybe I'll hear right back and perhaps have a new contract."

Gideon's attention moved to the imposing redbrick building.

"You don't have to go with me to the bank if you'd rather visit the mercantile or somewhere else," Ivy said.

"I'd feel better if you weren't alone."

For a moment, she'd almost forgotten he was here to protect her. "All right."

Since the telegraph office sat next door to the jail, they were shortly inside. In the morning sunlight, her brother's friend cast a tall, intimidating shadow. As Ivy's eyes adjusted to the dimmer light, Gideon made a low noise in his throat.

She followed his gaze. The counters and floor were covered with scraps of brown paper and newspaper. Except for the small patch on the desk where the telegraph machine sat, envelopes and letters covered every inch of the surface. No wonder she hadn't received Smith's wire. It might never be found in this chaos.

Elmer Wright stood in the far corner, pawing through a box. Full of more letters and telegrams!

The barrel-shaped man squinted through the haze of light and dust. "What can I do for you, Miss Ivy?"

"I'd like to send a telegram to the stage line manager in Boggy Depot, and I'm also looking for a recent wire from my brother."

The older man hobbled around a desk and came toward her. "Who's your young man?"

Why did everyone assume she and Gideon were a couple? "He's not my— This is Gideon Black, a friend of my brother's."

Gideon shook the man's hand as she studied the cluttered space. "It looks as if you might have trouble locating the message from Smith."

"No, no." Elmer shoved a hand through his thick gray-streaked hair, making it stand on end. He looked around helplessly. "It just might take me a while. I can't seem to find my spectacles."

"These spectacles?" Smiling, Ivy picked up a pair of glasses in plain view on the counter.

Giving her a sheepish look, he slid the glasses on and began digging through the clutter on the counter. He thumbed through a stack of correspondence, muttering.

Gideon stood quietly by, but Ivy moved about impatiently. "You should get some help in here, Elmer."

"Yes, yes. The sheriff's brother starts today after his schoolin'."

"That's good." Fifteen-year-old Coy Farrell was dependable and smart. And surely more organized than this.

"Aha, here it is." The older man smiled triumphantly and handed her the telegram.

It was indeed from Smith, and a quick glance confirmed everything Gideon had said upon his arrival. Though having the message in hand didn't much matter now that her brother's friend was already here, Ivy was glad to have it anyway.

"Now." Elmer cleared a stack of paper from atop the telegraph machine. "Let me find the information for the stage line office."

Ivy grimaced. "Are you sure you have it?"

"Yes, yes." He set aside a scribbled note and looked up, his blue eyes troubled. "I can do this, Miss Ivy. It don't matter what the mayor says. I can still run this telegraph office."

Though Ivy wasn't sure of that, she could see it meant a great deal to Elmer. She didn't want to hurt his feelings, but this was too important to mess up. What if he couldn't even get her message to the right place?

"It's okay, Elmer. I can just write a letter."

"No, no." His voice cracked.

Gideon leaned close. "Are you worried he can't tap out the right message?"

"Yes," she said under her breath.

"Let him do it. I learned Morse code during the war. I can tell if it's right or not."

She looked up at him in surprise, as much because of his knowledge as because of his kindness to the older man.

"Here it is!" the telegraph operator exclaimed.

"Okay." She leaned toward Elmer. "This is what I need to say."

Minutes later, Ivy and Gideon stepped outside and began walking to the bank.

Despite her disappointment that she hadn't received a quick response from the stage company, she tried not to dwell on it. She glanced at Gideon. "I can't believe Elmer didn't make a single mistake."

"He's probably done it for so long that he could tap those letters out blind."

They crossed the street and angled past Howe's Mercantile. As they neared the bank, Ivy spotted Conrad coming out of the saloon down the street.

When he started in her direction, she inwardly groaned. She had neither the time nor patience to deal with him today.

Gideon touched her elbow, sending a spark of heat up her arm. He tipped his head, showing that he had also spotted the stage driver.

Blocking her body with his, he opened the bank's tall front door for her. "I'll be right here. Take as long as you need."

Peeking around his broad frame, she saw Conrad turn and go in the opposite direction. "Thank you."

He nodded, his blue eyes warm on her face.

The look had her going soft inside. Aaargh! Flustered, she went through the door. The spacious interior boasted gray slate floors and stone walls. Three teller's cages, constructed of gold-trimmed wrought iron, greeted visitors. Each space had a desk, and on the wall behind was a wide vault door.

She approached the manager's office, her stomach knotting. She'd never asked for a loan. She'd also never been in this situation before.

A few minutes later, she was sitting in front of tall,

lanky Titus Rowland's desk. Her spine went rigid. "What do you mean, you can't loan money to a single woman?"

"It's bank policy, Ivy."

"But…but you know me." She curled and uncurled her reticule strings, her gaze falling on the tintype of Titus and his late wife, Lolly, on the wall behind him. "You've known me for years."

"I'm sorry." Sincere regret stamped his homely features.

"I was married longer than I've been a widow. Why should I be denied help just because I lost my husband?"

The gangly man shifted uncomfortably. "This isn't my decision in the end."

"I plan to use my farm as collateral, and I'm waiting to hear if I have a new contract with the stage line. That has to count for something." A greasy knot formed in her stomach. She couldn't just give up. "I see no reason why you can't help me."

Especially since she had put more sweat and effort into the stage stand than Tom ever had. Jittery with anxiety, she forced herself to remain seated, though she scooted to the edge of the leather chair. "I'll lose the business altogether and maybe my farm, too, if I don't get this loan. Please, Titus."

His shrewd gray eyes softened. "You've sure given a lot to make a go of it."

"And I'll continue to work hard. I *will* pay back the money. You know I will."

"I'll talk to the other members of the committee and try to convince them to waive the policy."

Ivy jumped up and snagged his hand, squeezing it. "Thank you, Titus. Thank you so much."

"Don't get your hopes up. What if I can't change their minds?"

"You will. And you won't regret helping me. I promise."

His smile transformed his gaunt features. "It will be a few days, but I'll let you know."

He walked her out of his office and across the slate floor, opening the front door for her.

She patted his bony arm. "Thank you again, Titus."

He lifted a hand in farewell as she stepped outside. Feeling more optimistic than she had since all the trouble at the farm had begun, she joined Gideon at the bottom of the stone steps.

The slow smile he gave her sent a tingle to her toes and made her skin prickle with awareness.

"You look like you got good news," he said.

"Not yet, but I think I will." As they started to the livery for the wagon, she explained what had happened with Titus.

"Sounds promising."

"Yes, I'm encouraged. Thank you again for that idea about contracting with the stage company on my own. Titus seemed impressed."

"I'm glad if I helped."

He had, she realized. In more ways than just this.

He did chores for no wages, protected her. Not only had he made sure her wire to the stage company was correct, he'd also managed to keep Conrad from bothering her. For that alone, she could kiss the man.

The thought jolted her, and she immediately pushed it away. She didn't want that with him. Well, maybe she did, just a tad, but she knew better than to let herself

be tempted by the idea. It might lead to being trapped
in another situation that would be difficult to escape.

    After finding Tug, it had been easy to lean on Gideon.
Too easy. She appreciated all that her brother's friend
had done since arriving, but she wouldn't—couldn't—
depend on a man ever again. She'd learned that the hard
way from her late husband.

Chapter Four

Smith's sister had grit. That had been impressed upon Gideon again yesterday in town. Ivy had lost a horse, her beloved dog and possibly her contract with the mayor. Rather than bellyaching, she had faced those problems head-on and tried to find a solution to what she could.

Had she become that tough and independent after the death of her husband? Or had she always been that way? Gideon didn't find a lot to admire in most women. Of course, that could be because he refused to share space with them longer than it took to learn their names. Ivy was different. Because of his promise to her brother, Gideon had already spent more time with her than he ever had spent with a woman, and that was only going to continue.

By midmorning the next day, both he and Ivy were busy with chores. Gideon had replaced two rotten slats on the back side of the corral. Now he stood at the chicken house, testing the sturdy latch he had just installed.

The pup chased a bit of fuzz blowing from a dandelion, running in a dizzying circle before plopping down in the grass and looking up at Gideon with dazed eyes. He grinned. This afternoon, he planned to white-wash the fence that encircled the house, but right now he wanted to check the woods in front of the place. He hadn't been out there since yesterday morning.

He rounded the barn, the pup trotting in his foot-steps. She stopped every foot or so to sniff another piece of grass or bat at a cricket. Suddenly, Thunder's ears pricked up. She gave an excited yelp and changed direction, racing toward the barn.

Curious, Gideon angled that way, too. The pup yipped again, and Gideon stopped in the barn doorway just as Ivy bent to scoop up the animal.

With a soft laugh, she managed to keep Thunder from licking her face.

Now that Gideon's eyes had adjusted to the dimmer light, he could see a large basket of laundry sitting on his bunk. Ivy spotted him then.

"Hello." She didn't quite meet his eyes. Putting the pup down, she reached back and gripped the edge of the basket. "Today is laundry day. Is there anything you want washed?"

"I can do it."

"It's no trouble, Mr. Black. You're not causing me extra work."

That was only one reason he wasn't interested.

She laid a hand on the mound of clothes swelling over the basket's top. "A pair of your trousers are in here and two of your shirts. If you give me the one you have on, I'll wash it."

No way in hell was he taking off his shirt in front of her. "I'm wearin' it."

Her gaze dropped to his chest, lingered as though

she could see beneath the garment. Damn good thing she couldn't.

"You could work without—"

"I've finished the latch on the henhouse door." He tried to keep his tone level. She didn't really know what she was asking of him. He hoped she would just leave it be. "I'm headed to the woods."

After a pause, she asked, "To see if the branch has been disturbed?"

He nodded.

"I hope you find it hasn't."

"Me, too." As he turned to walk out, he noticed the pup chewing at the hem of Ivy's gray day dress.

She looked down then, too, and bent to tug the fabric from Thunder's sharp teeth while scolding the animal in the least threatening tone Gideon had ever heard. It made him smile. He was still smiling when he reached the line of trees.

Breathing in the scent of pine, he wove his way around trees, pushed aside a clump of bush then another. He slowed as he neared the bois d'arc tree, his gaze dropping to the ground. The branch was broken!

Moving carefully, Gideon knelt and studied the boot print between what was now two pieces of twig.

Someone had been here since yesterday. What had they seen? How long had they stayed? Who the hell was it? From the shape and length of the boot and the depth of the imprint, he judged the visitor had been a man.

After pocketing the broken limb, he arranged another slender branch in the same spot and anchored it with a rock on either end. He headed for the house to show Ivy the halved branch. He was careful to watch where he stepped this time, searching for matching boot prints or other signs of a trespasser.

Between the woods and the house, the only identifiable prints he found were his own. He passed through the front gate and continued down the side of the house. A cloud of smoke drifted from the backyard.

The acrid smell of burning wood and the visible side of a black kettle confirmed Ivy was doing laundry. Just as he reached the corner of the house, the back door squeaked open then clattered shut.

"Miss Ivy?"

She glanced over as he drew even with her at the edge of the porch. Struggling to balance the overly full basket of clothes, she angled her body so she could see to step from the stoop.

"Here, let me help you." Gideon moved toward her, glancing down when he saw something in the thick grass. Something heavy. Iron.

Moving on pure instinct, he leaped over the object and lunged for Ivy. He wrapped an arm around her waist, grabbing a porch column to keep from falling.

Her breath whooshed out. The basket and laundry flew into the air.

Gideon's heel hit something hard, and there was a loud metal snap, sharp and startling in the quietness. Holding her tight, he got his legs under him and turned.

It was a trap. Someone had set an animal trap.

Ivy pushed at the arm he had locked around her waist. "You scared the daylights out of me! What are you doing?"

He loosened his hold a bit, angling her toward the spot where she'd stood.

The instant she caught sight of the snare and its

wicked teeth, she stilled immediately. Her voice came out in a choked whisper. "Is that a trap?"

"Yes."

"Someone put that there on purpose."

"Yes." The device had been arranged just so in the grass and the spring set.

If Ivy hadn't shifted to one side so she could see to step down onto the ground, Gideon probably wouldn't have glimpsed the object. A slick, greasy knot lodged in his gut.

She went limp as she made a sound like a sob. He started to put her on her feet, but she turned full into him, her arms latching around his neck.

Automatically, his arms wrapped around her. Trembling, she clutched him so tightly he felt her touch clear to his heart. That thing could've taken off her foot at her dainty ankle or mangled it beyond repair.

His chest felt strangely weak. Though glad she had escaped the trap, his relief edged quickly into a seething anger.

Ivy's heart was pounding so hard, he could hear it. Or maybe that was his. Her braid bumped the back of his hand. Beneath his touch, he felt the lithe tautness of her waist, the delicate line of her back. She buried her face in his neck. He felt like burying his face in her neck, too.

They stood like that for a long time. As he struggled to leash his fury, his pulse gradually slowed. The stinging smell of lye soap and woodsmoke drifted around them, but it was the subtle scent of her skin that settled him.

She wasn't hurt. She was all right.

"Gideon?" she breathed shakily. She lifted her head and stared at him with those midnight eyes.

What he saw there nearly made him swallow his teeth. No woman had ever looked at him this way—as if she had complete faith in him. As if she *needed* him.

No. Hell, no. Nothing good could come from that.

He slowly lowered her to the ground, clenching his jaw at the slide of her body all the way down his front.

She gripped his biceps and gave a wobbly laugh. "Give me a minute. I don't think my legs will hold me yet."

He didn't want to let go at all. Her breasts were full and soft against him, her magnolia scent teasing. Involuntarily, he smoothed an unsteady hand down her hair.

Her still-rapid breath brushed his chin. His gaze dropped to her mouth. He wanted to taste her. Even though his mind was fuzzy with relief and lust, he knew kissing her would be a mistake.

The sudden wariness in her eyes snapped him out of the moment. He stepped back, releasing her.

She wiped her hands down her skirts then wrapped her arms around herself.

Her beautiful features were chalk-white, her expression raw, vulnerable, just like when they'd found her dog. Gideon almost reached out to touch her again, but stopped himself. "Are you okay?"

"Yes, thanks to you." Her color returned slowly as she blanked her face. She seemed completely composed.

Did nothing put her off stride? Wasn't she angry? The attempt to harm her blistered him up. He knew she'd been rattled; she'd trembled so hard against him he'd thought she might shatter.

She stared across the yard for long seconds then moved jerkily toward the overturned basket and righted it.

He fought to rein in his temper. "I'll help you gather up the laundry. Then I'll take care of the trap."

"All right— Oh, Thunder!"

"She's probably fine, but I'll make sure."

"I'm glad she didn't follow me from the barn."

Gideon began to pick up sheets and shirts.

She glanced at him. "Were you looking for me earlier?"

His hands closed over a delicate nightgown, and he stared down at it for a moment. An image of her in the linen garment flashed through his brain. Desire tangled with the anger and relief still working through him.

"Gideon? Did you want me for something?"

He damn sure did, but he knew that wasn't what she meant. Reaching into his back trouser pocket, he pulled out the twigs. "Uh, yeah. I was coming from the woods to tell you the branch had been broken."

"You checked yesterday and the stick was undisturbed. It had to have been snapped last night."

He nodded.

"Whoever was in the woods is likely who set that trap."

The device had been placed in a spot that Ivy frequented. He saw when she put it together.

"They set that trap for me," she breathed out in horrified realization.

"That's what I think, too."

"Oh." The bit of color she'd regained disappeared, and her fingers curled so tightly on the lip of the basket that her knuckles turned white.

She looked wobbly. He reached out as if to steady her, but stopped when she drew back. "I'm all right."

"You sure?"

"Yes." She glanced back at the heavy iron snare. "Thank goodness you saw that thing. If I'd stepped on it—"

"But you didn't."

"No, I didn't." Her gaze met his. "Thank you."

"You're welcome."

There was no denying that someone was out for her, and they'd gotten closer to her than they should have. Gideon wouldn't let that happen again.

The anger he felt at her near injury didn't surprise him, but the sudden unfamiliar tide of possessiveness that welled inside him did. He didn't understand it. Ivy didn't belong to him; he didn't want her to. But the desire he'd been reining in rose to the surface.

Damn, he wanted her. Even more than he remembered wanting Eleanor.

The memory sobered him. He'd been blinded by his feelings before, and he wouldn't make that mistake again. He was here to protect Ivy, and that was all.

She was fine. Thanks to Gideon, Ivy didn't have even a scratch. Still, her nerves twitched at every noise, and it seemed as though just a hiccup might make her shatter.

Tears stung the backs of her eyes. Someone meant to do her harm. Who? Why? Did they want to kill her? Ruin her business? From the poems to the creepily detailed drawings, everything had grown more threatening. The dead animals, now a vicious trap.

With a shudder, she pushed the thoughts away. She

needed to stay busy. Not only to keep from losing her composure, but also to keep her mind off how she'd wanted to give herself over to Gideon when he had wrapped her in his arms. She'd felt safe and protected, and it vexed her. She didn't need a man for that or anything else.

An hour after her close call, Ivy was doing laundry. She had washed the bedding in the kettle kept hot by the fire beneath then rinsed everything in the big pot full of cold water. She focused only on the moment— the warmth of the sun on her neck, wringing water from the sheets.

Walking over to the clothesline that stretched between two posts a few yards away, she hefted the wet bulk of the linens. Tossing the heavy weight over the end of the line, she reached for the sheet on top.

"Let me help you."

At the sound of Gideon's voice right behind her, she jumped. Her heart gave a painful kick.

"Sorry." He ducked under the line to the other side. "I didn't mean to startle you."

"It doesn't take much," she said wryly.

Thunder bounded up to her, and Ivy bent to scratch behind the pup's ears.

Studying her, Gideon draped the sheet over the line. "Are you okay? From before, I mean."

"Yes." She lifted another piece of bedding. "I stripped your bunk, too."

He nodded, taking the linen from her and arranging it beside the other piece. "I hung that trap on the wall in the barn. Won't hurt anybody now."

"Thank you." She really didn't want to talk about this. Dwelling on it chipped away at her resolve not to cry. Drawing in his dark male scent, her gaze wandered to his big hands. He easily managed the unwieldy laundry. Just as easily as he'd handled her after snatching her out of harm's way.

Despite the size of his hands, his touch had been gentle. Reassuring. Just to be held without being expected to give anything in return had made her want to stay in his arms. That had rattled her almost as badly as the near miss with the trap.

It still did. She needed him gone from here.

"Thanks for your help. I think I've got it now."

"Okay." He thumbed his hat back, his blue eyes narrowed on her. "You sure?"

"Yes," she said tersely, then softened her voice. "I'm fine. Really."

He stooped to pass under the line and stand beside her. "I didn't find any tracks besides the ones in the woods."

The reminder of what had happened had her swallowing past a lump in her throat. Tension stretched across her shoulders. She wished he would go before her poise deserted her.

His gaze fixed on her face. "I'll be in the barn."

"All right." She managed a smile, knowing he wouldn't leave until he believed she was fine.

Finally, he seemed satisfied and walked back the way he'd come, the pup trotting behind. Relieved, she closed her eyes briefly then got back to washing clothes.

Slanting the washboard into the kettle of hot water, Ivy scooped up a handful of soap and began scrubbing her undergarments, corsets first. Each rinsed and wrung-dried piece went into the basket at her feet. It took all her focus to keep her attention strictly on her task, but she refused to let her mind wander.

"Miss Ivy?" This time, Gideon called from farther away.

Her pulse skipped, but she appreciated that he hadn't waited until he was right on top of her.

He walked up and leaned against the end post, crossing one booted foot over the other. The pup wasn't with him this time.

"I'm fixin' to mix whitewash unless there's something you'd like me to do first."

"I don't think so." She squeezed water out of a petticoat. She knew he hadn't come to tell her that.

"How're you doing?"

"I'm okay." Pinning the petticoat to the clothesline, she tried to temper her tone, but it came out short. "Please don't be so concerned."

"All right, then." He turned and strode across the yard.

She continued working, watching his long, easy gait until he disappeared around the corner of the house.

She did appreciate what he'd done for her and the fact that he cared for her well-being, but having him near made her want to lean on him. She didn't want to give in to the urge. She wouldn't.

Just as she pulled the last damp tablecloth out of the basket, she heard an approaching horse.

She draped the linen over the line then moved up the side of the house, reaching the porch as a buggy rolled up to the front. At the sight of the dark-haired couple in the carriage, she smiled. It was Sheriff Farrell and his wife, Meg.

Ivy was always pleased to see her friends, but their

arrival also gave her something to focus on besides the trap. And Gideon.

There was no sign of her rescuer. He must have already whitewashed his way around to the other side of the house.

Braking at the fence, Josh hopped out of the buggy and went around to help his wife out.

"Ivy!" Her petite friend hurried through the gate and across the yard toward her.

Badge glinting in the late-morning sunlight, the sheriff looped the buggy reins around the hitching rail and followed his wife. "McCain said you wanted me to come out to the farm."

Meg gave Ivy a quick hug. "The deputy also told Josh there was a big man with you in town yesterday."

She nodded. "Gideon Black. He's a friend of Smith's."

Josh stepped around his wife to give Ivy a hug, too. "Why the message? Is something going on?"

"Some strange things have been happening."

"Like what?" Pushing back his light-colored cowboy hat, the lawman's black eyes narrowed.

"Well, it started with these poems. At first, I thought they were from a secret admirer."

"And were they?" Meg's green eyes lit up.

Ivy sent her friend a look. The other woman had made no secret of wanting Ivy to find another man. She didn't want another one. "They weren't lover's poems. They were...odd."

Suddenly, her skin prickled. The air changed. She felt Gideon's presence before she saw him.

Glancing past Josh, Ivy saw her rugged guest round the corner of the fence and head their way. She pulled her gaze from his wide shoulders, the flex of muscle in his powerful thighs. "Then the drawings started appearing."

"Drawings?" Josh frowned.

Gideon reached the gate and stepped through.

"Pictures of my house," Ivy explained. "Growing more detailed each time."

"The inside of your house or the outside?" Josh asked.

Gideon reached them, and Meg turned. So did her husband.

A good three or four inches shorter than Gideon, Josh was brawny, as sturdy as a mountain. Gideon's gaze dropped to his badge as he moved to Ivy's side.

Meg smiled, but Josh studied the other man curiously.

Ivy waved a hand. "Josh and Meg Farrell, meet Gideon Black."

Josh offered his hand and after a slight hesitation, Gideon shook it. He glanced at Ivy. "Did you tell him?"

"I was getting ready to."

"Tell me what?"

"Someone tried to hurt her earlier," Gideon said flatly.

Josh's gaze sliced to Ivy. "Hurt how?"

"By setting an animal trap," Gideon answered. "The thing could have taken off her foot."

"Oh, my," Meg said.

Josh's jaw tightened. "How do you know it was for Ivy?"

"It was placed in her path, a spot where she would step down from the back porch."

"Anyone could step off there."

"True, but today is Friday. Laundry day. Anyone who's been watching the house would know that."

Josh looked at Ivy. "Do you do laundry the same day every week?"

"Yes. I have to keep clean linens for the stage passengers, so I work around the stage schedule."

Gideon scrubbed a hand down his face. "The trap wasn't there yesterday."

Alarm crossed Meg's gamine features as she turned to Ivy. "What exactly do these drawings show?"

"They're detailed illustrations of the house, front view only."

"Except for one," Gideon said, his deep voice prodding her.

Josh's brows snapped together.

"That one was a view of my bedroom," Ivy explained.

"Oh!" Meg squeezed Ivy's hand.

The sheriff stiffened. "How long has this been going on?"

"A few months."

"A few months!" Josh exclaimed. "Why didn't you say anything?"

"Until four days ago, I didn't feel threatened."

"What happened four days ago?"

Gideon answered in a tight voice. "One of the stage line's horses was killed. With a knife."

Meg gasped.

Ivy blinked back tears. "So was Tug."

"No," the other woman said softly. "I'm so sorry."

Josh's features went stone-hard. "Someone killed your dog?"

"Gideon and I found him a couple of days ago."

"Knife wound, just like the horse," he said.

"I want a look," Josh demanded.

Ivy nodded. "Tug's buried, but the horse is in a gully on the back side of the west pasture. I'll show you."

"I'll do it," Gideon said quietly to her. "The stench will be even worse than it was the other day."

After her close call this morning, Ivy wasn't sure she had the stomach to see the dead animal again. "All right."

Meg looped her arm through Ivy's. "Let's go inside and talk."

Ivy didn't want to talk about nearly getting her foot snapped off. Nor did she want to talk about Gideon, she decided as she saw her friend slide a sideways look at the big man next to Josh.

As Gideon started around her, Ivy touched his arm. "Thanks."

"Sure."

Gideon's arm burned where she'd put her hand. That same sizzle beneath the skin. The way he'd felt all over when he held her earlier. Realizing he was standing there like a half-wit, he turned to Josh. "The trap's in the barn. We'll stop there first."

The lawman nodded, keeping pace with Gideon as they strode across the thick grass toward the barn.

As he walked into the barn with the sheriff, Gideon recounted the story of where they'd found Ivy's missing dog and the pup he had protected with his own body. He gestured to the whelp sleeping beside Gideon's bunk in a crate. Ivy had switched the hay for fabric scraps.

Josh shook his head. "It's a real shame about Tug.

I bet his death hit Ivy hard. She and Tom raised that mutt from a baby."

"That's what she said." Gideon wanted to ask more about Ivy's husband, but he kept quiet. He didn't need to know anything so personal. It was none of his business.

Moving past the row of stalls and toward the opposite set of doors, Gideon led the sheriff to the wall where the tack was kept. Bridles, harnesses and bits hung neatly from nails along one wide section.

Josh halted in front of the trap, his eyes widening. He touched the wicked metal teeth of the trap. "Hell, that thing could take down a bear."

"Yeah." Gideon clenched his fists then unclenched them.

"Do you have any idea who could be doing this?"

"No, but it's a man." He pulled the pieces of broken branch from his trouser pocket, explaining how he'd found the campfire remains in the woods fronting Ivy's house. "And there's a tree that provides the exact view of the drawings she received."

"I want to see those drawings and the place where you found signs of the fire."

"All right, and on the way to the gully, I'll show you where the trap was set."

The sheriff's mouth tightened in a grim line. "She should've told me all of this from the beginning."

"It started before Christmas. I think the only person she mentioned it to back then was her brother."

"Confound it!" Josh's mouth flattened in disapproval as the two men left the barn.

Gideon stopped at the back porch and indicated the spot where he'd found the trap. He could still hear that screeching, brutal snap.

After a moment, he and the other man continued to the back fence. They walked through the gate and past the grazing Holsteins, moving across the rolling pasture toward the gully.

"It's lucky you showed up when you did." Farrell glanced over.

"It wasn't luck. Miss Ivy wired Smith. He couldn't come, so he sent me."

"How long have you and Smith been friends?"

"Two years." Tension coiled through Gideon's body. If the lawman knew anything about Smith's past, he would realize where Gideon had met Ivy's brother.

Josh's gaze leveled on Gideon, scrutinizing. Heavy.

Yeah, he knew. Spine rigid, Gideon waited, expecting a barrage of questions, wondering if the sheriff would accept that Ivy was being protected by a man who'd done time.

The other man's gaze fell on the Peacemaker slung low on Gideon's hip. He hoped Farrell didn't have a problem with an ex-convict carrying a gun, because he wasn't going without. Not when he was here to guard Ivy.

The lawman fell silent as they continued past stands of oaks and pines. Once they reached the gully, Gideon followed Farrell down the dirt walls to the bottom. The odor of death and decay hung in the air like a fog, and he jerked his bandanna up to cover his nose and mouth. Even bigger chunks of the horse's flesh and hide were missing than the last time Gideon had seen the animal.

"Ugh." Josh pulled his own neckerchief over his nose then knelt.

After examining the animal's carcass, he stood. "You're right. Killed with a knife. Long wide blade."

"Yeah." Overwhelmed by the stink, Gideon started back up the side of the gully, and the sheriff followed.

Once back on level ground, the other man's gaze swept the lush pastureland. "Where did you find Tug?"

"Beyond here, next to the river."

"I'd like to see that place, too."

"All right."

Several minutes later, after Josh had seen the tree hollow where Gideon and Ivy had found her dog, the men started back to the house.

"Was it the dog that made you decide there's a threat to Ivy? Or the trap?"

"Both. The missing chickens and the dead horse affect her business. The dog and the trap are personal." He stepped around a gopher hole, his anger sparking again. "I asked her if there was anyone who might want the land or just want to cause trouble for her. She said no."

"You found the campfire remains in the woods that border the road in front of Ivy's house."

Gideon nodded.

A thoughtful expression settled on Farrell's chiseled features. He and Gideon walked through the thick alfalfa and up the hill toward the house. The caw of a crow and the brush of grass against their trousers were the only sounds around them.

Josh glanced over. "That looks like a rope burn around your neck."

Here came the questions about prison. "It is, of a sort."

"What sort?"

Hell. He didn't want to talk about this, but if Farrell decided to find out anything about Gideon, it wouldn't be difficult for the lawman. "Strips of bed sheets braided into a rope."

"Prison sheets?"

Gideon tensed.

"Where were you?"

"Leavenworth."

Josh grimaced. "Why were you in?"

"For murdering a man."

"You did it?"

"Yes, and it wasn't in self-defense," he added before the sheriff could ask.

"Was the man posing a danger to someone else?"

The question took Gideon aback. Smith was the only person who'd ever asked that. "Yes."

"You served all your time?"

Nerves stretched taut, Gideon gave a short nod.

They passed through the back gate and walked around the house toward the woods beyond.

When the sheriff didn't ask anything further, Gideon frowned. Was that all the lawman wanted to know? "You ain't got no more— Do you have more questions?"

"Have you told Ivy about it?"

"Yes."

"Does she know you killed in defense of someone else?"

"No." And Gideon didn't want her to know. The less she knew about him, the better. Still, he couldn't stop the sheriff from telling her.

Josh considered him as they crossed the road. "Ivy should probably know everything."

The idea of that wound Gideon tighter than an eight-day watch. "My past is ugly, and it's done. I don't want any part of it to touch her. Besides, she has enough to handle with what's going on."

"True, but I still think you should consider telling her. Women are funny about things like that."

Women were funny about a lot of things, thought Gideon. Neither he nor Ivy needed to be tangled up in each other's lives more than absolutely necessary. He imagined she felt the same.

If his past put her at risk, Gideon might consider telling her everything, but she wasn't in danger because of him. "And if I don't tell her, will you?"

As they reached the edge of the woods, Farrell shrugged. "Your call, but I think it would be a mistake."

The thought of Ivy knowing how stupid he had been twisted his gut. Did he really need to tell her? He didn't know.

In short order, he'd shown the other man the spot where he'd found the campfire remains and the tree that provided a perfect view of the goings-on at the farm.

The lawman then examined the second branch Gideon had set in place near the bois d'arc tree using a small rock at either end. Josh rose, admiration glinting in his eyes. "I like how you rigged this up."

"You can still see the outline of the boot print. The size and depth of the imprint make it clear it belongs to a man."

"Who the hell is doing this?" Frustration laced Josh's words.

"That's what Miss Ivy and I are trying to find out."

"I'd say leave her out of it, but I know that would be like trying to rope the wind. I'm glad she has someone out here with her."

"I guess she's lived out here alone since her husband died?"

"Yeah."

Gideon wanted to know more. Even as he told himself to leave it be, he asked, "Did you know Powell?"

"Yes. After the war, he was never the same."

Sadly, Gideon could say the same about a lot of people. "How do you mean?"

"Tom didn't drink much before he left, but after he returned home, he liked his liquor."

That was probably why Ivy didn't hold with alcohol. "Was he a mean drunk?"

"I never saw that or heard it. I hope not."

Gideon recalled his questions to Ivy in the barn about her late husband. She hadn't wanted to talk about him at all. Because the loss was still too painful or for some other reason? She hadn't acted as if she'd been afraid of the man. She hadn't acted as if she missed him much, either.

She'd shut Gideon out at the first mention of Tom Powell. He hadn't been able to read her.

He and the other man walked through the front gate. Farrell lowered his voice. "Do you think she's all right after that business with the trap?"

"She says so."

The other man frowned. "But?"

"She was real shaken up." He had been, too. Rattled enough that he hadn't wanted to let her out of his sight. "But she gathered herself pretty quickly. Almost as if she wanted to pretend it hadn't happened."

"Hmph." The lawman didn't seem to know what to make of that.

Gideon sure as hell didn't. What he knew about women wouldn't cover the head of a nail.

"Black, I want you to contact me the next time something happens."

"All right."

"Can you show me those drawings?"

"Sure."

They went into the house and found the illustrations on the large kitchen table, where Ivy had left them after showing them to Meg. As Josh scoured the illustrations, Gideon watched Ivy. She was still pale, but that was the only sign of what had happened earlier. Was she really fine?

The sheriff put down the last sketch, frowning at Ivy. "Why don't you come back to town with us?"

Though Gideon didn't like the idea, it might be best for her.

"I've already tried to convince her," Meg said, frustration clouding her green eyes.

"There are two of us to keep watch." Ivy squeezed the other woman's hand. "Everything will be fine."

Neither Josh nor his wife looked convinced. Gideon could help ease their minds. "I'll be staying on the porch for a while."

He carefully watched Ivy's reaction, expecting a protest. When she didn't, he knew she was a lot more affected by her close call with the trap than she let on. The whole idea of it still shook Gideon to the core. The admission didn't sit well.

After Eleanor's lethal damsel-in-distress ruse had cost him so much, Gideon would be a fool to get close to another woman. But as long as he was here, nothing was going to happen to Ivy, no matter how close he had to get.

Chapter Five

All day and evening, Ivy managed not to dwell on nearly stepping into that vicious metal monster. Though it lingered in the back of her mind, she handled it. Just as she'd handled everything since marrying Tom. Finally, it was time for bed.

She was exhausted, but couldn't close her eyes. Every time she did, she heard that deafening metal snap, felt the tight, firm clamp of Gideon's arm around her waist.

Just when she finally started to drift off, a picture of Tug flashed through her brain, of the night his leg had been broken. His agonized scream echoed in her mind. And as always, when she recalled the dog's injury, she was swarmed by memories of the night Tom died.

She threw off the quilt and got out of bed. After lighting her bedside lamp, she tried to read *Moby Dick*. She started the same page five times before she gave up. The events of this morning hung over her like a cold, dark fog. She was not going to cry.

She rose to look out her window. Clouds covered the moon, making the night hazy and gray. Through the shadows and occasional peep of moonlight, she could make out the barn. She knew Gideon was on her front porch. Was he asleep? She couldn't deny she felt better knowing the big man was nearby.

Taking her lamp, she went into the kitchen and paced to the other side of the large room. She had mending to do, but couldn't bring herself to sit down. That trembly sinking feeling was back. If she returned to bed, she was afraid she might break down, and she'd managed to avoid doing that all day.

If she stayed in the house, she would never get the sounds, the images out of her head.

Carrying her lamp to the bedroom, she set it on the small table near her bed then took her wrapper from inside her wardrobe. She slipped on the lightweight cotton garment and belted it around her waist. She looked down the hall toward the back door.

Gideon had put the trap where it couldn't hurt anyone, but Ivy would just as soon avoid that spot. Plus, they had set up a can inside the back door so that if someone tried to get in, the container would fall and sound an alert.

She blew out the lamp then padded across the front room, her slippers making a slight scuffing noise. Quietly, she opened the door and peeked out.

"Miss Ivy?" In the shadows, she saw him get to his feet and come toward her. "Everything okay?"

"Yes. I couldn't sleep."

"I'm havin' the same problem." He moved in front of her. Moonlight sliced across the lower half of his jaw. His blue eyes glittered as he searched her features. The concern on his rugged face had her throat tightening.

His worry didn't annoy her, but she didn't want that from him. He would want to know how she was. She would be fine if she didn't have to relive what had happened.

She took a deep breath. "May I get you anything? A quilt? A pillow?"

"No, thanks. I'm fine. I've got my bedroll."

She stared out into the darkness. Just being with another person helped. "Have you heard or seen anything?"

"No."

"And you checked the woods?" She wrapped her arms around her middle.

"Yes, and the barn as well as all around the house." His voice was quiet, patient.

Her throat tightened. He was protecting her just as he had that morning.

She gathered her wrapper tighter around herself, her gaze probing the shadows. The croak of a frog sounded in an offbeat rhythm with the cows' bawling.

"You've got company."

"What?" She started, squinting into the night.

"The pup," Gideon said, a reassuring note in his voice.

She looked down to see Thunder wobble drowsily around Gideon's legs. Ivy scooped up the whelp and scratched her behind the ears. The pup climbed up Ivy's chest, sharp little nails pricking through the lightweight cotton of Ivy's wrapper. Once at her shoulder, the animal snuffled and closed her eyes.

Ivy smiled. "I wanted to show her to Meg, but we got to talking. Before I knew it, you and Josh were back. How did it go?"

"Fine."

She glanced at him. "Did he ask you about prison?"

"He asked how long I've known your brother. When I told him, he realized we'd met when we were both at Leavenworth."

"Did you tell him why you were there?"

"Yeah. He's the law. There's no sense keeping it from him."

She recalled their conversation during breakfast that first morning. "Did you tell him more than you told me the other day?"

"A little."

She studied him for a moment. So, Josh knew more about Gideon than Ivy did. While that chafed, it was for the best.

Tension pulsed from the big man beside her. "You want to ask me anything?"

"No." She was curious, but she didn't want him asking questions about her and Tom.

"Do you want to sit? You can use my bedroll so you won't mess up your...frillies."

She was properly covered, but was wearing no undergarments. A little shiver rippled through her. She knew it had nothing to do with the cool night air and everything to do with Gideon. He was fully dressed right down to his boots. In the darkness, he looked even more imposing. Broad shoulders, deep chest. Solid. Strong.

She should probably go back inside, but she wanted to stay out here with him. She *needed* to.

Despite that unsettling realization, she sank down on the top step, her nightgown and wrapper billowing out in a filmy cotton cloud.

He sat next to her, taking up all the free space. And air.

She felt his regard, steady and curious, before he looked out into the night. "You have a nice place here. Someday I want a place like this."

"I'm fortunate to have it. Hopefully, I'll be able to keep it running."

"When are you supposed to hear from the bank?"

"It will be a few days. The mayor, who's on the loan committee, is out of town." She drew in Gideon's clean male scent, a hint of leather. His hands were huge and rough-looking, but they were also gentle. His mouth looked hard, too. She wondered if it was.

Jerking her mind from the thought, she glanced at him. "You said you wanted a place like this. Do you want to settle down someday?"

He hesitated. "I'd like to own some land."

"Is there someone special waiting for you in Mimosa Springs or somewhere else?"

He gave a sharp laugh. "No."

The firm definitive way he said it sparked her curiosity. Had there been a woman in his past?

"Have you ever been married?"

"No," he snapped, then tempered his tone. "Maybe someday. That's not in my plans right now."

"Mine, either," she muttered darkly.

He gave her a sideways look, but didn't comment, which was just as well. She wasn't telling Gideon Black why she was so set against the idea.

Thunder squirmed her way to Ivy's lap and snuggled in. Stroking the dog, she thought back over how solicitous Gideon had been. Typically, having a man check on her repeatedly was annoying. For some reason, his concern hadn't bothered her.

In the half shadows, she could see the strong column of Gideon's throat, the stern line of his jaw. There was barely enough light to make out the scar there, though she could clearly see the one that ringed his neck.

What had happened to him? How long had he been scarred like this? She wasn't going to ask. She'd learned her lesson about that.

Several times, his attention drifted to her and lingered. He shifted beside her. For a long moment, they sat there surrounded by the chirp of crickets, the throaty call of an owl.

He looked as if he were piecing together a puzzle. Finally, he said slowly, "What happened today was scary. Are you all right? Truly?"

"I am." Why was he bringing this up? The pup let out a snore, her fur soft beneath Ivy's touch. "And I apologize for snapping at you this morning."

"That's okay." His gaze, silvery-blue in the dim light, moved over her, putting a hitch in her pulse.

Again she recalled the way he'd held her. And why he'd had to. The biting snap of the trap ricocheted through her mind, and the fear she'd kept at bay hit her like an arrow. Swift, stinging.

She began to tremble. She didn't want to think about it, but the scene looped through her mind. Tears stung her eyes.

"I can't believe someone would try to hurt me," she burst out. A chill worked under her skin. "The loss of the horse and my dog didn't run me off, so now this polecat wants to harm me. Why?"

Her voice shook. Along with the fear, the anger she'd

locked up since the incident broke free. As much as she hated crying, she couldn't stop it.

Covering her face with her hands, she sobbed. About Tug, the dead horse, the missing animals, her close call with the trap. The pup whimpered, and Ivy felt Gideon take the animal.

She wiped her face, but the tears kept coming.

"Oh, hell," he muttered helplessly.

She agreed. Embarrassed and irritated, she did her best to stifle more sobs. Forevermore! After another moment, she quieted.

Gideon awkwardly patted her shoulder. She dried her eyes with the sleeve of her wrapper. She couldn't bring herself to look at him. He was probably working on how to get away from her.

"I'm sorry for crying. It just got the better of me. I didn't mean to do that."

"What happened was damn scary." His voice was low and soothing. "Scared me, too."

Her head came up, and she searched his face. He was sincere.

"I'm so grateful you spotted that trap. Thank you again."

"You're welcome," he murmured. Suddenly, slowly, he reached toward her.

She held her breath, recalling the feel of his strong, steady arms around her. Wanting to feel them again.

But his palm settled on the wood floor beside her hip. The warmth of his body reached across to her.

She stared at his huge hand for a moment. It was nice not to be alone. Not to *feel* alone.

She pulled her nightgown and wrapper up to her calf, staring down at her ankle. Her undamaged ankle.

From the corner of her eye, she saw Gideon clench a fist. She glanced over to find him staring at her leg. The hunger in his face had her sucking in a breath.

His gaze traveled slowly up, over the folds of fabric to her breasts.

That look burned like a touch. It put a different, sharper sting in her nerves. Made her feel stripped raw.

She swallowed hard.

He finally met her eyes. "We'll figure this out, Miss Ivy. Find whoever's responsible for what's going on."

It was a vow. The determination in his face made her eyes well with tears again.

His brows drew together. "If you'd like, I can take you into town. To the Farrells'."

"No." This was her home; she wasn't leaving. She still felt wobbly, but it was passing. "I'm not running away from whoever is trying to hurt me."

"It's not runnin'. It's stayin' safe."

"I feel safe here." *With you,* she added silently.

Astonished at the thought and slightly panicked, she gathered the folds of her wrapper and stood. "I think I'll go in and let you get some sleep."

He rose, too, helping her up. She kept her hand in his warm, strong one longer than she should have. Finally, she pulled away.

As she turned for the door, he said, "I'll do my best not to let anything happen to you."

Her spine went rigid. "You don't have to rescue me, Mr. Black. I can take care of myself."

"Yes, ma'am, I surely know that, but it can't hurt to have someone at your back."

As much as she hated admitting it, he was right. It was even harder to admit that she was glad that someone was him. Despite her best efforts, she'd leaned on him and while she didn't regret it exactly, she couldn't do it again.

That little slip of a woman was dangerous. To his willpower, his resolve.

The next morning while working on the pump at the front of the house, Gideon finally admitted it. He'd known since their first meeting that she would get to him.

She was the reason he hadn't slept last night. He was a light sleeper and would've woken at the slightest noise, if he'd been able to even close his eyes.

On the porch in her nightclothes, she'd managed to worm some information out of him, though it hadn't been about his or Smith's prison time. No, Ivy had asked if he had anyone special. All he'd said was no, but he hadn't had anyone since Eleanor, and now he knew he'd never had her at all.

The biggest surprise had been Ivy asking if he'd ever been married. Had she asked about a woman in his life because she thought the sheriff might know something she didn't, or because she was genuinely interested?

He'd always figured he would marry. Even so, he'd never given much thought as to who it would be, just had a vague faceless woman in his head. Not now. Ever since Ivy had asked, he'd seen *her* face. Her body. Pictured the two of them together, naked and not naked.

He greased the pipe fitting before twisting it on.

Yes, he wanted her, but beneath the desire, there was something easy between them. Even with her tears, which had seemed to surprise her as much as they had him, being with Ivy felt natural, unlike when he'd been with Eleanor. And Ivy had sought him out, though not to use him as the woman in his past had done.

Gideon's first instinct had been to comfort her, hold her. In the end, all he'd done was lay a hand on her shoulder. It might have been enough for her, but not for him. He'd felt her body plastered to his after he'd grabbed her away from that trap. He wanted to feel her again. Still, he wasn't going to do a damn thing about it.

After giving the handle a couple of quick pumps to make sure it moved smoothly, Gideon took a clean bandanna from his back trouser pocket. He wiped the grease from his hands, glancing down the road. Though still quite a distance away, he could see the stage coming. The sun's position, as well as the gnaw of hunger in his gut, said it was nigh on noon.

Dropping the oily rag into the wooden box that also held a wrench, hammer and pliers, he hopped the fence and strode across the yard to the porch. The door was open, and the scent of cooking meat and yeasty dough drifted out.

He poked his head inside, and for a moment he watched Ivy. She stood over the stove, damp wisps of raven hair escaping from her low chignon to curl against her delicate nape. The pale blue dress sleeked over her curves like a glove, outlining slender shoulders and a slim waist that Gideon itched to span with his hands.

"Miss Ivy?"

"Yes?" She glanced over her shoulder, her movements measured and graceful as she turned sliced apples in one skillet while stirring a deep pot of something with the other.

How long was her hair? he wondered. The silky mass had to reach at least to the middle of her back.

When he didn't speak, she prompted, "Mr. Black?"

He recalled why he'd come inside. "The stage is coming. I'll wash up then help with whatever you need."

She nodded, using the edges of her neat white apron to move the pans off the heat to the back of the stove. Taking the tin of soap from the shelf above the dry sink, she walked toward him. Her face was flushed from the stove heat, her eyes dark and sparkling.

His gaze slid briefly to the rise and fall of her breasts. He took the soap, turning to go until she edged into the doorway with him. "Conrad thought he would have passengers today."

Gideon pushed his hat up with the back of his wrist, staring at the approaching coach. "Looks like at least one trunk or valise strapped to the top."

As the stage drew nearer, he could see a man seated inside, as well as a woman with a pink bonnet. "You need me to fetch anything?"

"Not yet."

He took a couple of steps then paused. "I'm going to send everyone inside as soon as they stop. I want to check Conrad's footprints."

"Against the ones you found in the woods?"

"Yes. I don't believe they'll match, but I want to make sure."

"All right." She moved out to stand beside him on the porch.

Beneath the aroma of stewing apples and cinnamon, he drew in her soft magnolia fragrance. His body went

tight the way it had last night. Careful not to touch her—
which was damn difficult seeing how close she stood—
he slid the soap tin into his back pocket and went out to
help with the horses and passengers.

"Whoop, Ivy!" Conrad called from his high seat.

She waved then smoothed her hair back. Gideon
strode out the gate and met the stage as the driver
braked near the trough and newly greased pump.

He held the harness between the two lead bays as
Conrad clambered down and opened the door, placing a mounting box beneath it so the passengers could
disembark.

A man with a jaunty straw hat atop thick gray hair
gripped the door frame and stepped down.

"How do," he said pleasantly to Gideon before turning and offering a hand to the woman wearing a pink
bonnet. And a pink dress and pink gloves.

When the couple moved to the side, Gideon blinked.
Neither of the pair stood even as tall as Ivy! He'd never
seen such diminutive people, especially a man.

The woman, her dark hair streaked with gray, walked
over to Gideon. Hazel eyes sparkled. "Hello."

"Ma'am."

Ivy glided down the steps. "Welcome. There's a hot
meal waiting."

"That sounds wonderful, my dear." The man drew
his companion forward. "Albert and Maude Hargrove,
at your service."

"Ivy Powell," she said with a smile that flashed a
dimple. "Nice to meet you. And this is Gideon."

The men shook hands.

A man wearing a bowler hat poked his head out then
stepped down. His three-piece suit looked hotter than

hell. He stood just under six feet and was shaped like a barrel.

He came forward and extended a hand to Ivy. "Porter Nichols. Nice to meet you. Conrad says your food is the best in the Territory."

"I hope you think so after you've eaten."

As the passengers made their way through the gate, Conrad tossed Gideon an imperious look. "Take care of my team, would ya?"

Ivy frowned and started to speak. Gideon shook his head. Better to get Conrad in the house now so Gideon could examine the man's prints before they became mixed with everyone else's.

"Change the horses?" he asked the stage driver.

"Just feed and water. We'll stop in Doaksville, and I'll change the team there."

By the time Ivy got everyone inside, Gideon had determined the stage driver's boot prints didn't match those in the woods. Neither did the others. He unhitched the horses so they could drink from the trough.

After putting out a bucket of grain, he soaped and scrubbed his hands then splashed water on his neck and face. He used the other clean rag in his trouser pocket to dry off then went inside.

Ivy stood at the opposite end of the table, setting down a steaming bowl of chicken and dumplings. Another bowl full of the same was at this end. Mr. Nichols sat at the foot of the table with Conrad on his right and the older couple on his left.

Ivy saw Gideon and indicated the chair at the head of the table. "I set you a place here."

He could feel the stage driver's glower as he made his way to his seat. When he reached Ivy, she arched a brow.

He shook his head no to her unspoken question about Conrad's prints. He sat, though she remained standing, making sure each dish was passed around the table.

Once the plates were filled, she took the chair to Gideon's right. Their knees bumped, and he waited for her to move away, but she didn't. For a few minutes, the only sounds were utensils scraping plates and the occasional creak of a chair.

Mr. Hargrove glanced at Gideon. "Where are you from, sir?"

All over, he thought, but said, "Mimosa Springs."

"That's farther west, isn't it? Past Doaksville?"

"Yes, sir." He leaned toward Ivy, saying quietly, "This is really good."

Her lips curved, and his head went a little fuzzy.

Albert Hargrove addressed the man at the foot of the table. "What about you, Mr. Nichols? Where do you hail from?"

"Texas. I'm scouting future railroad stops for the Katy."

Gideon knew that was the more common name for the Missouri, Kansas and Texas Railway Company.

As the older gentleman began asking questions about the railroad, Gideon glanced around the table. He hadn't eaten with this many people since prison. At least here no one fought over the food. There was enough for everyone, including Conrad's three helpings of chicken and dumplings.

Mr. Hargrove wiped his mouth with his napkin and spoke to Ivy. "I know a lot of stage stands have been adversely affected by the railroads. Has yours?"

Gideon felt her go still, but her tone gave away nothing of the trouble that had come to her door.

"No," she answered. "At least not yet. The railroad isn't near enough to impact." She glanced at Mr. Nichols. "There's been talk for a few years about the tracks coming through here, and nothing's happened. Is there a real possibility of that now?"

"Could be, could be." The man directed his attention to Gideon. "If the Katy were interested, would you consider selling this place?"

Gideon gestured to Ivy. "I'm just a ranch hand. She's the boss."

The agent's dark eyes settled on her. "No husband?"

"No." She angled her chin at him. "Would you refuse to deal with me because I'm not married?"

Gideon knew she was asking because the bank might do that very thing.

"Not at all."

"Well, then." Her shoulders relaxed. "If the railroad ever comes through, we might be able to come to an agreement. I might lease a stretch of land to you."

"Do you have an arrangement with the stage line?"

She hesitated briefly. "I'm currently trying to work out a new deal with them."

"Very smart," Conrad piped up. "I'll put in a good word for you, if you want."

"No," she said sharply, then softened her tone. "I mean, thank you, but I hope it won't be necessary."

Irritation flashed across his handsome features.

Mr. Nichols reached for more chicken and dumplings. "Mrs. Powell, your food is excellent, as Mr. Conrad said it would be."

Ivy flashed a grateful smile to the stage driver, who stared balefully at her.

Mrs. Hargrove touched Ivy's hand. "Do you offer overnight accommodations?"

"Yes, ma'am."

Conrad asked about the Katy's current progress in building its line from Kansas toward Texas. Nichols explained that a land grant in Indian Territory had been promised to the first railroad to reach a certain point on the Kansas border, but the Indian Nations were protesting that Congress had no right to grant the land at all.

After serving dessert, Ivy turned to the Hargroves. "Where are you headed after Doaksville?"

"On to Boggy Depot, then maybe up to Stringtown before we make our way to Perryville to see our daughter," Albert answered.

Maude took her husband's hand. "We'd love to stay here overnight on our return."

"I'd be happy to have you."

Gideon noticed how adoringly the couple looked at each other. He wondered if things had always been that way for them.

Mrs. Hargrove shared a secret smile with Ivy and Gideon. "It will be like a little honeymoon."

"We try to take one every year," Albert said.

Conrad pushed his plate away. "How long y'all been married?"

"Fifty-two years." Albert beamed at his wife.

Maude put her hand over his. "We've never spent a night apart."

Loud enough for only Gideon to hear, Ivy breathed, "It's a wonder you haven't killed each other."

He slid her a look, recalling what she'd said last night about not marrying again.

Now that he thought about it, Gideon realized he'd

seen her at Tug's grave every day since they'd buried the dog, but not once at her husband's grave site. Did she visit the man's grave at all?

Mrs. Hargrove gave Ivy a sympathetic smile. "I'm sorry for your loss, dear."

She looked blank for a moment, then understanding crossed her features. "Thank you."

"It's not easy being a widow."

Ivy murmured something, then asked about the woman's daughter.

It hadn't escaped Gideon's notice that she changed the subject whenever her husband was mentioned. He was starting to wonder if she had even liked Tom Powell, much less grieved when he'd gone.

Conrad rose, shoving his long blond hair over his shoulder. "That was delicious, Ivy."

"I'm glad you liked it."

He glanced around the table. "I'll hitch up the team and be ready to leave in ten minutes."

The passengers nodded, pushing away from the table. After a quick look outside, Gideon decided Conrad didn't need his help, and he began to clear the dishes.

Mrs. Hargrove handed him her plate. "Miss Ivy is lucky to have you. You make a good pair."

They weren't a pair at all, but rather than correct her, he just smiled.

At the thunder of approaching hooves, Ivy glanced at the door. Gideon peered out, not recognizing the dun galloping up the drive or the person on its back.

As the animal neared, Gideon could see the rider was a young man. He guided his mount past the stage team and to the other side of the trough. The lad slid out of the saddle and hastily looped the reins around the hitching post.

He greeted Conrad and the passengers as the stage driver helped Mrs. Hargrove into the coach, then her husband.

Ivy looked at Gideon. "Who is it?"

"Don't recognize him."

The black-haired boy, lanky with freckled features, walked quickly across the yard and onto the porch, where he stopped.

Nudging his hat back, he grinned. "You must be Gideon. My brother told me about you."

"Your brother?"

"Hello, Coy." As Ivy came toward them with a smile on her face, the boy snatched off his hat. "Gideon, this is Josh's brother."

"Nice to meet you." Coy offered a hand, pumping Gideon's hard, but his attention was squarely on Ivy. "I brought a wire from the stage line manager."

"Oh, good." She took the message. As she skimmed it, the boy's gaze never left her.

The kid looked purely besotted. Gideon wasn't surprised. If he weren't careful, he might fall for her, too.

Shifting his attention back to her, he saw her mouth tighten and concern crease her features. She motioned Coy inside. "Have you eaten? There's plenty left."

"Thank you. I'm hungry as a bear."

"You always are," she said good-naturedly, but Gideon could tell she was distracted.

As the boy sat and began to fill a plate, Ivy walked to the stove. Gideon followed.

"Bad news?" he asked quietly.

Irritation sparked in her eyes. "The stage line denied my request to contract directly with them."

"Did they say why?"

She shook her head. "No, blast 'em."

She poured a glass of water and took it to Coy. "I want to send a reply."

He nodded, mouth full.

As the stagecoach clattered away, she hurried into her husband's office and wrote something on the back of the message she'd received. After Coy finished his meal, she handed him the note.

Gideon waited until the boy had ridden off before he spoke. "I wonder why the stage line manager didn't give a reason for turning you down."

"I don't know, but I hope to find out. I reminded them that this is the only problem that's occurred during the entire time I've been contracted with the mayor. And I invited them to come here, see things for themselves."

Gideon nodded. "Good idea."

She began to clear the dishes, and he moved up the other side of the table to help her.

"That was nice of Conrad to offer to put in a good word for you with the stage line."

"If I'd said yes, he would think it meant more than it does and want something in return."

She sounded as cynical as Gideon was. "He seemed on better behavior today."

"I figured he would be."

Gideon gave a short laugh. "Why? Because he had passengers?"

"Because you were beside me. The last time he was here, that was all it took to keep him from becoming too familiar."

She walked to the dry sink, and Gideon stared after her. Was that why she'd given him a seat next to her? She'd used him? Not as harshly or blatantly as Eleanor had, but Ivy had manipulated him just the same.

Teeth clenched, Gideon forced himself to acknowledge that maybe *manipulate* was too strong a word. It had been a knee-jerk reaction.

For as long as he lived, he figured he would probably feel that instant, sharp wariness at the idea that any woman could work him the way Eleanor had.

But Ivy's using him as a buffer with Conrad was nothing to get blistered up about. Soon after the stage driver had arrived, Gideon himself had witnessed the way Conrad had stood too close for comfort to Ivy, not to mention put his hands on her. Gideon hadn't liked it then, and he would have taken a hell of a lot more exception to it now if Conrad had acted the same way today.

A sudden stab of possessiveness had Gideon expelling a mental curse. Ivy Powell was not his woman. He needed to remember that he was here for her brother, not her.

Chapter Six

Over the next three days, Ivy and Gideon fell into a routine that mainly consisted of working and eating. There had been no more late-night visits on the porch, few conversations about anything other than the farm or the pup.

Since the stage passengers had left on Saturday, Gideon had been different. She didn't know if he was keeping his distance the way she was, or if he was just focused on chores. Besides taking care of all of the livestock, he'd put a new door on her root cellar and repaired the steps leading down into it. Just an hour ago, he had helped her move the rugs outside for beating.

Now she was in the barn, feeding the pup. Her gaze fell on the animal trap that Gideon had hung on the wall, and she shivered. The stage was due back today for its Tuesday run. Gideon had told the railroad agent he was just a ranch hand. He was more than that, although she wasn't sure exactly how to define it or if she wanted to. Protector? Friend? Both?

He'd certainly rescued her from that vicious metal trap and offered her a shoulder to cry on, which she had done literally. She was grateful for it, had even felt close to him, but she had done fine without a man for years.

While Tom had been off fighting, she'd handled everything. Things hadn't been much different after he'd come home. Though he had tried at first, it hadn't been long before he'd begun to take refuge in liquor.

Gideon had been through hell, too, yet he hadn't turned to alcohol. To her knowledge. The man could have other vices she didn't know about, but if he did, they weren't obvious yet.

When the stage still hadn't shown up by midafternoon, Ivy and Gideon ate the sandwiches she'd prepared. Gideon had cleaned out the chicken coop then disappeared a while ago to wash up in the river.

Because of his height, he would have to go downstream to get into water that would reach higher than his waist. An image flashed of him in the altogether—water lapping low on his hips, brawny shoulders glinting with water, the flat iron-hard stomach she'd felt when he held her after snatching her from the trap.

She wouldn't mind taking a dip herself. She'd just spent ten minutes chasing Thunder, who wanted to play rather than eat, but that wasn't what had her so hot. It was the picture of a naked Gideon. She wondered if he had scars besides the ones on his jaw and around his neck.

Forevermore! She pushed away the thoughts and bent down to pick up the pup, who had curled up beside the milk bowl. Thunder blinked drowsily.

Ivy's attention turned to the bank. On Saturday, Conrad had said that the mayor was due back early in the week. She hoped he had returned. She needed to know as soon as possible about her bank loan, especially after her disappointing news from the stage line. That still irritated her.

Lifting her apron to dab at the perspiration on her forehead, she heard a sound behind her. Gideon. She started to turn. "How was the river?"

Something hard struck her on the back of the head. Pain burst in her skull. Another blow sent her stumbling. She went to her knees then crumpled to the ground, vaguely aware of the pup's sharp yelps before she slid into blackness.

The next thing she knew she was staring up into Gideon's face. He was on one knee, holding her against his solid chest.

Sharp pain arrowed through her head. "What happened?"

"I was hopin' you could tell me." Concern darkened his blue eyes. "Do you remember?"

"Someone came up behind me. I thought it was you."

She tried to ease to a sitting position. He flattened a hand on her stomach, keeping her in place. "Stay put."

"Go after them. You could probably catch whoever it was."

"I ain't goin' anywhere, and neither are you." He ran his free hand over her shoulders then arms. "What all hurts?"

"Just my head."

His touch skimmed down her legs, making her tingle. "Nothing's broken that I can tell."

"Except my head."

Still kneeling, he gathered her closer. Thunder wiggled next to Ivy and licked her wrist, whimpering.

Gideon moved a hand to the back of Ivy's head.

When he barely touched a certain spot, agony exploded in her brain and she winced.

"Easy," he murmured. He lowered his hand, blood streaking his fingers.

Suddenly she felt wobbly and was glad he was holding her.

"We're going to the doctor."

"I think it's just a bump."

His gaze scrutinized her face. "Did he say anything? Make any threats?"

"No." Thunder put a paw on her skirt then eased halfway into her lap. "How do you know it's a man?"

"Boot prints. Can't tell anything about them except they're large." Gideon's mouth tightened in a grim line. "I'm wondering if the reason he didn't say anything is because you might have recognized his voice."

She felt as if someone were driving tacks into her skull. She squeezed her eyes shut. "How long was I out?"

"Probably not long. I was already on my way back to the house when I heard the pup putting up a fuss. I ran."

Ivy noticed his hair was damp, as was his three-button shirt. The placket was undone, revealing a V of dark hair on his chest. He smelled of soap and fresh air. Ivy's light-headedness passed, leaving her with a piercing throb.

"I think I can stand."

Offering her a hand, he stayed on one knee as she got to her feet. He moved one big hand to her hip to steady her. After a moment, he rose, though his hand stayed on her hip, hot and heavy and possessive. Reassuring.

She straightened then cried out at the stab of agony. "Oh!"

"Enough of that," he growled. He carefully picked her up and carried her to his bunk.

She remained sitting up, afraid to move her head or neck. "Don't budge," Gideon said. "I'm hitching up the wagon."

"Is that necessary?"

He gave her a flat look. "We're going to town to see the doc, then Farrell."

She shut up, because she did want to talk to the sheriff.

After readying the wagon, Gideon went to the house and returned with every blanket she owned plus all of the pillows. He arranged them in the wagon bed, piled on top of each other like a fat cocoon.

He frowned at his handiwork. "You'll still get jounced around, but this should help cushion some of it."

Thunder lay at Ivy's side, her little head resting on Ivy's leg. The pup leaped down when Gideon bent to pick up her mistress. Once again he was careful as he handled her, easing her onto the plump mound of coverings and pillows. Thunder yelped, jumping on Gideon's leg. She bounced and pawed at his shin, yipping as though she wanted to go.

"Hush up," he murmured as he plucked up the dog and put her in the wagon beside Ivy. "You ain't helpin' Ivy's head."

Thunder quieted, curling up beside her. She had noticed Gideon's grammar worsened whenever he was angry or concerned about something.

He climbed into the wagon and guided it out of the barn.

Ivy closed her eyes, holding a pillow tight to her

head in an effort to lessen the piercing jabs of pain as the wagon bumped along the road.

He glanced back frequently. "I'm sorry for the jarring."

"It's okay."

"No, it's not, but I can't do anything about it."

After a ride that seemed interminable, they reached Paladin. She directed Gideon to the doctor's house on the outskirts of town near the gristmill. He braked the wagon and jumped down to come around for her. After lowering the wagon gate, he pulled the makeshift pallet toward him then gathered her up in his arms.

She wanted to sink into the shelter of his chest, the strong arms cradling her. "My head is better now. I don't think I need to see the doctor."

"There's blood." He barely spared her a glance. "You're goin'."

She'd had enough of men telling her what to do, and yet her temper didn't so much as spark. That blow must have been harder than she realized.

Resting her head on his shoulder, she squeezed her eyes shut against the burning ache in her skull. He smelled of soap and leather and a darker musky scent that was distinctly him.

"Doc?" Gideon's call brought Roe Manning to the door.

The tall, lean physician let them in, leading Gideon to a separate room with an exam table, a glass-front cabinet full of books and instruments.

Gideon put her gently on Roe Manning's exam table and explained what had happened.

"Where's Thunder?" she asked.

"In the wagon."

Dark hair waving over his forehead as usual, her life-long friend leaned forward to look into her eyes. "Did you lose consciousness?"

"I think so."

"Just a few seconds," Gideon answered. "I was almost to the barn when I heard the dog start howling, and Ivy had come to by the time I reached the barn."

Roe glanced over at Gideon. "Did you see who hit her?"

Gideon shook his head. "He was already gone, probably hidden in the woods, and I wasn't gonna leave her so I could chase after him."

The doctor ran his hands over her shoulders. "Are you nauseous?"

"No."

Roe's coffee-dark eyes fixed on her face as he carefully felt for the knot on the back of her head.

Gideon's features were grim, dark. Forbidding. "Ain't there somethin' you can give her for the pain?"

"I want to look at the wound first. You said there was blood." Roe's barely there probing felt like a skewer through her skull.

She winced, noting that Gideon looked away, a muscle working in his jaw. His concern had a strange warmth moving through her chest.

The doctor stepped over to the glass-front cabinet holding bottles, a bowl and pestle. A basin of clean water sat on top. Ivy noticed the spots of blood on his fingers.

After washing his hands, he returned. He examined her arms and legs just as Gideon had, but she didn't get that little tug low in her belly the way she had when Gideon had put his hands on her.

Her friend stepped in front of her, lifting his hand. "How many fingers am I holding up?"

"Three."

"And the date?"

She told him. She had no problem remembering things, but her head hurt like the devil. Especially with the late-afternoon sun streaming through the clinic's windows.

"You don't need stitches."

"I guess I really am a hardhead."

They shared a smile. Olivia, Roe's late wife and Ivy's dear friend, had often told her she was too hardheaded for her own good.

Roe squeezed her shoulder. "I think that knot on your head is the extent of your injury, but I'd feel better if you'd stay here overnight so I can keep an eye on you."

"No. I'd rather go home." What if something else happened to the farm or her animals?

Gideon moved to stand next to her. "If you're worried about the farm, I'll be there."

"I want to be there, too."

Roe shook his head. "Ivy—"

"I can keep an eye on her," Gideon offered. "What do I need to know?"

The other man's gaze went from her to Gideon, curiosity plain in the black depths. She could tell he wondered what, if anything, was between her and her brother's friend.

Though his mouth flattened in a disapproving line, Roe said, "Keep an eye on that bump. It shouldn't start bleeding again, but if it does, get her back here quickly. I think her head is only bruised, but I don't want to take any chances. If she becomes confused, nauseous or if her vision changes, bring her in."

Gideon nodded.

The doctor frowned. "I'll get a headache powder. Maybe that will help ease the discomfort."

Gideon shifted to stand in front of her, his gaze going over her solemnly, almost impersonally. Checking her over.

"I'm all right," she reassured him.

"Are you up for talking to the sheriff? I can do it, if you aren't."

She started to step down from the exam table. "I can—"

"No." He closed one big hand over her knee, causing a funny dip in her stomach. "I'll bring him here."

As badly as her head was throbbing, that was probably a good idea. "All right."

He waited until Roe returned then slipped out the door. Even though Ivy was careful when she turned her head to watch him leave, agony razored through her skull.

"Here, take this." Roe handed her a cup of water with tiny white granules swirling at the bottom.

She swallowed the bitter drink and returned the cup.

The doctor's gaze shifted to the window. "I like him. Looks like you've got some protection."

"He's a friend of my brother's."

"Seems to be a friend of yours, too."

"Yes," she said quietly, wondering exactly when that had happened. "He came at Smith's request."

Roe's gaze sharpened. "Why?"

She explained about the incidents of the past few

months, including the murder of the stage line's horse and her dog.

When she told him about the trap, his handsome features hardened. "Any idea why this stuff is happening?"

"No."

The door opened and Gideon stepped inside, followed by Josh.

The lawman came toward her, concern etched on his face. "Gideon told me what happened."

After assuring him she was fine, he agreed with Roe that she shouldn't go home yet. "If Meg were here, she would come out to stay with you, but she's in Doaksville until tomorrow."

Ivy knew she was checking on her sickly mother. "I'll be fine. Gideon will be there."

For which she was very glad.

Hands braced on his hips, the sheriff glanced at Gideon and Ivy. "I'll come by later to check on things."

"Thanks."

He turned to Ivy. "I'm glad you're not hurt worse."

She nodded, the throbbing in her head turning into a dull, widespread ache.

After Josh left, Roe gave Gideon several packets of headache powder, just in case Ivy needed them.

The doctor leveled a look on her. "You're leaving against my better judgment."

"I know, but I'll be fine."

He shook his head.

From the window, Gideon glanced at Ivy. "Will you be okay here for a few minutes? I want to send a wire to Smith."

"About this?"

"Yes." He leveled his gaze on her. "And don't ask me not to."

"I won't." It was good he'd thought of it; she hadn't.

Surprise lit his eyes. "Okay."

She sighed. "I guess I need to send a message, too. To my parents and my brother. I need to ask them for money."

Just the thought had her face heating in embarrassment. "I'll do it for you, if you're all right with that."

She nodded, feeling half-spent. Her head still pounded. "Thank you."

"You tell me what you want to say, and I'll get it right."

Lowering her voice, she gave him the message. Before he left, he checked her over once more.

"Stay put."

"I will."

Outside, Thunder howled.

"Oh, the pup," she murmured.

"I'll take care of her. Be right back."

Returning to the clinic less than ten minutes later, he helped Ivy down from the table, keeping one arm around her. Though she wasn't dizzy, her vision was a little blurred so she welcomed his help.

Roe followed them outside. "Nice to meet you, Gideon."

"You, too." He started toward the back of the wagon.

Thunder spotted them and barked, going up on her hind legs.

Ivy squinted against the glaring sun. "I'd like to ride up front."

Gideon's gaze moved over her face. "Doc?"

"If her head can stand it, I guess it's all right."

Gideon moved back to the front of the wagon and gently deposited her onto the seat. Thunder raced to the front of the buckboard.

Gideon caught hold of the pup and set her on the seat beside Ivy. She wasted no time crawling into her mistress's lap. Ivy stroked the animal's soft fur.

"Damn— Dang," Gideon said. "We didn't bring your bonnet from the farm."

"I'll be fine."

"Hang on," Roe said. "You can borrow one of Olivia's."

When he went inside, Ivy said to Gideon, "Olivia was his late wife. I didn't know he still had her things."

The doctor soon returned and handed over a faded blue-checked bonnet. Ivy took it, grateful to have some protection from the sun's blinding rays. The loss that had been in her friend's eyes since the death of his wife still lingered. She squeezed his hand.

He squeezed hers back.

"Ivy?"

She looked up to see Titus hurrying toward them from town. Gideon stopped, waited. Roe excused himself and went back inside.

When the banker reached the wagon, he frowned at the shingle hanging over the physician's door. "Are you hurt?"

"It's just a knot on my head." Anticipation swept through her. "Do you have an answer for me about the loan?"

He hesitated. "We can talk later. You look as if you're ready to leave."

"I need to know, Titus."

The older man grimaced, and she knew what he was

going to say before he said it. Her head started pounding even harder.

The banker looked miserable. "I wasn't able to convince the loan committee."

"I'm not getting the loan?"

"No. I'm so sorry, Ivy."

Even though she'd expected this, his words lashed at her. Her shoulders sagged. Now what was she supposed to do?

"How can they deny me? They know I'll pay back the money."

"I pointed that out several times," Titus said. "I argued more than once, but they just won't loan to a single woman."

"I appreciate your help, Titus." Her head felt like it might explode. On top of what had just happened, this was too much. Her legs felt like water. It was a good thing she was sitting down.

Gideon put a hand on her thigh. "You okay?" he asked gruffly.

"I will be." Though she didn't know how.

The distress on Titus's long features made him even more homely.

"It's all right, Titus," she said to her friend.

"If I had the money, I'd loan it to you myself, my dear."

"I know." She gave him a faint smile. Her stomach roiled, but she steadied herself. "Thank you for telling me and not waiting."

He shook his head, still looking distressed as he walked away.

Gideon hopped up beside her and gathered the reins.

He glanced over, pausing. "You sure you want to ride up here?"

No, she wasn't. Besides the ache in her head, the headache powder was making her queasy. "Maybe I shouldn't."

He came around to scoop her up then settle her in the back.

She gave him a small smile. "Sorry to be so much trouble."

"You aren't any trouble." He seemed to mean it. He eased her down gently onto the thick pile of blankets. "I sent a separate wire to Smith telling him about the attack. He can let your folks know. Shouldn't be too long before you hear from one of them."

"I hope not."

Gideon clucked to the team and lightly slapped the reins against the horses' rumps. The wagon lurched into motion.

She closed her eyes, uncertainty hammering through her with as much force as the headache. Her family was her last hope. If they couldn't help, she didn't know what she would do.

During the ride back to the farm, Gideon tried to leash his anger. Someone had just walked onto the farm and assaulted her. If it hadn't been for the pup's howling, he might have arrived after she'd been hurt worse. He'd nearly broken his neck in his rush to get to the barn and check out the disturbance.

Braking the wagon in front of the house, he scooted across the seat to hop down on the other side. He moved to the side of the wagon and froze, studying her. She lay so still, so pale that his stomach dropped.

"Ivy?"

The bonnet shaded her face, and after a moment she opened her eyes.

"We're home. How are you doing?"

"All right."

Pain still tightened her features, and she was wan. She started to push herself up.

"Stop that," he said, harsher than he intended. "Don't move."

"My head is the most sore thing on me."

"I don't care."

When she eased back onto the mound of quilts instead of arguing with him, he knew she hurt more than she let on.

He leaned over the side and smoothly pulled the bottom quilt toward him. He was able to move her without jostling, though that didn't erase the discomfort from her face. The pup whimpered, standing on her back legs to scratch at the side of the wagon.

Gideon set the dog on the ground. Thunder watched as he slid one arm beneath Ivy's shoulders and one beneath her legs then picked her up.

The specks of blood spotting her collar had him clenching his jaw tight enough to break a tooth. He reached down and flipped the gate latch with one finger then walked through.

Mixed with her soft magnolia scent were the smells of dirt and blood. And him.

"You can put me down," she said quietly. "I'm sure I can walk."

He shook his head. "I already found you on the ground once today. I ain't lettin' that happen again."

To his surprise, she rested her head on his shoulder

and slid an arm around his neck, her soft fingers resting gently on his scar. His nerves jumped. No one had ever touched the ragged mark that circled his throat. He didn't want *her* touching it, but what he wanted didn't matter right now.

He carried her inside. "Bedroom or sofa?"

"Bedroom, please."

Elbowing her door open, he set her carefully on her feet then eased away from her slowly, watching her closely. Rage nipped at him again, and he tried to stem it. "Do you feel like eating?"

"No." She touched the back of her head, wincing slightly.

Pain mixed with the fatigue in her voice, and there were dark circles under her eyes. Gideon hoped her eyes weren't blacking due to the blow she'd taken.

The sun sank low, painting everything in a fiery radiance. The light coming through the half-drawn shade in her room cast a soft amber glow over her pinched features.

She stood unmoving for so long that he started to worry. "Ivy? Do you need help?"

He hoped not. The last thing he needed was to put her in bed. His body was tight, humming with awareness just from carrying her inside.

"I want to change my clothes."

Oh, hell. He clenched and unclenched his fists, trying to force away the image of unbuttoning her green-striped dress and shucking her out of it. "Um."

"I can do it myself," she said testily.

"I don't want to leave you alone."

"I'll call out if I need you."

He hesitated then stepped outside. "I'm leaving the door open a bit. Just in case."

"All right."

As badly as he wanted to watch, and not only to make sure she was okay, he turned away and braced his back against the wall.

Her shoes thumped against the floor when she removed them. From the corner of his eye, he saw her hand go to her bodice.

"Did you see anyone running away from the house?" Her voice was faint. "When you found me in the barn?"

"No." He wasn't sure she should be talking.

"Did you find any footprints? Earlier, you said you thought the attacker was a man."

"I found boot prints, but I was in such a hurry to get to you that I ran over them. How're you coming there?"

"Fine."

"The prints weren't trackable so I can't identify them as the same ones I found in the woods." Gideon beat back the anger seething inside him. Who had hurt her?

"Did you find what he used to hit me?"

"No, sorry. I didn't come across rocks or pieces of wood with blood. *Nothing* with blood."

"He must've taken it with him."

"It's possible." The bastard might also have brought it.

Her skirts made a soft swishing sound, and Gideon imagined her stepping out of her dress. Then her petticoats. Then her chemise. A vision flashed through his mind of her raven hair falling down around her bare shoulders, soft plump breasts, the tight tuck of her waist.

Hell. He was getting himself worked up. She was

injured, for cryin' out loud! He cleared his throat. "I'm going to sleep outside your window tonight."

"No."

He straightened. "Listen here, I'll pack you up and take you to the doc."

"I mean, you're not sleeping outside on the ground. You can sleep in the house. There are three spare rooms on the other side of the front room."

Resting in a real bed sounded good, but he wasn't sure if it was the best idea. "Outside your window will put me closer."

"I don't want to be… Would you stay in the house? Please?" Her voice shook, and her next words were grudging. "It would make me feel better."

He understood finally that she didn't want to be alone; she just wasn't willing to say so.

"Yes, I'll bed down in the living room." Besides, being within steps of her, he would be able to see the door as well as the long hall leading to the back.

A barely audible moan sounded, then he heard the creak of the bed ropes.

"Ivy?"

"You can come in if you want."

He turned, seeing that she was in bed with the sheet and quilt pulled up to her chin. All he could see was her face and elegant neck. Her eyes were huge dark pools clouded with pain. Anger stirred again.

"You all right?" he asked.

"I will be. Did I already thank you?"

"For what?" His voice was taut. "Letting you get hurt?"

"Are you blaming yourself?"

He *was* to blame. There was no one else here.

"It wasn't your fault," she insisted.

He didn't agree, and he bet Smith wouldn't, either.

"The man walked up right behind me, and I never knew it. This is not your fault."

Maybe not, but it wasn't going to happen again. He turned away. "You should try to sleep."

"Mr. Black?"

"I'll leave the door open and stay right out here."

"All right." Her voice was wispy, as if her energy was waning fast.

After a moment, he moved, but he only got a foot from the door before his legs did some funny wobbly thing. Dragging a hand down his face, he braced a shoulder against the wall, a strange, dark emotion crowding his chest.

It took him a moment to recognize it was fear. For Ivy. His heart had flat-out stopped when he'd seen her lying motionless in the barn, so small and fragile. The pup pacing in front of her like a sentry.

She'd scared the hell out of him. He didn't know if he'd ever been that close to panicking about anything, including going to prison. He didn't even try to deny that she was coming to mean more to him than she should. Feelings like this were dangerous, and he had to get rid of them. Put some distance between him and her.

Which was going to be damn hard since the only way he knew to keep her safe was to stick to her like a burr.

Ivy made breakfast the next morning, then set about wiping out the glass chimneys of the kerosene lamps then trimming the wicks. Gideon helped her wash the windows, and she knew he did it so he could keep a close eye on her, but she found she didn't mind much.

Though the knot on her head hurt and there was an occasional shaft of pain, the headache powders had helped.

It was thanks to Gideon that she hadn't been hurt worse. For the second time, she was beholden to him, though she could've made her way to the doctor on her own if she'd been alone, provided the assailant hadn't hurt her more seriously. That was thanks to Gideon, too.

She was getting used to him, a man who actually pulled his own weight and then some, but deep down she was afraid it was more than that.

As she emptied a bucket of water out back, she heard the jingle of harness and the approaching *clop-clop* of horses. She walked up the side of the house at the same time Gideon stepped out of the barn. He joined her at the porch.

Shading her eyes beneath the brim of her bonnet, she saw a familiar buggy carrying Mayor Jumper. Conrad rode horseback and reined his bay to a stop beside the carriage.

Dread knotted her stomach. Jumper was here for the stage line's horses. She'd been expecting it. She just hadn't known when he would come.

"Mrs. Powell," the mayor greeted her from the buggy, his walking stick on the seat behind him. It was the one with the carved head.

She was hit all over again with the frustration she'd felt when the stage line had refused to do business with her. Had Jumper voted for or against her getting the bank loan?

Gideon didn't speak as he fell into step beside her. Again she found herself glad not to be alone.

Jumper eyed her from beneath the bonnet of his vehicle. "I've come for the horses."

"I kinda figured," she said under her breath.

The mayor glanced across the yard to the corral, where several horses roamed about. "Looks like they're all here. Except the one, of course."

"Yes," she said tightly. She'd boarded a total of ten here.

He gestured to the stage driver. "Conrad came along to help me get them to town."

"The livery will be hard-pressed to find room for them all. Are you sure you won't reconsider?"

"I'm afraid not."

"Fine," she said tightly before turning to Gideon. "Would you help them while I fetch one of my mares?"

He put a hand on her arm. "Are you really going to give him a horse?"

"I owe him one."

The anvil-hard line of his jaw said he didn't agree, but he didn't argue. As she'd asked, he stalked across the yard and into the corral to help Conrad.

Ivy headed for the back pasture. As she returned leading the brown-and-white mare she'd chosen, Conrad jogged out to meet her.

His hazel gaze moved over her. "Sorry about this. I tried to talk Leo out of removing the animals."

"I appreciate that." She tried to soften her tone. Conrad wasn't the one who irritated her at the moment.

He moved closer, though he didn't touch her. "Is everything all right? I stopped by yesterday, and no one was here."

"Things are fine."

He put a hand on her shoulder, causing her to stiffen.

"Elmer said he saw you at Doc Manning's yesterday. He thought you were hurt."

"It was nothing." Although her head had started to pound again when he and Jumper arrived.

The stage driver's gaze roamed her face and body, lingering too long on her breasts.

She narrowed her eyes, ready to lay into him. She had no patience for his nonsense today.

But when he spoke, there was only concern in his voice. "What happened? How were you hurt?"

"Just took a knock to the head."

"You're really okay?"

"Yes."

"Good." He sounded genuinely relieved. As they approached the corral, he took the lead rope from her and led the mare to the line of other horses already waiting. He slipped a bridle on the mare and tied the reins to the tail of the horse in front of her.

Gideon joined her. Watching Conrad, his face was like stone, his gaze hard and sharp. "He botherin' you?"

"Not really. He showed up here yesterday, and since no one was here, he wanted to know if everything was all right. He heard I was hurt."

"Who told him that?"

Surprised, she glanced up. "Elmer Wright."

Gideon's eyes narrowed.

"What's wrong?"

"I don't like that Conrad showed up after we left for the doctor yesterday. Did you ask him why he was so far behind schedule?"

"No." She could tell this really bothered him. "Do you think he's the one who assaulted me?"

"It's possible. He could've left the stage somewhere, walked here and attacked you then left."

"I've been assuming the same person who set the trap also hit me. Conrad wasn't around after the trap."

"That we know about," Gideon pointed out. "But he *was* around the day before your dog went missing."

"True," she said faintly as pain flared in her skull. She pressed a hand to her head.

Immediately, Gideon's blue eyes fixed on her. "You all right?"

"Yes."

He frowned, plainly skeptical.

Jumper scrutinized the horses then tossed Ivy a look. "Sorry it came to this, Mrs. Powell."

She doubted that.

Conrad mounted his horse and tipped his hat to Ivy as he led the string of horses away. As the mayor turned his buggy, the thunder of hooves had Ivy looking past both men.

Coy Farrell came tearing up on his dun mare.

Ivy's heart kicked hard. Maybe he had brought word from her family. If so, she hoped the news was good.

As Conrad and Leo left, Coy slid out of his saddle and jogged through the gate toward her. "Message, Miss Ivy. From your folks."

Sucking in a breath, she took it, vaguely aware that the boy also gave a piece of paper to Gideon. She unfolded the telegram and scanned the words.

They hit her like a punch to the stomach. Her heart sank, and tears stung her eyes.

"Ivy?" Gideon inched closer.

She wanted to scream, to turn into him, to run. She struggled not to do any of that.

Coy's concerned gaze slid tentatively to Gideon then to Ivy. "Do you want to reply?"

"Maybe later." Giving him a forced smile, she dug a penny from her apron pocket and pressed it into his hand.

After another questioning glance at Gideon, the young man went back to his horse and swung up into the saddle.

Anger and frustration made her want to scream. She managed to keep her anger under control until he rode off.

As dust plumed up from beneath the horse's hooves, Gideon turned, his blue eyes dark. "They can't help?"

She shook her head. Now what was she going to do?

"Is there anyone else you can ask?"

"No." On the edge of panic, she fought a crushing sense of helplessness.

He lifted his hand as though to touch her, then seemed to reconsider. "If I had enough money, I'd loan it to you."

She believed him, but it didn't really help her. "Thank you."

What was she going to do? Where could she turn?

Disappointed, discouraged, her temper snapped. "I can't believe the bank turned me down! All because I don't have a husband? Does having a husband mean I can repay a loan? I'm better with figures than Tom ever was."

Gideon watched her warily.

"I need that money. I've got to have it."

"Is there anything you can do? Do you have any ideas? I'll help if I can."

"If I want a loan from the bank, which right now

appears to be my only option, I'm going to have to marry somebody."

His head jerked back. "That seems desperate."

"I *am* desperate." She bit back a scream of pure rage. Another husband was the last thing she wanted, but if it allowed her to keep her home, then she would take one.

The whole idea made her skin shrivel, but it wouldn't be the first time she'd done something she didn't like in order to make things work.

Her mind raced, considering the possible candidates. Coy was too young. Titus was too old. Roe was too good a friend. He would still have to live here after she obtained a divorce—and she had every intention of getting one—which might hurt his reputation. It could damage hers, too, though right now she didn't care. She might need a husband in order to get her money, but she didn't need one for life.

All the other men she knew were spoken for. Except Conrad. Ugh. Just the thought made her shudder. She stared absently at Gideon, taking in the daunting width of his shoulders, the craggy roughness of his features. The scar ringing his neck. The massive hands that were deceptively gentle.

She stilled. The answer was right in front of her.

Why not? Gideon was already here. She wouldn't have to get used to someone else or put up with a second man. And there would be no danger of him wanting to stay once they discovered who was causing her trouble.

His allegiance was to her brother, not her. For just an instant, she wished Gideon felt that kind of devotion to her, but his loyalty to Smith could work in her favor.

Palms clammy, she shifted so that her back was to the sun and she could see his face, fully gauge his reaction.

"Mr. Black?"

"Yeah?"

"Could you help me?"

"Sure. What do you need?"

"I want—need… Oh, dear." She took a deep breath, her gaze locking with his.

Suddenly, he stiffened, eyeing her as if she were a coiled rattler.

She almost lost her nerve, but she forged on. "Would you marry me?"

Chapter Seven

His jaw dropped. "What?"

He'd heard her; he just wasn't sure he'd heard right.

"I *need* this loan. If I don't marry, I can't get it."

"I understand that part. What I want to know is why ask me?"

"You don't want a wife any more than I want a husband."

"That's true. Why is that?"

"What?" Her gaze shot to his.

"Why don't you want a husband?" He cocked his head, studying her. "You just asked me to marry you, and I know it's about the money, but I think I have a right to know why you're so dead set against marrying again."

She hesitated a long time. He stayed quiet, fascinated with the play of uncertainty then determination then stubborn refusal across her beautiful face.

Maybe she didn't want to go through the pain of losing someone so close to her again. But some of her past comments made Gideon think maybe there had been a problem between her and Tom.

Smith had never said anything about that, but Gideon could see why Ivy might not have told her brother if there were problems in her marriage. She was one independent woman. Besides, what could Smith have done? Fetched her home? Gideon didn't see Ivy walking away from a commitment she'd made, no matter how much she might want to do just that.

"Let's just say my marriage wasn't ideal."

"Because he drank?"

Her eyes narrowed. "How do you know about that?"

"Josh told me."

She hesitated. "Yes. It was bad because he drank. And I would rather not say more about it. Please."

Which was fair enough. It wasn't as if they would be marrying for love or even forever. "We'd be legally wed?"

"Yes." Ivy frowned, looking troubled. "The bank will expect you to sign the loan papers. That means you'll be responsible for half the loan. I don't like asking you to do that."

He wanted to smooth the furrow of worry between her brows. "Is there another way you can get the money?"

She shook her head then stilled, her midnight gaze weighing him. "You said you wanted a place like this someday."

"I can't buy it."

"In exchange for marrying me, I'll deed half of the farm to you."

"What? No."

Tears welled in her eyes. "I have nothing else to give you."

She had herself, but he knew better than to say it.

"This is a chance for you to get what you want. For both of us to get what we want."

He'd never thought about getting it this way. "What happens when we figure out who's causing problems and it's time for me to leave?"

For a moment, she looked startled, almost as if she'd forgotten his stay was temporary. "Well, you can either deed it back to me or you can hold on to it."

"If I kept it, I'd want to stay. You'd let me do that?"

"I owe you a great debt, plus we work well together." She shrugged. "We don't get in each other's way."

He found himself wanting to get in her way more every day.

"And I know you won't expect anything from me." She looked down.

"Anything like what? Something physical?"

"Yes." She swallowed hard, her face flushed. "That."

Gideon shouldn't push her, but he couldn't help it. His gaze dropped to her mouth. He wanted to kiss her, had been wanting to for a while. "What happens if one of us decides we want…*that*? A true marriage?"

"We'll renegotiate," she said.

He nearly swallowed his teeth. He'd expected her to shoot the idea to hell. "You *are* desperate."

"Yes, and you've got me over a barrel, Mr. Black. You can just about name your terms."

"Really?" He liked the sound of that. From what he'd seen, she wasn't often backed into a corner. Another man might take advantage. Or a man who didn't know how good she was with a pistol.

Her gaze flicked to his mouth then away. She turned bright pink. "Within reason."

She was offering him his own place, roots. Everything he'd ever wanted except... Gideon realized with a sudden jolt that *she* was what he wanted. And if he let on, she'd run faster than a six-legged jackrabbit.

"Are you sure about this?"

"Not really, but I need to do something, and right now this seems to be the only option. I know I'm asking a lot for you to give up your freedom."

He noted again her attitude about wedlock. There was no denying she didn't have much use for it.

He knew she wouldn't ask him to marry her if she didn't absolutely have to. She had no gauzy pink hopes of happily ever after.

Like Eleanor, Ivy wanted to use him for something, but that was the only similarity. This situation with Ivy was straightforward, no manipulation.

"If you help me out, there's a lot of responsibility involved," she said. "I don't want or intend for you to pay this loan, regardless of you signing the papers, but if something happens to me—"

"It won't," he said fiercely, determined not to let her get hurt again.

"If it does," she went on quietly, "I want the record to show half the farm is yours. My half will go to my family."

"Nothing's going to happen."

"Someone's already tried to hurt me twice. I'll feel better if things are handled this way."

"All right." He wanted to touch her, but didn't know if he should.

She put a hand on his arm. "If you want time to think about it, I don't mind."

"I don't. I said I'd do it, and I will."

"Are you sure?"

"Are you trying to talk me out of it?"

"No. I just want you to understand there's a risk here."

"I understand."

He was quiet for a long moment. She held his gaze, her fingers tangling in her skirts. Uncertainty and hope mingled in her midnight eyes.

She'd been attacked, refused a loan from the bank and had her last hope squelched by her family's inability to help her financially. Hell, he'd had better days than this in prison.

"If we're gettin' hitched, I guess you'll have to start callin' me Gideon."

Shocking him and maybe even herself, she jumped into his arms, hugging him around the neck. "Thank you! Thank you so much!"

He froze, holding her tight, feeling every inch of her down his body. Especially against his arousal. He wanted to kiss her so badly that his mind blanked for a moment.

Her loose inky-black hair slid over his wrists to the middle of her back. His face was buried in the silky, fragrant mass, his mouth so close to her neck that he could almost taste her. And he wanted to. He wanted to run his hands, his mouth all over her.

He should let go of her, but he couldn't make himself.

She drew back to look at him. She must have seen the desire in his face because her eyes widened, yet she didn't pull away. All he had to do was dip his head to brush his lips against hers.

For a heartbeat, she went soft against him then pain etched her features. "Oh, my head," she groaned.

He cursed. "It was the jumping."

"Maybe so." Her face was suddenly wan, her voice faint.

Still holding her, he walked into the house and eased her onto the couch. "What can I do? Get a headache powder? Will a cool rag help?"

"I think I just need to sit for a minute."

Gideon went to the cupboard. Taking out a square of linen, he wet it with water from the pitcher covered with cheesecloth to keep out dirt and bugs.

Sitting beside her, he laid the damp cloth across her forehead.

"Thank you." A faint smile traced her lips, but her eyes were still closed.

She looked so fragile. He wanted to settle her in his lap and just hold her.

So that he wouldn't, he rose and walked to the window. "Want me to pull the shade?"

"That's all right."

Compelled to do something, he lowered the isinglass anyway. Though the light dimmed, Gideon could still see her just fine. He wasn't leaving her like this. Not until some color came back into her cheeks.

After a moment, she opened her eyes, saying sheepishly, "Sorry."

"Is it better?"

"It will be."

"Do you still want to marry?"

"You haven't changed your mind, have you?" Her expression alarmed, she sat straight up, wincing.

"No." He closed the distance between them, holding up a hand. "Be still."

"Okay," she breathed in plain relief.

The soft smile she gave him sent his pulse into a jerky rhythm. Hell.

He returned to the end of the sofa. "When do you want to do this?"

"Now. The sooner, the better."

"What about your head?" He didn't like the idea of putting her in the wagon when she was in obvious pain.

"If I don't feel better in a bit, we'll put it off until tomorrow."

He nodded. Her eyes opened slowly, thick dark lashes fanning her cheeks. One dainty hand went to the cloth on her forehead. He could still feel the burn of her fingers against the scar on his neck. She hadn't acted as if she'd even noticed the ugly puckered flesh.

After a couple of minutes, her gaze cleared of pain. "I already feel better."

He didn't think they should go to town today, but he knew she wouldn't settle inside until they did. "Sit tight and I'll hitch up the wagon."

"All right. Thank you."

"Be right back."

On his way out the door, she stopped him. "If you'd said no, I don't know what I'd do. I know you don't want to marry any more than I do."

Maybe it hadn't been his idea, but he was nowhere near as opposed to it as she was. Although when he'd vowed to stick close to her, he'd sure never imagined this.

Gideon could hardly take it in. Ivy was going to be his wife.

Wife.

The word stunned him like a kick to the gut.

His deal with her brother hadn't touched on anything like marriage. He hadn't accepted her proposal because he'd promised Smith he would protect her. Or because he wanted to keep her safe. Gideon had said yes because he wanted *her*.

Thank goodness he'd said yes. Ivy's relief was overwhelming. If they found the preacher quickly enough, they could marry and make it to the bank before closing.

No one could've foreseen that she would need to marry, but Gideon hadn't blinked. Not for the first time, she was glad Smith had sent his friend.

As they drove to town, the ache in her head dulled. Lush pasture and trees flashed by, broken occasionally by the small purple flowers hidden among the alfalfa. They entered Paladin, and she directed him to the white clapboard church.

After braking the wagon under a leafy oak, Gideon came around to help her down. Big hands wrapped around her waist, sending a jolt of sensation through her. Her gaze locked with his as he set her on her feet. His blue eyes were deep, intense, hot. Rattling her composure for a moment.

The man set off a flutter inside her entire body. Or maybe that was caused by her delight over being able to get the loan.

Across the way, the school yard was quiet, the children back inside after their noon break. The rest of Paladin hummed with voices as people conducted business, punctuated every so often by the ring of the blacksmith's hammer against iron.

Reverend Simmons wasn't at the church, so Ivy led Gideon to the pastor's house situated behind the small building and up a slight rise.

Gideon's knock on the door was answered by the preacher, Haywood Simmons. The slight man with his warm blue eyes and ever-present smile invited them inside.

Gideon palmed off his hat, looking serious and slightly uneasy. Was he having second thoughts? Ivy hoped not.

Anxious to get to the bank, she introduced the two men then explained to the reverend what they needed. A smile wreathed his ruddy face, his eyes twinkling.

He gave her a quick hug. "Congratulations, my dear. I had no idea you were considering remarriage."

Turning to Gideon, he pumped his hand. "You're new here."

"Yes, sir."

"And evidently smarter than most of the men in Paladin, if you've already seen how special our Ivy is." Haywood gave her another squeeze. "I didn't know anyone was courting you. Dot will be tickled." He smiled at Gideon. "Dot's my wife."

The big man nodded, his expression still uncertain.

"I bet your family is happy. You're much too young to remain a widow. How did y'all meet?"

"Gideon is a friend of my brother's." She hadn't considered that people might take this for a love match. It didn't matter. She and Gideon knew what it was. "Haywood, can you marry us now?"

He chuckled, sharing a conspiratorial look with Gideon. "Don't want to waste time, eh?"

"No, sir," her intended said quietly.

Did he think she should set the preacher straight? She didn't care what the older man believed as long as they got on with it. "Haywood?"

"Yes, yes." The older man's bushy white brows drew together. "And who's to stand up with the two of you?"

Oh, bother. Ivy didn't want anyone standing up with her. Finding someone would only delay things.

Next to her, Gideon shifted. "I don't know nobody—" He broke off, clearly frustrated. "Can't you be the witness for us both?"

The preacher ran a hand through his shock of white hair. "I guess there's nothing says I can't."

"Oh, good." Ivy exhaled in relief, her patience stretching thin.

Her friend motioned at them. "Come into the parlor, then."

They followed him into a room off to the side. On the back wall, white muslin curtains fluttered at the window, hanging over a raised oilskin shade. A small sofa and crocheted rug gave a cozy feel to the space. In one corner sat two chairs angled toward each other with a table between.

Reaching around the kerosene lamp there, Haywood picked up a Bible and motioned them over to stand in front of him.

Ivy's stomach fluttered. She was really getting married after she'd sworn she never would again. But this would be nothing like her marriage to Tom. It certainly wouldn't end the same.

As she replayed the night he died, a sudden frisson of guilt rippled through her. She pushed it away. No, her second marriage certainly wouldn't end like her first one.

The preacher flipped through the Bible, glancing at Gideon. "Do you have a ring?"

"No, sir." Looking taken aback, his gaze shot to Ivy's.

She hadn't thought about a ring, either. She and Gideon were joining forces, not their hearts.

"That's all right," she said quickly. "I don't need one."

"Very well," the preacher said. "Let's begin."

Beaming, he began to speak the words that would make them husband and wife. Ivy barely heard him.

This was so different from her first wedding. Back then, she'd been married in a fancy white dress that reflected her hope and anticipation for a bright future, which had ultimately disappointed.

Her sister-in-law, Caroline, had stood up with her back then, and Smith had stood with Tom. She and Tom had been a love match, though it hadn't lasted long.

Today, she wore red calico. Tidy and practical. Just as her marriage to Gideon would be.

Reverend Simmons jolted her out of her thoughts when he firmly put her hand in Gideon's. Her intended's fingers closed over hers. His grip was gentle, but she felt it like a brand. Her pulse skipped.

She stared down at their joined hands. Hers was tiny next to his, pale against the sun-burnished darkness of his skin.

Haywood's voice dimmed, and Ivy became increasingly aware of the man beside her. He exuded a leashed power, a barely contained intensity. Unwavering control.

She turned to face him, suddenly realizing that he had washed up before leaving the farm. My, he looked nice. His dark hair was slightly damp, and he wore a clean shirt and trousers. The sleeves of his blue work shirt were rolled back to reveal corded forearms dusted with dark hair. She caught a whiff of soap and leather.

Her gaze moved over his broad shoulders, his strong neck, finally meeting his blue eyes. The molten heat there disconcerted her, forcing her attention back to the ceremony. Soon, she would sign the loan papers and have the money to keep the farm going.

After the preacher said a few more words and a short prayer, he smiled at Gideon. "Young man, you may kiss your bride."

Kiss? Ivy froze. She hadn't considered that at all. From the shock on Gideon's face, he hadn't, either. She inwardly groaned. This was what she got for letting her friend believe she had feelings for Gideon.

As the moment stretched out, Haywood frowned. Well, how bad could it be? Ivy thought. It wasn't as if she hadn't been kissed before.

Before things could turn awkward, she rolled up on tiptoe, intending only a light kiss to move things along. Something hot and fierce flared in Gideon's eyes, and he bent his head to meet her.

Their lips brushed, and the bottom of her stomach dropped out. Despite how hard his mouth looked, his lips were soft. That was her last conscious thought.

The world narrowed to only him. She drew in the clean male scent of him—spicy and dark and heady.

His mouth moved on hers. Gently at first, then decisively. It was slow. And devastating. The ground shifted beneath her feet. Dimly, she was aware of his big hands settling at her waist and was glad of the support. Even though Gideon didn't deepen the kiss, she felt herself surrendering.

She didn't know how long they stayed that way, perhaps only seconds. When he lifted his head, she could still feel his breath against her lips.

Warmth spread through her limbs like honey, and she struggled to open her eyes. No one had ever kissed her like that. As if they just liked kissing.

Though in a daze, she became aware that she was leaning into Gideon, her breasts pressed to the solid wall of his chest, her palms flattened against him. Beneath her hands, she could feel the steady thump of his heart. And that wasn't all.

He had pulled her right up against him, and he was hard. All over.

Heat flushed her body. Her own pulse skittered wildly as she stared up at him.

Dark color streaked his cheekbones, and his eyes blazed with desire. A breath shuddered out of her, and she slowly pulled away, hazily realizing she wanted him to keep kissing her.

The thought spurred her to step back. She couldn't believe she'd responded to him the way she had. Her entire world had been Gideon.

Feeling as if she were spiraling out of control, Ivy barely kept her composure enough to enter her name in the reverend's record book. Her mind raced as she and Gideon thanked the preacher and left.

Vaguely, she was aware of going to the bank, of telling Titus why she was there, but she felt outside of herself. Her lips still tingled, and she could feel the imprint of Gideon's hands at her waist. Oh, forevermore!

Reminding herself that this was a business deal did nothing to quell the flutters in her belly. She and her new husband waited while the bank officer drew up the papers. Ivy's mind raced.

She had never known a kiss could make you feel hot and tingly and…wanting. Tom had never been much for kissing. She reminded herself that her kiss with Gideon was really just a step in her quest to get a loan.

By the time Titus put the papers on the desk in front of her, she had managed to focus. Mostly. She carefully signed her new name, noticing that she and Gideon each had a separate signature line rather than him signing for them as a couple.

That was his doing, she realized. He'd made sure to list them separately, which would make it easier for her to deed half of the farm to him. Or for it to revert back to her if something happened to him. It made her want to kiss the man again.

After finishing the deed release that ceded half her farm to Gideon, Titus gathered all the papers, his gaze darting cautiously around the marble-floored building.

He leaned toward them. "Miss Ivy, I feel you should know that some committee members, like Joe Howe or the mayor, might think you and Mr. Black have married strictly so you can get a loan."

She didn't understand why those men would care about the reason she'd wed again as long as they weren't lending to a single woman.

Titus lowered his voice. "If you're planning to have the marriage dissolved after receiving the money, it will be considered false representation. The loan could be recalled."

"That's ridiculous," she snapped.

"Yes, ma'am, but I thought you should know."

"I appreciate that, Titus. As long as the loan is repaid, I don't see why anyone should care."

Before she could say more, Gideon slid a hand to

the small of her back. She stilled, acutely aware of his touch.

He nodded to the older man. "We have no plans to change our arrangement, Mr. Rowland."

"Glad to hear it."

After bidding the bank officer good day, he steered Ivy toward the door. She realized then what her husband had actually said.

They stopped on the landing, Gideon settling his hat on his head.

She nudged him lightly in the ribs. "You said we wouldn't change our arrangement. You meant between the two of us, not our deal with the bank."

"That's right."

She hugged him. She couldn't help it. "Thank you for everything."

"You're welcome." One arm curled lightly around her waist. He stared down at her, his blue eyes soft.

Her stomach dipped. Barely able to recall anything except that kiss, she fought to gather her thoughts along with her composure. She took a deep breath to steady herself. "You'll never know how much I appreciate this. I know you did it for my brother."

"That's why I came." He tipped her chin up with one finger. "That's not why I married you."

Her eyes widened, and she couldn't think of a single thing to say to that. With a crooked grin, he cupped her elbow and steered her down the street.

He measured his steps so she could keep up. Hit with a startling realization, Ivy shot him a look.

She had attributed her giddiness and excitement to

finally getting the loan, but now she knew some of it was because of Gideon. The man. His kiss.

She had the money now. She should've felt more secure. Instead, her whole world had gone topsy-turvy.

Chapter Eight

Gideon could not look at her. If he did, he would kiss her again. And again.

From the bank, they went to the telegraph office and sent a wire to Smith informing him of their marriage. As they walked out, Gideon readjusted his hat and offered Ivy a hand to help her step into the street. He steered her toward the south end of town, past the jail then the livery.

Her skirts brushed against his trousers, the line of her thigh teasing his. He wanted to pull her into him, hold on tight, but didn't trust himself to release her. He also wasn't sure how she wanted to inform people about their wedding.

Sliding a sideways look at her, Gideon replayed the press of her lips against his. When he'd realized she intended to kiss him, he had expected some perfunctory peck, but he'd gotten more. He'd gotten a response. A taste of her. He wanted another.

Teased by her soft magnolia scent, the feel of her sleek curves against him, Gideon hadn't been able to keep his body from reacting. And she hadn't backed away. For a few seconds, she'd looked just as dazed as he'd felt.

The sun's rays began to soften. Ivy glanced back toward their wagon in front of the church. "Where are we going?"

"I thought we could eat supper in town." He nodded toward the restaurant that sat on the lushly treed banks of the Kiamichi River.

Her eyes widened in surprise. "At The Wildflower?"

"Is that a bad idea? I heard it served the best food in town."

"It's also the most expensive."

"All right."

She frowned. "I can fix something at home."

"We're going to celebrate." He guided her up the slope of green grass to the white frame building. "That means no cooking."

"What are we celebrating? Oh, you getting half the farm." She smiled up at him.

"And you getting the loan. And maybe our marriage."

"You want to celebrate that?" she asked in disbelief.

"Why not? It's a good thing for both of us."

"Right. Why not?" she murmured.

He wasn't about to hint that he didn't have the willpower to be alone with her just yet. His body was still tight from the feel of her against him, and all he wanted to do was peel her out of that red calico and whatever she had on underneath.

Her lips curved, and Gideon found himself smiling, too. She was so beautiful, her eyes sparkling like polished onyx, a slight flush on her cheeks. As they neared the eating establishment, she drew him to a stop.

"Are you sure you want to eat here?" She gestured at the white two-story building with green shutters. "I don't want to be rude, but…can you spend the money?"

"Are you asking if I can afford it?"

She flushed, but nodded.

"I actually have some money," he said dryly. "From working for your family and other jobs."

"Oh. Good. I hope I didn't offend you."

"You didn't." He wondered if she had reservations about being seen with him. "If you don't want to eat in town, we don't have to. I just thought it would be a nice end to a nice day."

"It would. Very nice."

He pressed a hand to the small of her back, and they stepped up onto the columned porch that faced town. A second one with matching gingerbread trim overlooked the shimmering water of the river. As they made their way around to the rear of the restaurant, Ivy pointed at the extension on the north side of the building.

"The Tollisons, who own this place, are adding on a hotel in response to all the people coming to this area now."

Stella Tollison, the owner and cook, welcomed them and showed them to a table that was next to a wide window. After being introduced to Gideon, the short, rotund lady with a rat's nest of gray hair hurried off.

Square and rectangular tables of varying sizes were covered with white tablecloths and polished silverware. The hardwood floor shone with beeswax. Outside, the river gleamed like gold-streaked silver, spilling over rocks with a faint rushing noise. Only a few tables were occupied. Gideon and Ivy had this area almost to themselves.

When Stella returned with menus and coffee, Gideon ordered a steak and urged Ivy to get whatever she wanted. Some minutes later, the food arrived and he cut into his meat. It was tender and juicy. Ivy seemed to enjoy her smaller cut of beef.

About halfway through the meal, Mrs. Tollison came to their table with an older balding man who wore spectacles. "Mr. Black, this is my husband, Butch."

"Call me Gideon." He started to stand and shake the man's hand, but Mr. Tollison waved at him to stay seated.

"Pleasure to meet you, Gideon." Butch peered through his thick glasses. "How's the food? If anything isn't to your liking, we want to know. We'll try again."

"Everything's good," he said. "Best steak I've had in a long time."

Ivy murmured her agreement. Stella put a hand on the younger woman's shoulder. "We don't see you in here nearly enough. Is this a special occasion?"

"We're celebrating." Ivy dabbed at her mouth with a snowy-white cloth napkin.

"Oh!" Stella's blue eyes lit up. "What's the happy occasion?"

When Ivy hesitated, Gideon said, "We had some good news today."

Maybe she wasn't ready to tell other people about their marriage. This was her town, her friends. He'd follow her lead. "Congratulations," Butch boomed.

"Congratulations for what?" Mayor Jumper walked over from a corner table, carrying his silver-headed cane as usual. "Hello, Mr. Black. Mrs. Powell."

"It's Mrs. Black now," Ivy corrected with a smile.

So Gideon had been wrong about why she'd hesitated. He was glad.

Leo's eyes widened. "You two are married!"

"Yes." Ivy gave Gideon a shy smile that had him thinking about that kiss again.

His brain went fuzzy for half a second. Stella squealed and hugged Ivy. Butch pounded Gideon on the back. Disapproval streaked across Jumper's features before he blanked his face.

"Well." The mayor slowly extended a hand to Gideon, saying in a stiff voice, "Congratulations, indeed."

He wondered why the other man would disapprove. He was fairly certain that Paladin's mayor didn't know that Gideon was an ex-convict.

"Thank you," Ivy said.

Stella smiled warmly. "We'll leave you two to your wedding dinner."

"Yes." The mayor offered a tight smile. "Enjoy."

He tipped his hat and walked across the dining area. Gideon watched him hold the door open for an arriving couple. "Jumper didn't seem that pleased."

"No, he didn't," Ivy agreed. "Maybe he's heard about the loan and wonders if we're planning to divorce shortly."

"Like Mr. Rowland warned he might," Gideon said.

She nodded.

"I guess we'll find out."

They both turned their attention to supper. Gideon's mind raced with thoughts of the wedding, his bride, their trip to the bank. The deed she'd filed.

For the first time in his life, he had roots. A home that was truly his. Satisfaction filled him, and he let himself enjoy it.

He had been working toward this since he was fifteen. All those years he'd spent sweating and laboring for someone else's ranch before going to war. Surviving that to start working and saving again only to be interrupted by his years in prison. Now he'd gotten a place to belong.

His gaze wandered to Ivy. She'd worn her hair up for their trip to town, and he wanted to get his hands in it, wanted to see it down. From holding her hand during the ceremony earlier, he knew her skin was as soft as a cloud. He bet she was that soft everywhere. Her neck, her throat, her breasts. He wanted to find out.

He wanted her. A hell of a lot more than was smart.

She looked up, and twin spots of color dotted her cheeks before she shifted her gaze to the dining room.

She knew he wanted her. There was no way she could be mistaken about that because he'd pulled her flat up against him when they'd kissed. She wasn't ready to admit that she wanted him, too.

Ivy dabbed daintily at her mouth with her napkin then folded the cloth in her lap. "I'm glad you thought to wire my brother. The news will be better coming from him."

"Better for who?"

"My parents."

Would Emmett and Viola Jennings have a problem with Gideon marrying their daughter? Would Smith? Gideon had no idea how Smith would react to the news that his sister was now married to his ex-convict friend.

She tilted her head, studying him as if she knew his thoughts. "Smith will understand. It's strictly business."

Business wasn't what Gideon had felt when Ivy had kissed him back there in the preacher's house.

"My parents will appreciate that you helped me, and I'll be forever grateful."

If her gratitude came with more kissing, Gideon figured he could suffer through.

They had just finished their meal when Meg and Josh Farrell entered the restaurant. Seeing Ivy and Gideon, the couple made their way over.

The petite brunette gave Ivy a hug, her green eyes lighting up when she greeted Gideon. "We saw Titus, and he said y'all were in town. We thought we'd come say hello. What are you two doing?"

Before they could answer, Stella rushed up to clear the dishes away. Butch appeared behind her holding a single-layer chocolate cake on a large white platter, which he placed in the center of the table.

"What's this?" Ivy asked.

"It's our gift to you," Stella answered. The older woman suddenly looked uncertain. "Unless you don't like chocolate."

"I like it," Gideon and Ivy said in unison.

Stella grinned. "Be right back with a knife and plates."

Butch followed his wife back to the kitchen.

Meg pulled out a chair and plopped down next to Ivy. "Why is Stella giving you her best dessert?"

Ivy glanced at Gideon. "We were married today."

"Married!" Meg squeaked. She lowered her voice. "Ooh, tell. Right now."

Grinning, Josh touched his wife's shoulder. "Hon, they might want to be alone."

"No, it's all right." Ivy gestured toward the dessert. "We can't eat this by ourselves. Please, join us."

The sheriff looked at Gideon. "You sure?"

"Yes." Even though he did want to be alone with his bride, he wasn't about to do anything that might take that smile off her face.

Josh eased down into the chair to Gideon's right as Stella returned with the promised plates. Ivy served everyone a piece of cake.

After her first bite, Meg looked from Ivy to Gideon then back again. "Well, I guess congratulations are in order."

"Thanks," Gideon said.

Eyes narrowing, the brunette pointed her fork at Ivy. "Why didn't you say anything? You never even hinted."

"It happened suddenly." She lowered her voice. "Gideon agreed to help me get a loan from the bank."

"*That's* why you got married?" Meg frowned, looking so disgruntled that Gideon bit back a smile.

Josh cut off a large bite. "The bank won't lend to a single woman."

"That's right." Ivy sipped at her coffee.

"Did Haywood perform the ceremony?"

"Yes."

"So it's legal."

"Of course."

As the women continued to talk, Josh gave Gideon a long, measuring stare. "That was real generous of you."

"Not really. We worked out a mutual arrangement." He saw no reason to share every detail of his agreement with Ivy.

"After Ivy was assaulted in the barn, I'm glad you're sticking close. Although this is a damn sight closer than I would've figured."

Gideon had been just as surprised. "It's what she needed," he said gruffly.

Did the sheriff disapprove? It was too bad if he did.

A grin playing at his mouth, Josh eyed Gideon. "You ever been married?"

"No. First time."

"You'll get used to it," the other man said with a laugh in his voice.

"Josh Farrell!" Meg swatted him on the arm.

Gideon grinned and pushed his plate away as Josh finished his own dessert.

After a sip of coffee, Josh shot a look toward the women and lowered his voice. "Has anything else happened at the farm?"

"No."

Meg asked Ivy a question, catching Gideon's attention when she mentioned his name.

Though he continued to talk to the sheriff, he listened as much as possible to his wife's conversation with her friend.

"I'm glad you married again," Meg said. "Josh and I both wondered if you ever would."

"It's just business, Meg."

"It could be more."

Ivy didn't answer.

The other woman put a hand over Ivy's, and Gideon could barely hear her next words. "Are you afraid you won't be able to feel for another man what you felt for Tom?"

His wife looked distinctly pained before her expression flickered with what Gideon swore was loathing.

He didn't understand that at all, but he could see she didn't want to answer her friend. Rising, he caught her eye. "We'd better start back so we can make it home before dark."

She gave him a grateful smile. "And we need to check on Thunder. She's been in that crate for quite a while."

He nodded. "I'll take care of the bill."

When he returned to the table, he frowned. "They wouldn't let me pay for the cake."

"I told you it's a wedding gift," Stella said from behind him. She swept around the table and transferred the remainder of the dessert from the china plate to a tin one. After covering the sweet with a cloth, she handed it to Gideon.

"Thank you, Miz Tollison."

"Stella. I insist." She patted his arm. "You bring your wife here again, all right?"

He nodded, pulling out Ivy's chair. She stood along with her friends, and they all left the restaurant. As they walked back to the church, Gideon cupped her elbow, pleased when she didn't pull away.

After another minute of conversation with the Farrells, they said goodbye. Gideon helped Ivy into the wagon then climbed in and snapped the reins against the horse's rump. The animal lurched into motion.

The sun began to set in a wash of pink and orange as the wagon bumped along the hard-packed dirt road. Ivy's soft floral scent was faint beneath the smells of horseflesh and earth. She'd been quiet, and he wondered if she was thinking about the conversation with her friend. Gideon was.

Beside him, she clasped her hands in her lap. After a moment, she gripped the seat, then fiddled with her skirts. She sure was fidgety. Nerves? Or misgivings?

His knee bumped hers as they rolled home. When

she shifted again on the seat, he glanced over. "Are you having second thoughts about the wedding?"

"No, none." Her gaze met his, her midnight eyes earnest. "If I gave that impression, I didn't mean to."

He could still see her ambivalent expression at the restaurant. "I heard part of your conversation with Miz Farrell."

"You did?"

"About why you were set against marrying again."

She stiffened. "What did you hear?"

"Are you afraid you can't feel for another man what you felt for Tom?"

"I hope I never feel that again," she said fiercely before looking out over the rolling landscape.

He got the impression she wasn't talking about love. He wanted her to tell him more, but after a long moment, he realized she wouldn't.

She wasn't ready to tell him. She might never be. Something had happened between her and Powell, and Gideon wanted to know what. For now, he gritted his teeth and let it be.

They reached the farm about ten minutes later. Gideon reined up in front of the gate and jumped out of the wagon to help Ivy. He clamped his hands around her waist and lifted her from the seat, setting her on her feet.

The evening sunlight gave her velvety skin a golden hue. Her bodice sleeked over full breasts then nipped in at a waist he knew he could easily span with his hands. Despite her dainty frame, he knew she was stronger than she looked.

Her hands rested on his forearms as she stared up at him. If he bent his head, he could kiss her again. And for just a split second, her eyes said she would let him.

Then she pulled away and stepped around him, jittery as a spooked horse.

"Wait." From the wagon seat, he took the cake and gave it to her.

He didn't know much more about her first husband now than he'd known before he'd asked, except that she went skittish whenever anyone brought up the subject.

Ivy started through the gate.

"I'll unhitch the wagon and take care of the horses."

"Oh." She turned, looking sheepish. "I can help. I wasn't thinking."

"No need. I can do it."

She nodded, biting her bottom lip. He'd never seen her do that. What was bothering her? Was it him? She was certainly ready to get away from him. He should probably leave it be, but he couldn't.

"Hey," he said softly, "are you worried about something? Is it me? I'm not going to do anything you don't want me to."

"I know that. I'm just tired, I guess. Thank you again for today. Not just for…helping me get the loan, but for all of it."

"You're welcome." Her practical dress gloved her lithe curves.

He watched the sway of her hips as she made her way up the front walk to the porch. Hard want thrummed in his blood, but that wasn't all he felt. Again there was that odd weakness in his chest. Damn, he wanted her.

The only reason she had married him was to save this place. He'd almost forgotten that earlier when their kiss had knocked the sense clean out of him. But he had his wits now.

This union was still business to her, but not to

Gideon. She didn't belong to him, not yet, but that was what Gideon wanted. And he wanted her to come to him. Which meant he would have to let her decide if she wanted more from their marriage. He hoped the waiting didn't kill him first.

She couldn't say anything else about Tom. After Gideon had asked her about what he'd overheard at supper, a tight pressure banded her chest. The knot on her head began to ache.

She had wanted to tell someone ever since it happened, but not with this same burning need. It wasn't only so she could selfishly unburden herself, but also because she felt she shouldn't keep secrets from Gideon.

That made no sense because she knew he was keeping some of his own, specifically what had happened to him and her brother in prison, as well as what had caused him to commit murder in the first place. But she couldn't tell him.

What if he reacted badly? There was no telling what he would do or say. That alone was enough of an uncertainty to keep her quiet. There was too much risk.

It was close to dark by the time she fetched Thunder from her crate and let her out the back door. Ivy waited to go inside the house until she saw the pup reach Gideon, who was coming out of the barn. He glanced down at the little dog trotting beside him and said something that had the animal's tail wagging enthusiastically.

Ivy stored the remainder of the chocolate cake in the pie safe. After mixing bread dough, she set it aside in a covered bowl to rise for the next morning's biscuits.

Gideon stepped into the house and put the pup down. Thunder rushed across the room to Ivy, and she leaned down to scratch the animal. Gideon closed the door, hanging his hat on the wall peg.

He watched her carefully. "I checked the woods. No one's been here. The branch hasn't been broken."

"Good."

"Doesn't look like anyone's been around the house, barn or chicken coop, either."

She nodded, relieved. As long as their absence had been today, she wouldn't have been surprised if Gideon had found more unidentifiable boot prints. Thank goodness he hadn't seen any signs of a visitor.

Ever since she'd blurted out what she had about Tom, her nerves had been raw. What if Gideon asked her more questions? What if she said something else?

She opened the cupboard and rearranged some plates she'd already stacked. Moved a covered butter dish from one shelf to another.

Gideon took a step toward her. "Anything I can do to help?"

"No. I'm tidying up." She gave him a bright smile. "I just finished the dough for tomorrow's biscuits."

It had been a long day—Jumper coming for his horses, learning her parents couldn't help financially and marrying Gideon. He'd been steady and calm, and she'd enjoyed their supper at The Wildflower. Until Meg had brought up Tom. And Gideon had followed suit.

She had to be careful. Gideon hadn't asked her anything else about Tom, but Ivy was afraid he might.

Exhausted and on edge, she closed the cupboard. "I'm going to turn in. Do you need anything?"

"No." He gestured toward the bedroll he'd stowed in the corner beside the fireplace. "My bed's ready whenever I am."

"You should sleep in one of the guest rooms."

"I feel better if I stay out here."

She tried to smile, feeling as if the walls were closing in. "Shall I put the dog back in the crate?"

"No. She can stay up with me for a while, and I'll take her out again before I hit the hay."

"Thank you."

She walked to her bedroom, acutely aware of his gaze on her. "Ivy?"

Putting a hand on the door frame, she looked over her shoulder.

"Are you sure you're okay? That you ain't bothered by somethin'?"

"I'm just tired."

He was plainly skeptical, but he didn't push. She didn't want him to think he was the cause of her unease. Her gaze met his. "Gideon, everything you've done has been wonderful and much appreciated. I really don't know what I would've done without your help."

"You're welcome." A muscle worked in his jaw, and he looked as if he were fighting the urge to say something. *Do* something. Was it about Tom?

Ivy didn't want to find out. "Well, good night, then."

"Good night." His deep voice stroked over her, somehow soothing and arousing at the same time.

She slipped inside her room and shut the door, standing there for a moment with her head against the wood. He hadn't asked, thank goodness.

It was a wonder she hadn't blurted out something else.

Frustration and dread had risen steadily inside her since Gideon had asked her about Tom. She didn't want to think about her late husband, but she couldn't seem to stop.

How relieved and giddy she'd been when the war ended and he'd come home. She'd looked forward to starting their married life, which had barely begun when it had been interrupted by the fighting. But Tom hadn't been the same.

At first, it was nothing she could define, but as time passed, she realized he was changed. He wasn't the man she thought she'd known, the man she thought she'd married.

Telling herself to stop thinking about him, she pushed away from the door and walked over to light the lamp on her bedside table. She took her pistol out from under her pillow, double-checked that it was loaded and laid it next to the lamp within easy reach. In short order, she undressed and slipped into a soft light blue nightgown.

Pulling back the quilt and sheet, she sank down on the edge of the mattress. Tom had been home barely a month when he began disappearing for hours at a time. If she asked him about it, he grew surly. Sometimes he even left again.

She had told herself he just needed time. That she had no idea what horrors he'd seen on the battlefield, how he might have suffered. But his moods grew darker, and then he began to drink.

Head aching, tired to the bone, Ivy's frustration boiled over, and she slid under the covers. Why did she have to think about him? No matter how she tried, she couldn't squelch the flood of memories or the sharp-edged guilt.

When he was drunk, there was nothing of the man

she'd married. He'd become short-tempered, grim and downright mean sometimes. After a while, she began to keep her distance, but the night he'd died, she hadn't been able to, and she would always pay for that choice.

Giving herself a stern mental kick, she blew out the lamp, settled on her back and attempted to blank her mind. Moonlight streamed in through her window, and she stared up at the play of silvery shadows on the ceiling until she felt her body relax.

Her eyes closed, and she let out a big sigh. An image of Gideon flashed through her mind. How ruggedly compelling he'd looked at their wedding, the dark sapphire of his eyes. The way his mouth had felt against hers.

Suddenly, abruptly, that picture was fractured by an image of Tom and her on the front porch that night.

She forced away the memory and gradually relaxed until she hovered between sleep and wakefulness. Tom's face floated in front of her, then his broken body. The night around them was heavy with summer heat and the scent of wildflowers, underlined by a hum of foreboding.

She felt the sharp slap of his hand against her face, the crack of her head against the wall. Tug growled, lunging for Tom; Tom kicked the dog, hard enough to break his leg.

"Damn you, Tom!"

The words snapped her fully awake. Before she could gather her thoughts, she became aware that someone was in her room. A huge masculine shadow loomed over her. She fumbled for her pistol and thumbed down the hammer.

"Whoa! Ivy, hold up!"

Gideon. She slowly sat up in bed, releasing the hammer and letting out a deep breath as she returned the gun to the bedside table.

"What the hell?" He sounded more confused than angry.

"Sorry."

He stepped closer, into the moonlight, and she could see the alarm creasing his features. Shoulders rigid, his gaze searched the shadows and corners of her room.

"You startled me," she said with a half laugh.

"*You* startled *me*."

"What do you mean?"

"You yelled out in your sleep."

She had? She realized then what had happened. She had cursed Tom, not waking fully until Gideon was in her room. "Did I wake up Thunder?"

"No." His gaze locked on her face. "You were upset. Were you dreaming?"

"No." Her hair had come loose from its braid, and she pushed the wisps out of her face.

"Are you all right?" he asked quietly.

He was barefoot, his shirt untucked from his trousers. The four buttons of his placket were undone, and she could see the muscular plane of his chest and the dusting of dark hair there. Her pulse thudded hard.

"Ivy?"

"Yes." She dragged her attention to his face. "I'm all right."

"You don't sound it. Something was wrong, still is."

"No."

He moved another step closer. Close enough for her to draw in his dark masculine scent. Close enough to touch if she'd had the courage. She fisted her hand against her leg.

His gaze moved over her slowly, heatedly, stripping her bare emotionally.

The tenderness in his eyes was almost her undoing. She wanted so badly to tell him her secret, but she couldn't.

Even so, she wasn't sure she could keep her mouth shut. He had to leave now. "I'd like to go back to sleep."

"Can I get you anything?"

"No, thank you." She eased back against the headboard, pulling the covers up to her chin.

Gideon didn't move, just watched her with a piercing intensity that made her feel as if he knew the truth. But he didn't. No one did.

Thoughts of Tom had bombarded her because of her conversation with Meg then Gideon. A deep, gnawing guilt pinched her gut. She'd managed many times to bury it, keep it inside, but beneath Gideon's prolonged silence, Ivy felt her resolve crumble.

"Good night," she finally said.

He reached toward her and very lightly brushed a knuckle against her cheek.

Her throat tightened. She wanted to grab his hand and hang on, fold herself into him, but she stayed still.

"You've been crying," he said huskily, pulling his hand back.

"What?" She swiped at her face and forced a laugh that she could tell didn't fool him. "No, I haven't."

Backing up, he stared at her. "Are you sure you're okay?"

"Yes. And I'm sorry for pulling the gun on you."

One corner of his mouth quirked up. "Guess I'd better be more careful in the future about startling you."

She nodded, urging him silently to go, even though what she really wanted was for him to climb into bed with her and hold her.

He stepped out of her room and pulled the door partially shut. "I'll be right out here."

She nodded.

"I'm going to leave the door open a bit."

"Okay." She eased down onto her side and watched as he gave her a last once-over then disappeared from sight.

Smoky yellow light from the lamp still burning in the kitchen area spread into her room, eating away at the darkness. She closed her eyes, feeling one tear then another spill down her cheeks.

More than anything, Ivy wanted to tell Gideon what she had never told another soul. The tender look on his face had gone straight to her heart. He would never look at her that way again if she told him that she'd killed her husband.

Chapter Nine

Everything at the farm had been quiet last night. Except Ivy. Gideon hadn't heard her cry out again, but he was still concerned about what had happened.

When he came in for breakfast after milking the cows and feeding the horses, she was putting a basket of fluffy biscuits on the table. He inhaled the yeasty scent of bread and the rich aroma of coffee. It wasn't the savory juiciness of frying meat that had his mouth watering. It was his wife.

The dress she wore was blue-and-white checkered with a square-cut neck that showed a hint of golden skin. The sleeves ended just below her elbows, revealing the delicate bones of her wrists and forearms.

Her hair had been plaited then coiled around and upswept into some pretty do that bared her dainty ears, and the tender bit of flesh behind her ears where he wanted to press his mouth.

Whoa, slow down.

As she put two plates on the table, she gave him a fleeting smile, not meeting his eyes. Was she embarrassed or upset about what had happened last night?

The pup whined and scratched at her crate. "Thunder, no," Gideon said firmly.

She whined again, but stopped clawing at the wooden slats.

He palmed off his hat and hung it on the peg, glancing at Ivy. "Smells good."

"Have a seat. It's ready." She went to the stove and returned with a platter of fried bacon.

He took it and watched as she fetched the coffeepot from the stove burner. There were dark circles under her eyes, and she was quiet.

"Did you sleep?"

"Yes." She didn't look as though she had.

Staying alert in case she cried out again, Gideon hadn't gotten much rest himself. She might not want to talk about last night, but the memory hung in the air between them. He recalled the vehemence in her voice, the near hate when she'd cursed Powell. Just like she'd sounded in the wagon on the way home yesterday when he'd asked about her feelings for her late husband.

He couldn't help being concerned. "How are you holding up?"

Her gaze shot to his as she set down a plate of eggs.

"After last night, I mean."

Her mouth tightened. "I'm fine."

"You're sure?"

"Of course."

The pup yelped, making it plain she wanted out of her crate. At the same time, Gideon and Ivy told her to hush.

He pulled out Ivy's chair, and after she sat, he eased down into the seat beside hers. "You said last night you didn't have a nightmare."

"I didn't."

"So why were you cursing Tom?"

"Eggs?" she asked pointedly, scooting the platter toward him.

"Ivy?"

She forked several pieces of meat onto her plate.

He clamped down on the urge to push. Why wouldn't the woman tell him anything? "Did things between you go bad?"

Though her face closed up, there was plenty of emotion in her dark eyes. The torment there tugged at something deep inside him.

She looked away. "I thought you weren't going to do anything I didn't want."

"You mean, ask questions you're not inclined to answer?"

She gave a sharp nod.

Hell. Why had he gone and said that? "So you won't tell me about it."

"No."

Every part of him wanted to press her, wanted to know what would put such scorn in her voice.

Despite his frustration, Gideon left it alone. There were things he didn't want her to know, either. "All right."

Even though she stared down at her plate, he felt her surprise at his agreement. "Thank you."

He nodded, digging into his breakfast. Maybe if he gave her some time, she would tell him. But if she did, it wasn't going to be today, Gideon realized as they finished their meal and she rose to clear the dishes.

He stood, too, and carried his plate to the dry sink. Scraping the remains of their meal onto a tin plate, he took it to Thunder and let her out of the crate. The pup attacked the eggs then the bits of bacon.

When he rejoined Ivy, the dishes were stacked in a tub. She barely spared him a glance. Her frame was rigid, unease vibrating from her. She acted leery of him. Was she waiting for him to ask more questions?

"I'll pump some water," he said.

"Thank you."

He returned with a full bucket, and she began to wash the dishes.

"Want some help?" he asked.

"No, I'll do it," she said quickly. "I mean, I don't mind doing it."

In other words, vamoose. "All right. I'll take the pup. We'll be around the farm."

She nodded. "This afternoon, I need to go buy a horse."

"To replace the one you had to give the mayor?"

"Yes."

"All right. Where are we going?"

"The Roberts's place. Marcus Roberts and his brothers breed and sell the best horses around."

"Do you want to ride or take the wagon?" Gideon asked.

"Ride. It's been a while since I have."

"Let me know when, and I'll saddle our mounts."

"Thank you," she said softly.

He didn't want her damn thanks. He wanted to know what last night had meant. Clamping down on his frustration, he went about his chores. He checked the woods and around the house, glad to see there were no signs of anyone besides them. No missing, injured or dead animals.

When he joined her for the noon meal, she held herself stiffly aloof. Last night, Gideon had wanted to hold her, soothe her. He still did, but he was determined to keep his hands to himself. And keep his mouth shut about her late husband.

It was midafternoon before they set out for the horse ranch. Ivy rode astride in those damn pants he'd seen once before, and Gideon was hard-pressed to even hold up his end of the conversation, minimal though it was.

He did a lot of nodding as she told him that the Roberts family raised and trained the best horses in the Territory. Ivy led the way through the pasture behind her house and across the river, heading north.

She gestured toward a stand of pecan trees, pointing out the spot that marked the beginning of the large Roberts spread. Their mounts moved through thick green alfalfa as they came within sight of a sprawling two-story stone home that looked like a mansion to Gideon.

They passed a barn full of hay then another, sectioned into feed bins, then a paddock outfitted with a cattle chute at one end.

Across the rolling countryside, horses dotted the landscape. Small pink and yellow flowers pushed up through the ground in random clusters. The sky was a clear blue, the sun a buttery-yellow that flickered off the surface of a small creek that ran alongside their route. Off in the distance, hills rose into mountains thick with timber.

Gideon found it nearly impossible to pay attention. He was acutely aware of Ivy's perfect backside in those britches and the smooth, easy rhythm she had with her mount.

They came up on a corral with about a dozen fine-looking mares and geldings. A sandy-haired man who looked younger than Gideon walked out of the barn to meet them.

He was dressed in a blue shirt that had probably been spotless when he'd started work this morning. Pulling a bandanna from his back pocket, he wiped his hands on the cloth as he moved toward them. "Ivy! Hello."

"Hello, Marcus." She reined up at the horse trough just outside the corral.

Gideon eased his mount to a stop next to hers as she introduced the two men.

Sturdy and standing about six feet tall, Marcus Roberts had the sun-weathered face and hands that bespoke a life of ranching and outdoor work. Gideon slid off his mount and shook the man's hand before moving around to help Ivy down.

He had to force himself to release her, especially when he noticed Roberts eyeing her in those britches with the same frank male interest that Gideon had. He had a fierce primal urge to claim her as his, an urge that wasn't satisfied even after Ivy announced they were married.

Gideon stayed close even though it played hell with his resolve to keep his hands to himself. When she stepped up on the bottom rung of the corral fence, he put a hand low on her back and left it there, glad that she didn't stiffen or move away.

It didn't take her long to choose the horse she wanted. She pointed at a black-and-white paint. "Is she saddle-broke?"

Roberts nodded. "Buggy-broke, too. She's a good worker."

Ivy glanced at Gideon. "What do you think?"

Surprised she'd asked, he studied the animal. The mare was well-formed with good lines and a proud carriage. Her black eyes were intelligent. "She's a beauty."

Ivy smiled, jerking his world to a stop for a moment and putting him off balance. He wanted to kiss those soft pink lips.

The feel of her taut waist, the slender line of her spine, the beginning swell of her hips made him want to shuck her out of her clothes. He wanted to *see* her, all of her.

He was relieved when they left shortly after purchasing the mare. He held the new horse's lead rope, and she trotted easily alongside him.

Ivy appeared much more relaxed than she had all day. Gideon wished he was. His body was tight, and there was a prickly heat beneath his skin.

When they finally reached the farm, Ivy dismounted before he could help. He joined her at the fence, where she stood stroking the new mare's velvety nose.

"You're a pretty one," she murmured.

It was on the tip of his tongue to say the same to her, but he refrained.

From inside the house, he could hear Thunder yelping. Ivy turned to him with a smile. "I'll take care of her."

"I'll put up the horses and feed them."

"All right. Come in when you're finished. I'll fix supper."

She gave the new mare a pat then hurried up the walk into the house. Gideon gathered the other horses' reins and started for the barn. He slowed for one last look back. Ivy's sleek curves were haloed in the last of the sun's golden-pink rays.

By the time he brushed down the horses, fed them and washed up, it was twilight. The early April air was comfortably cool.

Gideon stepped into the house, where Ivy was frying ham as well as potatoes. The savory aromas made his stomach growl.

"Need me to fetch anything?" he asked.

"Plates, please."

He retrieved plates and cups then set places for Ivy and himself. The cake they'd brought home last night sat at the corner of the table. The tempting smell of chocolate was too powerful, and he couldn't resist pinching off a piece of the dessert.

The sweet practically melted in his mouth. He reached for another bite.

"Stay out of that," Ivy exclaimed. "You'll ruin your supper."

He was hungry enough to eat two meals plus an entire cake. Glancing over his shoulder, he dug out forks and knives from the small silverware chest in the cupboard. He placed a pair of utensils beside each plate, unable to resist filching another bit of cake.

Suddenly beside him, Ivy swatted at his arm. "Did you hear what I said? Supper is almost ready."

"What say we eat this first?" he asked hopefully.

"No." She reached for the dessert plate.

He snagged her hand. "Hey, what are you doing?"

"Just moving it out of temptation's way."

"Or so you can keep it all for yourself," he teased.

"Maybe I will." Her eyes danced.

"Oh, no, you won't." With a mock scowl, he reached for the plate.

She lunged for it at the same time. "Give that to me!"

He hooked one arm around her waist and pulled her into his side to keep her pinned in place. Her breasts pressed against him; her silky hair tickled his chin.

He was distracted enough that he didn't feel her make a grab for the plate until she had her hands on it. Laughing, she tugged it away from him.

"Okay, I give," he said, enjoying the smile on her face as she leaned around him to push the plate across the table.

"Now, leave that be until after supper."

He nodded, still holding her, taken with the slight color in her cheeks and the intent way she suddenly looked at him. As if she wanted to touch him. His pulse thudded hard when she did just that.

She reached up and flicked at something on his chest. "You got crumbs all over you."

Her fingers stroked down his throat then lowered to his chest, brushing away the dessert.

"There."

Her smile turned him inside out, and his attention went to her lips.

The moment shifted from lighthearted to a thick, pulsing awareness. Gideon involuntarily tightened his hold. Her gaze locked with his as her expression sobered.

And when she turned her focus to his mouth, raw desire seared him. He bit back a groan.

He went hard against her. The deep flush on her cheeks said she felt it, too. Gideon fought the compulsion to crush his mouth to hers.

She shifted, her body settling into his. One hand rested on his chest. She looked up at him with curiosity and longing and clear intent. She was going to kiss him, and he was going to kiss her back.

C'mon, sweetheart.

Her breath feathered against his chin as she studied his mouth. He didn't know how he managed to keep from taking her mouth the way he wanted.

Every muscle coiled as he fought the urge. She licked her lips and lifted to him. Not boldly, but enough that his heart kicked hard. One long second pulsed between them, then another.

Just when he thought she might close the distance, she drew away. Only a fraction, but enough to shatter the moment. His heartbeat pounded in his ears. She was still close enough so that all he had to do was dip his head and their lips would touch. But he needed her to make the move.

She wanted him. It was there in her eyes. But still she waited. Watched. Considered.

Finally, nerves raw, he said hoarsely, "I won't put up a fight."

She studied him for another second then wiggled out of his hold. He bit back a curse at the feel of her body sliding down his.

She stepped back, flushed, her pulse jerking in her neck. "I'll get supper on."

No! He stood motionless, struggling to get his body under control. It didn't work. He knew she was just as affected as he was; his body seemed to have trouble processing that. Finally, the haze of desire cleared even though his body burned. He needed some relief.

"Uh…I'm going to the river."

She took another step back, her brow furrowing. "You don't have to go all the way down there to wash up."

"I know." His voice sounded gravelly.

"But it's only the beginning of April. The water will be freezing."

"That's the point," he ground out.

Her attention moved down his body then stopped at his groin. "Oh," she breathed.

"Yeah," he muttered.

Having her eyes on him there made his trousers painfully tight. His muscles coiled against the need to reach for her. He physically hurt.

He had told himself he would let her decide if she wanted their marriage to be more than a business arrangement. Right now, that sounded like the most addlepated idea he'd ever had, and he wasn't sure he could hold to it. He had to get the hell out of here.

Gideon wasn't the only one who needed to cool down. After he left, Ivy wet a cloth and pressed it to her overheated cheeks and neck. She had really wanted to kiss him. Or wanted him to kiss her. She didn't care; she had just wanted it.

At least he hadn't pressed more about Tom. He would at some point, she knew. Another day, two at the most.

As the days passed, they both stayed busy. Ivy made sure of that. Anticipating more questions from Gideon had her nerves growing more raw every minute.

Friday was laundry day. The stage made its regular stop on Saturday and again on Tuesday. Conrad expressed his dislike about her marriage to Gideon, but the stage driver didn't linger. Each day, Ivy braced herself for Gideon to press her about her late husband.

She expected him to become angry and short with her, but he didn't. She thought he might try to blackmail the information out of her by maybe refusing to perform the chores he'd taken over. He didn't do that, either.

He didn't do anything she supposed he would—things Tom had done after he started drinking. Though Gideon didn't avoid her, he seemed to be around only for meals and at night.

He began to train the half wolf–half dog to give the cows a wide berth and to be respectful of the horses. And he regularly checked the woods and kept an eye on things, watching out for her. Protecting her. Thankfully, there had been no more incidents at the farm.

Gideon took care of the livestock, doing everything from working with the new mare to doctoring any animal in need to making sure the heavily pregnant cows stayed close to the barn.

As the week passed, Ivy could barely imagine the farm without him. Which was ridiculous. She'd done just fine on her own before he came.

As soon as they figured out who wanted to harm her and they dealt with that person, she and Gideon would divorce. That shouldn't bother her, but it did. A great deal.

She knew why. What she felt for him had more to do with want than gratitude or even needing his help.

She found herself being seduced by the idea of a future with him. She didn't understand that at all. She'd been fooled by Tom and sworn she would never again be taken in by a man.

What if Gideon wasn't the man she thought he was? What if he wasn't showing his true self? So why couldn't she get the idea of *them* out of her head?

The nights were the worst. Her infernal imagination

continually replayed the moment she'd nearly kissed him. Why hadn't she just done it?

Even though it had been for the best, she had regretted her inaction every day for the past week. Especially when she caught him several times looking at her with undisguised hunger blazing in his eyes. It was obvious Gideon wasn't going to do anything until or unless she decided it was what she wanted.

The problem was that she did want it. She couldn't stop wondering how it would feel to be with him.

Their current arrangement was straightforward, simple. Becoming intimate with him would complicate that to no end. Still, that didn't ease the ache that seemed to bore deeper each time they were together.

Between her anxiety over whether Gideon would press her about the night she'd cursed her late husband and her sharpening awareness of her current husband, Ivy felt as if the walls were closing in on her.

Frustrated and confused, she kept reminding herself that she didn't know him. Not the real him. That their marriage was temporary.

None of it seemed to matter. She wanted him in a way she had never wanted any other man, but she wasn't going to do anything about it. She'd meant it when she said she didn't want another husband. The only reason she had one now was because it had been the sole way to get a loan for the farm.

On Thursday evening, a week after their near kiss, Ivy stood on the back porch looking for Gideon. They had eaten supper, then he had disappeared. Tomorrow was laundry day. When she had gone to the barn to gather his clothes for washing, she'd thought she'd find him there, but no. The sun set in a burst of gold as her gaze scanned the yard then the pasture beyond where the cows grazed.

Hearing a bark, she shaded her eyes and saw the pup leaping and pouncing in the alfalfa a healthy distance from the cattle. She let out a series of short yips.

"Thunder!" Ivy warned sharply.

The whelp carried on, darting away when a cow stepped toward her. The black-and-white-spotted animal lowered her big head and eyed the little noisemaker.

Though the cow regarded Thunder as a minor annoyance and not a threat, Ivy stepped off the porch and picked up her skirts, hurrying toward the back fence. Opening the gate, she called again for the dog. The pup ran toward her, slowed by the thick grass.

Ivy bent toward the animal. "Leave the cows alone."

Giving a playful bark, Thunder attacked her skirt hem then scampered away.

"Come here." She tried again to pick up the dog, but the pup escaped her reach and raced toward a flat, well-grazed area of the pasture.

Grabbing up her skirts, Ivy chased Thunder across the short and tall grass and through the line of trees bordering the river. By the time the dog plopped down in front of a stretch of trees and undergrowth, she was breathing hard and so was Ivy.

She approached slowly, hoping the animal was give out. The nearby water rushed and gurgled over the rocks. She drew in the scent of pine and wildflowers. A splash alerted her to what was probably a deer or some other creature. The pup leaped up, but before she could bolt again, Ivy grabbed her.

"Gotcha." Smiling, she straightened.

From the corner of her eye, she caught a movement

and searched through the trees. Her gaze skimmed the water that glinted gold in the setting sunlight. Thunder squirmed, and Ivy tightened her hold as she finally caught a glimpse of something. No, she corrected. Some*one.*

Dark wet hair. Strong nape. And a bare masculine shoulder. Gideon.

Her breath caught. Sleek and wet, he faced away from her and plucked a towel from a tree branch. Thanks to the underbrush, she caught only a flash of a naked hip and tight buttocks, the line where his sun-burnished back gave way to the lighter golden color of flesh that rarely saw the sun. But it was enough to scramble her pulse.

Oh, mercy.

He lifted a hand and dried his hair with the towel then swiped the cloth across his chest, muscles flexing in his arm as he moved. Ivy inched closer, absorbed by the glimpse of lean flanks, powerful thighs, the well-hewn plane of his stomach. He was beautiful. Masculine and sculpted and strong. Desire tugged low in her belly, and she went soft inside.

Dimly, she registered the pup squirming in her hold, but she couldn't take her eyes off the big man half-hidden by the trees. Her husband.

She'd assumed his frequently damp hair the past several evenings had been the result of him washing up at the house pump. Had he been coming here instead?

As Gideon pulled on his trousers, her gaze moved over him again—the arch of his spine, the strength in his massive shoulders. Sunlight speared through the trees and washed over him in a haze of gold, revealing a crisscross of puckered skin across the entire expanse of his back.

Ivy frowned. What was that? Horror stole her breath as she registered what she was seeing. Scars.

Extensive scars. Everywhere in view. His back, his waist and sides. On the back side of his upper arm.

Tears filled her eyes. Had someone done that to him, or were those cruel marks the result of some kind of injury?

She or the dog must've made a noise because suddenly Gideon spun in her direction. A hammer clicked on a gun as his gaze probed the trees. "Who's there?"

She felt as if she'd been spying on him, the same way someone had spied on her. It was pure reflex that had her turning and rushing back to the house.

This was why he never worked without a shirt. Once in the house, she tucked Thunder into her crate and flipped the small door bar into place. Only then did she realize she was crying.

She scraped away the tears, wondering what she should do. If she should do anything.

After scratching around a bit, the pup curled up on the rags Ivy had used to line the makeshift bed. Ivy was torn. She wanted to go to Gideon, but should she? She burned to know what had happened to him.

Hands shaking, it took her two attempts to light the lamp on the corner of the dry sink.

"What were you doing down there?" His quiet voice behind her nearly made her jump out of her skin.

She didn't turn around, tried not to move at all. The door closed, and his boots scraped against the floor as he came up the short hallway.

He moved up to her back. "Answer me."

"I didn't mean to— I wasn't spying on you." She was afraid to turn around, not because of his scars, but because she didn't want to do anything that might make him uncomfortable. "Thunder. She was bothering the cows and wouldn't come when I called her. I chased her to the river."

"How much did you see?" His voice was grim.

"Enough to know you were in the altogether." Oops.

A sudden silence descended then he said flatly, "You saw 'em."

"Yes." Hands tangling in her skirts, she stared down at the floor. She had no idea what to do or say.

"I'm sorry you had to see that," he said gruffly. "I know they're...ugly."

He thought she was disgusted. He couldn't be more wrong. She turned then, noticing how his damp shirt clung to his deep chest. Now only the scar encircling his neck and the one on his jaw were visible.

From this angle, the lamplight cast half of him in shadow. She wanted to touch him, but didn't know if she should. "I didn't even notice your scars at first."

"You don't have to spare my feelings," he snapped.

"I'm not! I didn't see them because I couldn't take my eyes off your— Oh." She'd almost told him exactly where she'd been staring. Intense heat flushed her body.

He arched a brow, waiting. Tense.

"Your scars weren't what I noticed first," she repeated primly. "But I did notice. There are so many. What happened?"

He turned to go. She snagged his hand, his work-roughened skin slightly cool from the water. "Please, don't walk away."

She was fully aware that she was asking him to talk

about something painful, something he might never want to discuss, but she had to know.

He stood there, his wet shirt skimming over trousers that were now buttoned. He was naked under there, she knew.

She shouldn't be thinking about him naked, not right now. She took a step closer, halting when he drew back. Her heart twisted. "Won't you tell me?"

His face went carefully blank, and Ivy felt a tug of regret at asking him. Suddenly, she didn't want to know. Not if it would cause him to relive painful memories.

"I'm sorry. I shouldn't have asked." She started to release his hand.

His grip tightened. Not bruising, but too strong for her to break easily. "I was whipped," he said brusquely. "The first ranch I worked was run by a mean bastard, and if you didn't do what he wanted or work as fast as he ordered, you got a whippin'."

Hadn't he told her he had struck out on his own when he was twelve? He'd been a child when he'd received those lashes.

Recalling the expanse of mutilated flesh, she winced. "Do they ever hurt?"

"No." He released her then.

She found herself in front of him, close enough to feel his body heat, to draw in the heady scent of male and soap and a dark musk. "How long did you work at that awful place?"

"Three months. I took off after that flogging."

She wanted—needed—to touch him. Carefully, slowly, she laid a hand on his chest.

He grabbed her wrist. "What are you doing?"

"I didn't mean to embarrass you or bring up bad memories, but when I saw you—"

"You couldn't stand the sight." The matter-of-fact way he said it had her chest tightening.

"Only because it was horribly obvious how much pain you suffered."

Still holding her wrist, he searched her eyes as if trying to decide whether she told the truth.

She reached up to cup his cheek. He looked startled, but didn't pull back.

"I hate that you went through so much. That anyone could do such a thing." Her fingers gently touched the thin jagged line on his left jaw. "Is that how your face and neck were scarred, too? From a whipping?"

"That was in prison." His voice was emotionless, but Ivy saw plenty of emotion in his eyes. How much had he endured?

"Did you go to prison because you killed the monster who did that to you?"

"No." A muscle flexed in his jaw. There was a wealth of pain in that one word. And an unyielding tone that made it clear he wasn't going to explain why he'd been sent to Leavenworth.

It seemed natural to go up on tiptoe and brush a kiss against his stubbled jaw. How strong he was to have survived such brutality, especially so early in his life.

"What do you want, Ivy?" His grip grew a little tighter. "For me to tell you about the whippings so you can feel sorry for me? It's over and done."

He was right. She shouldn't pry. "I'm sorry. You don't have to tell me anything if you'd rather not."

His nostrils flared, and dull red color rode his cheeks. Anger? Arousal? She wasn't sure.

Before she knew what he was about, he hauled her close. "Say I answer your questions?"

"All right," she answered breathlessly. His body cradled hers, and a sharp ache unfurled inside her.

"What if I want you to talk?"

Her spine went rigid. She knew what he was going to say.

"Tell me what the other night was about. Why you were cursing Powell."

She'd walked right into that. How could she refuse when he'd just shared something that brought up horrific memories for him?

"Ivy."

He was the one holding her hand now, keeping her near when she was torn between moving closer or running. It wasn't right to take so much from him without giving something of herself. But this felt like she was giving everything, completely baring herself emotionally.

And if she told him the truth, then what? It would likely squelch whatever was growing between them.

She swallowed hard. Emotions churning, she tugged her hand from his and turned away.

Behind her, he cursed, moving back.

He'd taken two steps when she finally said in a low voice, "I was glad when he was gone."

"You feel guilty for that?"

She heard the scuff of his boots, felt him return. So close she could lean back into him if she wanted. "That's not how a wife is supposed to feel."

"Did you have a fight before he was thrown from the wagon? Did you have words?"

"Not exactly."

Gideon's big hand settled on her shoulder, his thumb making small circles on her upper arm. Despite his soothing touch, she couldn't look at him.

"You were crying the other night. If you weren't angry, you were hurt in some way. What did he do?"

She wanted to turn into the wide shelter of Gideon's chest, but she didn't deserve comfort. Not after what she'd done.

"Did he cheat on you?"

"No." If he had, she wouldn't feel so bad about what had happened.

Gideon went still, his voice rough with leashed fury. "Did he hit you?"

Something tight inside her cracked open. "He tried."

"Damn." The word was clipped, vicious.

"When Tom drank, he was mean."

Despite the ferocity in his tone, Gideon gently smoothed both hands down her arms, embracing her from behind. "Josh said Tom started drinking after the war."

She nodded. "One night when he was drunk, he became angry about something and took it out on me."

Her husband had swung at her with his fist, which she'd managed to duck, but then he'd grabbed her arm, hard enough to leave a bruise. "Tug attacked him and he kicked the dog. Repeatedly."

"That's how Tug's leg was broken," Gideon said softly.

"Yes. Tom lunged at me, pulling my hair and trying to get his hands around my neck. I…"

The word stuck in her throat. She'd never confessed to anyone the whole truth of that night. She wasn't sure she could do it now.

Gideon turned her to him. "Tom attacked you, then what?"

She didn't think she could bear it if he looked at her with contempt, but she knew she had to tell him.

"I killed him."

Chapter Ten

Gideon's eyes widened slightly. "You killed him."

"Yes. I shoved him off the porch." The words choked out of her. Her legs almost buckled from the sheer relief of finally saying it aloud. Tears filled her eyes, and she buried her face in her hands.

"Hey," he said softly, pulling her into his chest. His big arms went around her, and she held on for dear life.

Her throat was tight with a combination of dread and uncertainty. What was he thinking? Had she done the right thing in telling him?

As the moment dragged out, her anxiety grew. She drew back a fraction, forced herself to examine his eyes for scorn, revulsion. There was only steadiness, acceptance in his blue eyes. "I've never told anyone before."

"Not even Smith?"

"No. My family thinks Tom was killed because he was thrown from a wagon." A breath shuddered out of her. "I let them think that."

He held her to him with one arm; his other hand rubbed her back in soothing circles. He hadn't withdrawn from her. Instead, he'd wrapped her up in his strength, his unshakable calm.

"It sounds like you acted in self-defense."

"I could've run. Or held him at gunpoint until I could get away."

"Did you have time to think?" The words rumbled deep in his chest.

"I just reacted."

"Because you were threatened." He tilted her chin up. "You have nothing to feel guilty about."

"I wasn't sorry after it happened. I felt as if I'd been rewarded!" She brushed away the tears on her cheeks. "That's not how a wife is supposed to feel."

"It is if she's been in danger from someone who's supposed to protect her. Love her." Gideon took her shoulders in his hands, holding her gaze. "Tom breaking his neck when you shoved him was an accident. It wasn't premeditated. If you'd really wanted him dead, you would've shot him. You don't miss with your gun."

She'd never thought about it that way. It didn't absolve her, but it did ease the guilt slightly.

She wiped at her damp eyes. "It feels good to tell someone. To tell *you*."

There had been any number of times in the past several years that she could've confided in Meg or Smith or their parents. Yet she hadn't.

For some reason, she'd shared her secret with Gideon. Telling him the truth made her feel as if she'd escaped a trap every bit as vicious as the one someone had set for her.

Here in his arms, she felt stronger. Her fingers slid gently down the side of his face. The hand at her waist tightened.

"Thank you," she said.

"For what?" he asked gruffly.

"For not condemning me. For not bolting. For not dismissing it."

"No one would find fault with what you had to do."

"Some would."

"Not someone who's been threatened. Not me." He looked so fierce, so protective that she almost smiled.

Her gaze dropped to his mouth, and she lightly grazed his lower lip with one finger. His eyes darkened.

She'd thought about that missed kiss for a week. And every day she had regretted not doing it when she'd had the chance. She wasn't going to miss this one.

Rolling up on tiptoe, she rested a hand on his chest. His heart thumped steady and reassuring beneath her touch.

He stilled. "Ivy?"

"I wish I'd kissed you the other night."

Desire flared in his eyes, but he didn't pull her closer, didn't lean toward her. He gave her no encouragement at all.

Moving her palm to his strong, corded neck, she tried to bring him to her. He wouldn't budge. She let out an exasperated breath and threw back his words of the other night. "You said you wouldn't put up a fight."

He went hard against her, his entire body. This time, when she tugged at him, he dipped his head to meet hers.

A voice in the back of her head sounded a warning, but her need was stronger. This man touched her deep inside where no other ever had. She felt a bond with him, a completely unexpected bond. She needed more of that connection.

Their mouths touched, and a sudden near despera-
tion filled her. She wanted another slow, thorough kiss
like the one he'd given her at their wedding, but that
wasn't what she got. This one was demanding and deep,
hungry. And every bit as devastating as their first one.

A simmering mix of relief, longing, hunger swept
through her. A burning urgency to be as close to him
as a woman could be to a man.

He filled this emptiness inside her, the hollow ache
of loss that she'd carried even when Tom was alive. The
only thing she cared about was being close to Gideon,
satisfying the fiery itch in her blood.

She wanted him. All of him. *Now.*

He slanted his head at a different angle, moved his
mouth from hers to her cheek, then nipped lightly at
her earlobe.

She shivered. It was a good thing he was holding her
because the starch went right out of her, and her legs
nearly gave. She clutched him tighter.

His breathing ragged, Gideon pulled away. "You're
goin' to my head. We'd better stop."

"No."

"Ivy?" His voice was hoarse, his muscles drawn taut
with restraint.

She didn't want restraint. "I want you," she whispered.

Desire sharpened his features, then a pained expression crossed his face. "You gotta be sure."

She had confessed her deepest, most awful secret
to him. She wanted to share all of herself. Going up
on tiptoe, she nipped at his lower lip then pressed light
kisses along the scar on his jaw.

That got him moving. He swung her up in his arms,

and by the time they reached her bedroom, he had her bodice undone. The glide of his hot mouth down her neck only fueled her impatience to feel his naked flesh against hers.

He laid her on top of the blue star quilt, pushing her blouse off. Her skirt and petticoats followed, falling to the floor along with her drawers. His callused hand moved between her legs, and he gently slipped one finger into her silky heat.

Arching against him, she tugged his shirt over his head.

When she touched the hot, supple skin of his chest, he froze.

Her finger traced a web of scars beneath the dark hair on his chest. The wounds were barely visible in the shadowy light. "Is this okay?" she whispered.

He gave a sharp nod, ridding her of shoes and stockings. She ran her hands over granite-hard shoulders, palms skimming ragged patches of flesh. Each stroke had her heart aching.

His mouth skimmed down her throat, moved to her breasts as he tugged the ribbon of her chemise and anchored her to him so he could shove off the undergarment.

When she lay there without a stitch, his gaze locked on her with an awe and appreciation that sent a rush of heat through her entire body.

"I've never seen anything like you in all my born days," he breathed reverently. His eyes were hot with a raw need she'd never seen in another man.

She kissed him again, fumbling with the button on his trousers. He shucked off his boots and socks then his pants. He came down on top of her, his hair-roughened legs nudging hers wider. His big hands glided up her sides to cup her breasts, his thumbs teasing her tight nipples before he put his mouth on her.

Sliding her arms around his hard shoulders, she moved beneath him, unable to help the plea in her voice. "Gideon, don't wait."

He lifted his head, his chest heaving against hers. His skin was sheened with sweat and shadow.

His clean male scent had her nuzzling his neck. "Now."

Staring into her eyes, he smoothed her hair back and slid inside. She cried out at finally connecting with him, the moment unexpectedly poignant. His eyes blazed with such naked emotion that her chest tightened. Something huge and scary rolled through her, and for an instant she felt emotionally raw, completely vulnerable.

Then her body took over. They moved together in a blur of heat and pleasure. She held on tight as Gideon drove her up a dizzying peak. Her hips met every stroke of his body. He possessed her, silently demanding she surrender every bit of herself. It sent her over the edge and he joined her, his muscles bunching beneath her hands.

He collapsed against her, his face buried in her hair. At some point, he had unraveled her chignon. She hadn't even noticed.

He rolled to his back and brought her on top of him. His heart beat heavy and quick beneath her, slowing as they lay together.

Gideon kissed her shoulder. "That was somethin'."

There was no complaint in his drowsy voice. She certainly had none. She had never known marital relations could be like that. Exciting, yes. Consuming, almost frightening? No.

She eased away slightly, looking up when he didn't protest. He was already asleep. His clean soap scent teased the air. Out back, a cow bawled. Down the hall, she could hear the pup's snuffling snores.

She tried to quiet her mind, but she couldn't. Making love to Gideon had been more than she'd imagined. More delicious, more intense, more…disconcerting.

The entire time he had kept his gaze on her, and she had been unable to look away. He seemed to see all of her, and he wanted everything. It scared the daylights out of her.

Not only had she seen desire in his blue eyes, but also tenderness and what she feared was love. Love would ruin everything.

She had reached out to him on impulse. Though she wasn't sorry for it, she was on the edge of a risk she didn't want to take. Ivy had shared her entire self with Gideon, but had he done the same? She had no idea.

Trusting another man completely, wholly? She couldn't do it. She couldn't let herself be caught in that quicksand again. No matter how much she might wish things were different.

When Gideon woke the next morning, he lay there enjoying the feel of his wife against him. In the hazy state between asleep and awake, he drowsily savored the softness of her sleek curves. Her hair, an inky curtain of silk between them, tickled his chest. The scent of their loving mingled with a subtle whiff of magnolia from Ivy's skin.

She lay quietly, snuggled into him. After her initial reference to his scars, she hadn't mentioned them again. She hadn't seemed bothered by them, either. Then again, their lovemaking had been fast, urgent, more so than he had wanted, but it did mean she hadn't dwelled on the vicious marks on his body.

The mattress gave a little, and she slipped out of bed, waking him fully. He opened his eyes in time to see her drawing on her blue wrapper. He propped himself up on one arm, admiring one bare shoulder and the gorgeous fall of her hair.

"Morning," he said.

"Oh!" She jumped, turning with a sheepish smile. "You startled me."

"Sorry." He glanced at the watery sunlight creeping under the oilskin shade. "Do you have to get up so early today?"

"Laundry day." She threw him a quick smile, belting her wrapper.

He itched to turn her right around and unwrap her. Sitting up instead, he swung his legs over the edge of the mattress, reaching for his trousers. They were half-hidden under the bed.

He snagged them and pulled them on as he stood.

"Oh," she breathed behind him.

He tensed. Was she looking at his scars? When he turned, she quickly shifted her attention, but he felt the heat of her gaze. What he saw there was appreciation, not revulsion or disgust.

If he thought he stood a chance, he'd toss her back on that bed, but he could tell she was ready to get moving.

He buttoned his trousers then tugged his shirt over his head. "I'll see to the livestock and come back in to help you with whatever you need."

"Thank you."

He moved around to her side of the bed for his socks and boots. She ducked out of the bedroom and into the kitchen area. As he finished dressing, he stared at the rumpled sheets on the bed.

He was smiling when he strode out of the bedroom and found her lighting a fire in the cookstove.

"Need me to bring in some water?"

He thought she hesitated briefly before nodding. "Yes, please."

On his way past her, he stopped and stroked a finger down her cheek. "Did you sleep okay?"

"Yes." She offered a smile, but it didn't reach her eyes.

A sudden disquiet needled at him, and he didn't know why. "Be right back."

He jogged outside to the pump. Ivy appeared to be of the same mind about their marriage as he was. A sense of contentment rolled over him, a satisfaction he'd never experienced before.

After breakfast, he offered to help her clean up, but she shooed him off. He made his morning check around the farm and the woods, glad to see there were still no signs of any trespassers. Though he wanted to believe there would be no more trouble, he wouldn't bet on it.

Shortly following the noon meal, he made his way to the backyard, where Ivy was doing laundry. The pup trotted alongside him. His wife had changed into a gray day dress and was bent over a tub of water, scrubbing at a garment on the washboard. Her bodice pulled taut across her back, outlining her slim waist.

She had braided her hair and coiled it into a low chignon, exposing her elegant neck. Gideon could still feel the velvety softness of her skin. Remembered that she tasted like sweet cream.

She rinsed what he now saw was one of his shirts. The dog raced up to her with a happy yip. He closed the distance between them, his boots making no sound on the grass.

"You need any help?"

Ivy jumped, frowning at him as she wrung out the garment. "This is the last of the wash."

"I can hang it for you."

She seemed to hesitate before giving the damp shirt to him. After draping it over the clothesline, he turned to find her struggling to tilt the kettle onto its side.

"Here." He reached her in two steps and tipped the cast-iron pot over, draining out the water.

"Thank you," she said quietly.

"Anything else I can do?"

"Not right now."

"Okay."

The dog stayed close to Ivy when Gideon returned to the barn and began to muck out the stalls. Less than an hour later, he saw her wrestling a rug from one of the guest rooms. It took some doing, but she managed to drape it over the porch railing then began to beat out the dirt and dust.

This time when he offered assistance, she refused. If he didn't know better, he'd think she didn't want help or anything else from him.

Later that afternoon, when he saw her spreading fresh linens on the beds in the guest rooms, he decided to test his theory. This time, he didn't ask. He just stepped into the room and moved to the opposite side of the bed, snagging a corner of the sheet she'd unfolded.

She frowned. "What are you doing?"

"Helping."

"But—"

"You don't need help," he finished drily. "I know."

He tucked the linen in at the foot of the bed then smoothed it across the mattress before Ivy spread the quilt over it. When she moved to the next room, so did he.

"I really can do it myself." Her voice was soft, even, but she wouldn't look at him.

He finally understood. What she meant was that she *wanted* to do it herself. He studied her for a moment. Her gray dress was wrinkled, and wisps of hair, damp from perspiration, curled around her face. Her features were drawn, weary.

Maybe she was just tired. She'd been working since sunrise. No lingering in bed for her, even though he hadn't seen the harm.

"All right," he said. "I'll leave you to it."

He moved around the bed and out into the hall, seeing the pup curled up asleep under the dining table. What was going on with Ivy? Gideon wondered.

All day, she had stayed close to the house, been careful not to touch him if he were nearby. If the dadgum woman had let him help today, even just once, maybe she wouldn't be so tired.

As he entered the front room, he spied the platter of fried chicken covered with a white cloth. Covered dishes of beets, bread and cake shared space on the table.

They could have a picnic down by the river. That would get Ivy away for a bit, and she wouldn't have to worry about the dishes.

After gathering the food, he started past the dry sink, aiming for the root cellar and a jar of pickles.

"What are you doing?" Ivy asked behind him.

He glanced over his shoulder. "I thought we could take a picnic to the river. There are plenty of leftovers from lunch."

"We can eat here."

Frowning, he turned. "Everything's ready, and you won't have to worry about cleanup."

She threw a longing glance at the meal he'd put together. Good, he thought. She wanted to do it.

"I don't think so," she said.

"What? Why not?"

"We can just eat here."

"That's not an answer."

She angled her chin at him. "I just don't think it's a good idea."

Not a good idea? What the hell? "I thought it would be nice."

"It would."

"Then what's the problem?" He stilled as a thought streaked through his mind. She'd avoided him today whenever possible. "You don't want to be alone with me."

"I never said that."

"You're not saying anything," he growled, shoving a hand through his hair. "Do you think I'm going to try to get you out of your clothes?"

She colored, her gaze skittering away.

She did! The idea sounded good to him, but even a half-wit could see she didn't agree.

Was she embarrassed because they'd been intimate? Surely not. She wasn't a virgin.

It was something else. Something to do with him, but what? It had never mattered much to Gideon that he couldn't fathom a woman's mind, but it sure would come in handy right now.

She was withdrawn, aloof, acting as if he hadn't seen and touched every inch of her body. And *that* was the problem, he realized with a flash of anger. "You regret that we consummated our marriage."

"Don't put words in my mouth."

"I asked you straight out if you were sure you wanted to be with me, and you said yes."

"That's right. I did."

"So tell me why you don't want me around today."

"I didn't mean to cause a fuss. Your idea of a picnic is good. Let's go."

"No. I want to know what's going on." He folded his arms across his chest and stared her down. "Why are you pulling away? Acting like last night never should've happened?"

It wasn't because of his scars. She hadn't recoiled from those at all. "Answer me," he said. "Are you sorry about last night?"

After a long moment, she said, "We probably shouldn't do it again."

That caught him right in the gut. "Why the hell not?"

"I haven't changed my mind about having a husband, staying married."

"We're good together." When she blushed, he shook his head. "Not just that way."

"It's not you." Her voice cracked.

He stepped toward her. "It's Tom. You haven't told me everything."

"You won't understand."

"I want to."

She studied him for a long moment.

"He changed after we married."

"How? In what way?"

"He became lazy, barely helped around here. Blamed me when things went wrong. I thought I was marrying a man who wanted to be my partner."

"Instead, he wanted you to take care of him."

"I could've dealt with that."

"Then what?"

"He was always opposed to liquor, but after the war, he couldn't get enough."

As gently as he could, Gideon said, "Honey, a lot of soldiers turned to drink. Things we saw, the things some men had to do were just too much. Sometimes liquor is the only thing that will dim those images."

"I know that. And I hate what he suffered, what all of you suffered, but Tom was vehemently opposed to alcohol. Both of his parents were drunks. Their negligence caused the death of his sister. Tom swore he would never drink, but he did."

"When he started, he couldn't stop?"

"That's right. And he became mean, violent. After a while, I didn't know him at all."

"Is that what you think about me?" Gideon struggled to understand. "That I'm hiding my true self?"

"I don't know, and that's the problem. I don't trust—"

"You don't trust me? What have I done to make you feel that way?"

"It isn't you. I don't trust any man. That's not fair, but it's the truth."

His frustration ebbed. She needed reassurance. That was all. He closed the distance between them. "There are no surprises I can spring on you. You know *everything* about me."

"That's not true."

He went still inside.

"I know you went to prison for killing a man, but I don't know why you killed him."

"You know I did it, though. Why does the reason matter?"

"Because you know every single thing about me. You know why I killed Tom."

His skin felt too small. So did the house. How had they gotten on this topic? "Ivy, the point is, you know the worst thing about me."

"I thought I knew Tom, too."

I'm not him! Gideon bit back the words. As much as he didn't want to share this story, he was going to. Considering what she'd just told him about her late husband and her desire to know everything about Gideon, he didn't want her to think he was hiding anything.

"All right, then."

A sudden heavy rustling noise erupted outside, startling them both. Thunder jumped up and faced the door, growling. Something struck a piece of wood with a sharp hammerlike *thwap*.

Gideon's gaze shot to Ivy's.

"Someone's out there," they said together.

Chapter Eleven

Drawing his gun, Gideon started for the back door. "Stay here."

"I can help—"

"No." His voice was harsh, but he didn't care. Not when they were talking about her safety. "It might be the same person who hit you on the back of the head."

Though she looked as if she would protest, she nodded. "All right, but I'm getting my gun."

He quietly opened the door and slipped outside, working his way up the side of the house. A swarm of squawking birds flew from the direction of the woods fronting Ivy's house. That explained the rustling noise they'd heard. In the corral, the horses jostled each other, crowding against the gate. One or more of them must have kicked the slatted walls in their earlier panic.

Gideon scanned the area around the barn, then the front yard. His gaze shifted to the woods. Was whatever had disturbed the animals still in those trees? The birds and horses had settled, but unease still hummed at the base of his spine.

He started for the woods then decided he should

tell Ivy what he was doing. He turned back toward the house. A gunshot cracked the air.

Gideon pivoted just as a bullet slammed into his left shoulder. Searing pain blazed through him. From the house, he heard Ivy scream. The pup barked frantically. The birds burst into flight again.

Scrambling for cover, he skidded toward the far corner of the corral. The horses shied, bumping and pushing at each other. Cows bawled from the pasture.

The shot had definitely come from the woods. Where was the bastard? Gideon scanned the trees then squeezed the trigger on his own weapon, trying to draw fire so he could determine the shooter's position. There was no return round.

His upper arm burned like blue blazes. Blood plastered his sleeve to his skin. It was pure luck that he'd turned toward the house. If he hadn't, he would've been hit dead center in the chest.

He pulled the trigger a second time. Again, no answering gunfire. Suddenly he felt a slight vibration in the ground, then heard the pounding of hooves heading away from the house.

Was the shooter leaving? There had been only one gunshot, and it had come from one place. A single shooter? Just as Gideon decided the gunman was gone and eased down against the corral post, he saw Ivy racing toward him.

His heart jumped to his throat. There had been no more shooting, but Gideon didn't care.

When she reached him, he grabbed a handful of skirts, yanking her to the ground.

"Get down, woman!" Cold sweat slicked his palms

as anger and fear nearly choked him. "I told you to stay inside."

"I saw you'd been hit!"

"You could've been, too."

"Whoever it was rode off."

He peered through the last of the sun's rays and saw no movement. Heard nothing. The surrounding area was quiet, and he was fairly certain the shooter was gone. Still, it didn't steady his stuttering heartbeat. "You shouldn't have come out here."

"I had to." Her eyes, stormy with worry, searched his. "I knew there was a possibility you could get hurt if we were somewhere together, but I never thought they would target you."

Distracted by the agony clawing through his arm, Gideon hadn't gotten that far in his mind yet, but she was right.

A look of horror crossed her face. "They tried to kill you because we're married."

Ivy didn't think she took a full breath until the front door was closed and Gideon was seated at the dining table. Leaving the shade down, she moved the lamp in the center of the table toward him.

He had a hand clamped to his upper left arm. Blood covered his fingers and soaked the sleeve of his gray work shirt.

Her hands were trembling as she reached for him. She gently plucked at the fabric stuck to his skin. "How bad is it?"

"Not deep, but I think the bullet's still in there." His jaw worked.

Ivy grimaced. "We should get you to the doctor."

"I can get it out."

"You? No!"

"The slug has to come out."

He was in a lot of pain. Ivy licked her lips, feeling slightly nauseous at the thought of what she must do. "I'll get it out."

Gideon must have noticed her hesitation because he said, "I can do it."

"No. I'll do it." It was the least she could offer after he'd come close to dying for her. She fought a surge of red-hot rage at whoever had done this.

Her movements sharp and jerky, she gathered up a knife, a pair of pliers and scissors, two basins of water and several cloths. When she returned to the table, she pulled the lamp closer and turned up the flame.

As she washed her hands and the tools, she stared at his arm. "Can you get out of your shirt, or should I cut it off?"

He glanced down at the red-stained sleeve. Blood spattered his shirtfront, too. "Do you think you can get the blood out?"

"Probably not all of it."

"Just cut it off, then."

Dragging in a deep, calming breath, she ripped his sleeve where the slug had torn a hole, then snipped off the whole thing. She grimaced as she got her first full look at the ragged hole in his flesh.

Blood streaked his arm, stained his fingers and hands. Thank goodness he'd turned back toward the house. She reached for a cloth and wet it, her fury bubbling up again. Why hadn't she agreed to go to the river for a picnic?

"Ivy, are you okay to do this?"

"Yes."

He set a hand on her waist until she looked at him. "You're angry."

She searched his eyes for blame, resentment, but she found none. "I thought this was all about me, but they hurt you this time."

"That tells me that whoever is behind your troubles is after something besides you."

"The farm?"

"Yes." Pain etched his features. His skin was waxy, sweat beading on his forehead.

Here he was, reassuring her when he was the one who needed help. "I'm sorry. We can talk about this later."

Trying to steady her hands, she cleaned the wound as gently as she could. Finally, she saw the bullet. Gideon was right. It wasn't very deep, and luckily it hadn't hit any bone, but she would still have to dig it out.

Picking up the pliers, she stared down at the ragged hole, steeling herself. She didn't want to hurt him, but this was going to hurt like the devil.

She grimaced. "I don't have any laudanum or liquor. Do you?"

His eyebrows shot up. He couldn't be any more surprised at her question than she was. "You said you don't hold with drinking."

"I don't, but you need something to dull the pain. Alcohol could help, and I don't have a drop."

"Neither do I."

She bit her lip.

"Ivy." At his labored tone, she met his gaze. "It's okay."

"It's going to hurt."

"There's no help for that. Do what you need to. I'll stay still."

"All right." The sooner she got this done, the better.

Fresh blood seeped out of the wound. Pliers in hand, she took a deep breath and shakily reached in for the bullet.

The muscles in his arm rippled and veins stood out in his neck, but he didn't move. Ivy worked as quickly as she could.

His upper arm was just like the rest of him—hard, solid muscle. Though she gripped the lead ball on her first try, the tool was slick with blood and the bullet slipped out.

Gideon made a noise deep in his throat, and she knew he must be in agony. Sweat trickled down his temple. His free hand gripped the table so forcefully that his knuckles were white.

She tried not to tremble. After what seemed much too long, she worked the lead out then cleaned the wound again and pressed a clean cloth firmly against it. "Hold that tight."

He did, panting slightly. His dark hair stuck damply to his forehead.

She gave him a wobbly smile. "The hole isn't too deep."

"Do you think I need stitches?"

Oh, she hoped not. She didn't know how much longer she could keep her composure.

He lifted the soiled rag and studied the tear in his flesh.

"Do you think I should stitch you up?"

"If I say yes, are you going to faint?"

"No," she huffed, relaxing when she saw he was teasing her. "I think I've done a pretty good job so far."

"You have." His lopsided grin belied the shadows of pain in his eyes. "I don't think I need to be stitched up."

"All right. Until the bleeding slows more, I don't want to bandage you."

Taking another clean cloth, she handed it to him, and he held the pad firmly against the wound. She carried the basin of red-tinted water down the hall and dumped it out the back door. When she returned, she gathered the items she'd used and began to wash them.

She glanced over to find him watching her intently. Sensation fluttered low in her belly. "Do you need anything?"

He shook his head, his gaze warm on her. "Our conversation was interrupted."

"Forevermore, Gideon!" Her head jerked around. "You don't have to tell me now!"

She hadn't really expected him to share, much less bring it up himself.

"It was right after the war." His voice was low and gravelly. "Her name was Eleanor."

Ivy went still. He had killed another man over a woman? She wasn't sure she wanted to hear more.

"I was courting her. Or thought I was."

Turning to tell him to stop, she saw his face, taut with agony as he stared at a spot on the floor. Ivy realized he was talking to distract himself from the pain.

"Her daddy owned a big spread in Kansas, and I worked for him." He gave a grim smile. "She said I 'rescued' her from her previous beau."

Laying the wet tools on a dry cloth, Ivy used another to dry her hands.

"We were supposed to go for a buggy ride one night, but she said she didn't feel well."

Ivy walked over to him and carefully exchanged the bloodied pad for a clean one.

He pressed it to the wound, and she slowly pulled away.

"After taking care of some business in town for her father, I came upon her and her old beau just outside of town. Just as I rode up, he hit her. Backhanded her so hard she stumbled. I didn't think. I just jumped off my horse and punched him. We fought until he went down. When I turned around to check on Eleanor, she came at me, clawing and hitting."

Ivy drew in a sharp breath, easing down onto the edge of the table.

"I managed to get her off of me, then Doyle hit me from behind with a whiskey bottle."

"Is that how you got the scar on your jaw?"

"Yeah. He tried to hit me twice, but I shot him. Killed him."

"Good," she said vehemently. "But it was self-defense. Why were you sent to prison?"

"Eleanor wouldn't back my story."

"You were trying to help her!"

"She was enraged that I'd interfered."

"Stupid woman! You might have saved her life."

"She told the sheriff I'd been 'taking liberties,' and when Doyle tried to defend her, I shot him. So I was arrested."

Ivy fought the urge to stroke his hair. "Did you get a trial?"

"Yes, but it didn't matter. Nobody was going up

against Eleanor's daddy or Doyle's. Between the two of them, they owned everything in town."

She checked his wound, glad to see the bleeding had slowed. Cutting a cloth into strips, she folded one length into a thick pad. "So you were sent to prison."

"The judge thought their story was suspect, but he had no proof. He sentenced me on a lesser charge, though I still had to do time at Leavenworth." He shifted in the chair as she laid the bandage against his wound then began wrapping the longer piece around his upper arm. "Now you know every last thing about me."

"Why are you telling me?"

"I said I would."

She kind of wished he hadn't. If he hadn't shared that part of his history, it would've confirmed her belief that he wasn't showing her his whole self, that there were parts of himself he was hiding. Instead, he seemed willing to let her know everything.

"And because I'd like to stay."

Aware of how long he had wanted his own place, she had expected that. What she hadn't expected was the pleasure that spread through her at his words. Tying off the end of the dressing, she surveyed her work. "As my partner."

"As your husband."

"But…I don't want a husband." She stood, her fingers tangling in her skirts. "That's why we shouldn't make love again. It will only complicate our arrangement."

Gideon snorted. "We already complicated it. We complicated the hell out of it last night."

"That was just one time. It was a mistake."

"No, it wasn't." He reached up, skimming his thumb

along her lower lip. "Can you forget about it? I can't. I won't."

"We should." A blush heated her cheeks.

He spoke carefully, calmly. "I told you I won't do anything against your wishes, but I want more from this marriage and I think you do, too."

"What if I don't change my mind? What if I'm never ready?"

"Just say you'll think about it."

She didn't refuse, although the word was on the tip of her tongue.

He was slowly, steadily chipping away her resolve to stick to their arrangement.

At first, Ivy was too wound up over Gideon's being shot to think much about him staying as her husband.

The image of that bullet hitting him was seared into her brain, and her stomach was still queasy. She hadn't wasted her breath trying to get him to leave; she knew he wouldn't go.

After cleaning everything up, they went to the woods to look for signs of the shooter. Sure enough, the branch Gideon had arranged was broken and there were clear boot prints, as well. But they still didn't have any idea who they belonged to.

Even though there had been no more trouble, Ivy didn't sleep well. Her mind began to churn with thoughts of the shooting and Gideon's desire to make their marriage permanent. Unable to bear the idea of him lying on the floor with his injury, she insisted he take a bed in one of the guest rooms. He had finally given in and agreed, though he didn't like the idea of the front room separating them.

She lay in bed, restless, finally getting up to check on him. Relieved when she saw he wasn't bleeding, she stood beside his bed for a few moments.

The moonlight washed silver over the lines lashing his torso. Last night when she'd first seen them, she'd wanted to cry, but she hadn't. He would have hated that. And the truth was, once he touched her, she hadn't thought about them. They were just another part of him, like his blue eyes and dark hair.

Remembering how Gideon had made her feel last night, the expression on his face when he'd been deep inside her, she'd been afraid she might be falling in love with him. The memory sent her back to her room.

The next morning after she'd changed his dressing and they'd had breakfast, she began preparing lunch for the few stage passengers they might have today. She put a pot of beans on the stove then mixed up filling for a pecan pie.

She slid the dessert into the stove. Hearing Gideon whistle for Thunder, she went to the front window. The sling she'd fashioned for his left arm fit snugly. As he checked the corral posts for damage from the horses' panic, his tan work shirt stretched across his massive shoulders. Shoulders that she had touched and kissed. Just as she had touched and kissed the rest of him.

There was no denying she wanted the man or that his lovemaking made her feel things she never had. Even though the urge to give herself over to that was staggering, she couldn't let their intimacy cloud her judgment.

Turning away from the window, she checked the beans and added bits of ham. He'd been right. She did want more from their marriage. But she knew how deceptive that thinking could be. She'd learned that from Tom.

What she felt for Gideon wasn't love. It was a combination of gratitude, affection and attraction. She needed to listen to her head, not her heart. Gideon didn't make it easy on her, though.

Like yesterday, when he had tried repeatedly to help her. He was always willing to lend a hand. And it had been so sweet of him to suggest a picnic, though she'd rejected that offer, too.

The reason she'd said no wasn't because she was worried he might try to get her out of her clothes, but because she wanted to get him out of his! She'd never fancied such a thing in her life.

The fact was she couldn't hold a thought when the man was around, which was a shame because she liked spending time with him.

Her thoughts were interrupted by the rumble of wheels. She went to the front door and saw a stage-coach bearing the same insignia as the one Conrad drove. It pulled up at the fence, but Conrad wasn't in the high seat.

Ivy stepped out onto the porch just as Gideon walked up the steps to her.

"I tied Thunder in the barn." He pushed his hat back. "That's not Conrad."

"I know. I wonder if something happened."

"Guess we'd better find out." Resting his hand in the small of her back, he walked down the steps with her and out to meet the visitors.

The driver, a burly younger man with sun-streaked brown hair, opened the coach door and an older gentleman got out. Short and round, his features were even more weathered than the driver's. He came toward her, doffing his cowboy hat.

"Miz Powell?" he asked.

"It's Mrs. Black now, but yes."

Gideon eased closer, his touch both reassuring and enticing.

The two men came through the gate, followed by a man Ivy recognized.

"Mr. Nichols?"

The railroad agent, again dressed in a three-piece suit, removed his bowler hat as he reached them. "Mrs. Powell, I mean Mrs. Black. Let me offer my congratulations to you both."

"Thank you," Gideon said quietly.

The other two visitors stood back as Gideon and Ivy shook hands with the barrel-chested man who had stopped here not too long ago.

Porter Nichols beamed at them. "Never would've guessed there was something between the two of you when I was here before."

"What brings you back this way?" Gideon stayed close, which was fine with Ivy.

She knew he was wondering, just as she was, if the railroad might be considering Paladin as a stop.

The scout for the Katy railway smiled. "I had some business to discuss with these two gentlemen. And you, too, once you have a minute."

He introduced the older man, who offered a hand to Gideon. "Hal Davis. And this is my son, Kirby."

"Mr. Davis." Ivy checked the stagecoach and the name painted there. "Territorial Stage Company. You're the stage line owner."

"Yes, ma'am," Kirby said. "After receiving your invitation to see your operation for ourselves, we decided to do it."

The elder Davis eyed her for a moment, hazel eyes shrewd. "Are you still willing to show us around?"

"Absolutely." She gestured to Gideon. "You've met my husband. If you'll excuse me for a moment, I need to take a pie out of the stove then we can begin."

"I can show them around until you join us," Gideon offered.

"Thank you." She squeezed his good arm before addressing the other men. "I'll catch up with you."

The men nodded their acquiescence. As Gideon led them toward the corral, Ivy hurried back into the house and checked the dessert. She left it to cook for a few more minutes and covered the beans with a lid, moving them off the hottest part of the stove. The corn bread could be made after she and Gideon finished with the Davises.

Excitement fluttered. If they were here to evaluate the stage stop, that meant they were reconsidering a deal with her, didn't it?

She hurried out the front door and down the steps, meeting the men as they left the barn.

"Your stalls are some of the cleanest I've seen." Kirby Davis sounded bemused.

Ivy shared a look with Gideon, who shrugged. They walked toward the back pasture.

"Mrs. Black," Hal Davis said. "I just told your husband that you have some fine horses here. All healthy, all strong."

"My wife has an eye for good livestock," Gideon said.

Ivy wasn't sure if it was the rumble of his deep voice

or the compliment that sent a rush of warmth through her. "The Holsteins give plenty of milk, so that's fresh every day. It makes good butter, and we have our own chickens that provide a ready supply of eggs."

Gideon pointed out the lush alfalfa where the cattle grazed then the river that bordered the farm. The father and son examined everything thoroughly, asking a lot of questions.

As the visitors stopped at the pump near the house, Ivy leaned toward Gideon. "They're checking everything!"

"They act almost like they're surprised at what they find."

Ivy nodded. "They were really impressed that all the chickens are alive."

"And that the livestock is well fed," he added.

"I don't understand." She kept her voice low, too. "They seem to expect poor conditions or sickly animals."

Gideon nodded in agreement.

Hal Davis turned from the pump to them. "You have a fine operation here, Mr. and Mrs. Black. Better than any we've seen."

"Thank you." Ivy smiled. "Conrad should arrive just in time for lunch. I'll be serving if you'd like to stay."

"We would. Thank you."

While she went inside and stoked the stove fire, Gideon fetched soap and toweling so the visitors could wash up. With the aroma of nuts and sugar filling the front room, she poured corn bread batter into two skillets. Thunder's yips sounded faintly from the barn.

As the bread sizzled on the stove, Ivy set out plates

and utensils. Gideon showed their guests the rooms available for overnight accommodations.

She filled two large serving bowls with beans and placed them on the table, returning to see if the corn bread was done. It was, so she sliced it and put the pieces in a large basket, covering it with a cloth.

"It's ready." She set a plate of butter at each end of the table.

Gideon pulled out her chair, and the men remained standing until she took her seat. After the first bite, the visitors didn't speak at all. They seemed to enjoy the meal, and when she served the pecan pie, they complimented her effusively.

Under the table, Gideon squeezed her knee, and she smiled at him. Had the Davises reconsidered signing a contract with her? She wished they would say something.

When the older Mr. Davis pushed away his plate, he gave Ivy a broad smile. "Miz Black, that was excellent."

"Thank you."

"And it's the one thing we were told about your place that's true."

She frowned. "What do you mean? Has someone been talking about my stage stop?"

"We've heard some things, most of them not complimentary."

"What!"

Kirby spoke up. "We were completely misinformed."

"But why—" Ivy broke off, stunned.

"Who would do something like that?" Gideon's mouth tightened. "Where did you get that information? From a passenger?"

"We'd rather not say," Hal answered. "But we're glad you invited us to judge for ourselves."

The younger man set his fork on his plate. "We were given the impression that your animals were poorly cared for, your place becoming a shambles."

No wonder they hadn't wanted to do business with her. Furious, Ivy could barely keep her voice from shaking. "I think I have a right to know who's telling such lies about me."

"I really can't say. It was told in confidence." Hal gave her a sympathetic smile. "However, now that we've seen what a fine operation you and your husband run, we'd like to discuss contracting with you if you're still interested."

"We are." She seethed. Who had slandered her reputation? It had to be the same person who was trying to run her and Gideon off.

Mr. Nichols excused himself and went outside so Ivy and Gideon could discuss business with the Davis men. They quickly worked out a lucrative agreement with the stage line owners. They all shook on the deal as the railroad agent returned to the room.

When Hal and Kirby asked to see the horses again, Gideon took them out to the corral.

Mr. Nichols helped Ivy carry dishes to the dry sink. "The Katy is seriously considering making Paladin a stop on the railroad. If that happens, it won't be long before we start laying tracks. Would you consider leasing your land, as we discussed when I was here?"

"I would."

"Good. I'm headed into Paladin to speak to Mayor Jumper and the other city leaders about the possibility.

After that, I'll have a better idea about what to propose to you."

"Hullo!"

Recognizing Conrad's voice, Ivy went to the door. The stage driver braked at the fence behind the other coach. He lifted a hand in greeting. As the Davises walked over to speak to him, Gideon made his way up the steps to her.

Nichols slipped past them. "Excuse me for a moment."

He hurried down the steps toward the father and son. "Hal, I can probably catch a ride into town with Conrad, and that way you won't need to go to the trouble of taking me out of your way. You can head on back home."

Gideon leaned slightly toward her, murmuring, "No passengers again. If Conrad knew yesterday that Nichols wouldn't be riding with him, he could've returned early and hidden in the woods."

"And shot you," Ivy finished angrily. She walked down the steps with Gideon, calling out to the stage driver. "Conrad, there are beans and corn bread left from lunch."

"Are you doin' what I think you're doin'?" Gideon asked in a low voice.

"If he'll climb down, you can compare his prints to the ones we found."

Conrad waved. "That sounds good, Ivy, but I need to get on to town." His gaze shifted to the railroad agent. "Porter, I appreciate you letting me know early that you wouldn't be taking my stage today. That way, we both stayed on schedule."

"Could I hitch a ride into Paladin with you?"

"I stopped by to see if you needed one."

After goodbyes all around, Conrad set off down the road toward town. Hal and Kirby Davis again stated how pleased they were to have a contract with the stage stop then left in their own stage.

As they drove away, dust plumed beneath the wagon's wheels. Ivy waited until they were down the road a bit.

Bracing her hands on her hips, she spun toward Gideon. "Who do you think told all those lies?"

"The same person who's caused all the other trouble." His voice was hard.

"It has to be someone who knows something about my operation. And who's met with Hal and his son."

"There probably aren't too many people who fit that bill."

"Could it be Conrad?" Ivy hated the thought, but she wasn't surprised at the possibility.

Frustration creased Gideon's features. "It could be."

"Is there someone else?" Stung by a thought, she frowned. "What about the mayor? He could still be angry about his horse being killed here."

"Maybe," Gideon said slowly. "Or maybe we aren't the only people Nichols has told about the railroad's plans to move forward. Jumper is the only other person we know of who's familiar with your operation and has contact with the stage line owners."

"Would he or Conrad want my farm badly enough to kill for it?"

"I've seen men kill for less."

"We may never get a look at Leo's footprints. I don't think I've ever seen him walk anywhere except in town. Anytime he has business outside of Paladin, he takes a buggy or the stage."

"He doesn't ride at all?"

She shook her head. "How can we find out about his prints? What are we going to do?"

"Hey. Don't look so worried." He stroked her cheek. "We'll come up with a way."

"I'm so glad—" She stopped. She'd almost said she was glad she wasn't alone. "I'm so glad we worked out a new deal with the stage line."

"It's a nice one, too."

She smiled.

The sound of Thunder's barking had Gideon starting for the barn. "I'd better untie her before she gets the horses rattled."

Ivy watched him go, feeling a surge of affection and satisfaction and an emotion she didn't want to name.

He was a good man, and she really was glad she wasn't alone. After Tom, she had believed she would never feel that way again. It was unsettling.

As unsettling as Gideon saying he wanted theirs to be a real and permanent marriage. Ivy didn't doubt his commitment for a second. She just wasn't sure she could make the same one to him.

Chapter Twelve

The rest of the day passed quickly. Gideon and Ivy stayed up later than usual, talking about the contract with the stage line and their suspicions of the mayor and Conrad.

Smoky amber light from the lamp spread across the dining table where they sat. She had included Gideon in all the decisions today, but he didn't know if that was because she was a fair businesswoman and he owned half of the farm now, or because she was considering a future with him.

She rose from her seat and picked up the lamp. "We'd better get to bed."

He wished they were going to bed together, but he didn't react to her phrasing.

He stood, too, and walked over to the opposite corner where he kept his bedroll.

"You're not sleeping on the floor. You should be in a bed."

Maybe so, but pillowed on that plump mattress last night, his head had been filled with memories of being there with Ivy. Staying on the floor tonight might be more uncomfortable, but he wouldn't be reaching for her as he'd done on waking up this morning.

He gestured to the area in front of the fireplace, which shared a wall with her bedroom. "I'd rather sleep out here. Closer to the door." And to her.

She shook her head. "What about your arm?"

"I'll be careful."

"Why you want to be on the hard floor rather than a mattress is beyond me."

Using his good hand, he spread out his bedroll.

Ivy shook the pup awake from her spot under the table. Thunder stretched and yawned before finally getting up to follow her mistress down the hall to her crate.

Gideon took off his boots, setting them beside his blanket as Ivy returned.

"Do you have any ideas about what we can do to find out if Conrad or the mayor are behind what's been happening?"

"Not yet, but tomorrow I think we should go to town and talk to the sheriff. He needs to know what's going on, and we can tell him about our suspicions."

"Maybe he'll have an idea."

Gideon nodded. "You said the mayor never walks anywhere, that he always stays in the buggy."

"Yes."

"I've seen him use that cane, and he doesn't have a limp."

"What's your point?"

"Maybe he does walk, just not anywhere outside of town."

Realization spread across her face. "Where no one would be able to distinguish his prints from anyone else's."

"Right. We need to figure out a way to get footprints from both Conrad and Jumper."

"Maybe Josh will have an idea about that, too." She paused in her bedroom doorway. "I'm really glad you're here."

Heady words from a woman who hadn't wanted anyone around just weeks ago. Warmed by what she'd said, he eased down onto his blanket, folding his good arm behind his head. Maybe she was coming to accept the idea of him staying as her husband?

The throb in his arm reminded him of the attentive care she'd given him. For the first time in his life, he felt as if he belonged somewhere. His life before Ivy seemed bleak. He had been empty, searching and not understanding why until now.

It was too soon to ask if she'd made a decision about their marriage, and he wanted her to come to him on her own. The truth was, he was loath to ask because he wasn't sure he wanted to hear her answer.

He filched a pillow from the nearest guest room and lay back down. It felt as if he'd only just drifted off when a series of sharp barks jolted him awake.

Thunder.

Gideon pushed up on his elbows, cursing when pain razored down his injured arm. Clamping a hand on the wound, he sat up, looking toward the hall.

Thin ribbons of gray mist snaked out from under Ivy's bedroom door. Not mist, smoke! The pup clawed frantically at her crate.

"Ivy!" Gideon bellowed. He jammed his feet into his boots and jumped up, crashing through her door. "Ivy, wake up!"

She sat straight up, blinking sleepily at him. "What's going on?"

"Fire!"

Even as he spoke, alarm widened her eyes, and before he could reach her, she flew out of bed. Pulling on her brown work shoes, she coughed.

Smoke thickened in the room, and Gideon saw orange flames licking around the window above her bed. The fire hissed then snapped as it ate through wood.

He started to pluck her up and run for it, but she grabbed his hand and bolted down the hall. Gideon seized Thunder's crate, barely aware of the agony in his arm. He pushed Ivy out the back door ahead of him.

They raced for the nearest pump, the one next to the corral. The horse trough was full of water Gideon had pumped for the horses before dark. He released the dog so she wouldn't be trapped if they couldn't contain the fire.

Grabbing two of the closest buckets, Gideon filled both and ran to throw water on the blaze. The flames spread quickly, climbing up the wall. They had to stop it before it reached more of the house.

Ivy's window shattered. She hurried up behind him, her nightgown fluttering around her as she tossed her own bucket of water on the fire.

He beat her back to the trough, scooping up water and dumping it on the blaze. The horses neighed, the whites of their eyes showing in the darkness. All of the animals crashed to the back of the corral, as far from the flames as they could get. Some of them reared, their hooves striking out at the air or another horse. A splintering crack of wood told Gideon the animals had kicked down a section of the pen. He couldn't worry about that right now.

The flames writhed toward the roof, giving off heat like an inferno. Gideon and Ivy concentrated their efforts on that section. She half jogged, half walked back to him with another full bucket, trying to spill as little water as possible.

"Trough's getting low," she yelled above the sound of wood splitting and crackling.

He spun, rushing for more water. Ivy was at the pump, working the handle as hard as she could. Water gushed out, and Gideon scooped up two more pails of water then dashed back to the house. Smoke stung his nostrils, his chest hurt, but it looked as if the fire was dwindling. It had shifted direction and was now headed sideways rather than up toward the roof.

Alongside Ivy, Gideon continued to drench the burning wood. The flames began to sputter and die. Ivy pitched more water on an ember that kept rekindling. Finally, the glow disappeared; the blaze died. Water soaked the ground around Ivy, dripped from the eaves and the side of the house.

Intending to further wet down what he could, Gideon started toward her with two more buckets of water. A creak sounded overhead, and he realized it was a weakened beam. That would have to be fixed. Ash fluttered down. The acrid odor of smoke bit the air. The charred screen of wall began to crumble and sway. Toward Ivy.

"Move!" he bellowed. "Ivy!"

She looked over her shoulder and sprinted forward. The side of her bedroom collapsed, crashing down on her. She screamed and stumbled, falling facedown.

Cold, piercing fear shanked his spine. Not even aware he'd moved, he found himself clawing at the charred wood, breaking and slinging pieces of blackened lumber out of the way. He could see her pale nightgown beneath the torched planks.

Ignoring the sting of heat and splinters on his hands, he muscled the wall off her. His heart pounded so hard he thought it would burst out of his chest.

She pushed herself up, her gown muddy, her hair wet and streaming over her shoulders. Her dazed eyes met his. "Gideon?"

Finally, he reached her. He knelt and gathered her up, carrying her several yards away from the broken glass and smoldering timber. The pup raced toward them from the direction of the woods.

A huge searing knot lodged in his chest. Gideon coasted his hands gently over his wife. "Where are you hurt? Are you bleeding?"

She shifted in his lap so she could sit up more fully and check herself.

"I'm okay. I'm not burned at all," she said in a half whisper, staring up at him in wonder. "My back's a little sore, maybe scratched, but nothing feels out of place."

Unable to draw a full breath, he examined her as thoroughly as he could. The capped sleeves of her nightgown were torn and a few scratches raked down the silky length of her arm, but he saw no other injuries.

He couldn't believe it. He carefully angled her face so he could see her neck and shoulders. Aside from the scrapes, soot and mud, she looked fine. She felt even better.

She cupped his face in her hands. "I'm all right. Truly. How's your arm? It has to be paining you after all that."

"It's fine." It hurt like the devil, but all he cared about was that she was here in his lap, and she was okay.

Moonlight spilled down on them, illuminating the

singed table and lamp next to her bed, the scorched back side of the headboard.

He hugged her to him.

She drew back, her face streaked with ash and soot. Apprehension clouded her eyes. "Somebody did that on purpose."

"Yeah," he said grimly.

"Do you think it was intended for both of us?"

"Yeah." He thumbed away a smudge of black on her cheek. "They probably thought we were together in the bedroom."

A whine behind them alerted him to the pup's presence. Gideon glanced back, glad to see the animal looked unharmed. "C'mon, girl."

Thunder crept warily toward them. Ivy laid her head on Gideon's shoulder, coaxing the dog near until it finally crawled into her lap.

The animal stared up at Gideon, nosing his chest in a plea for a scratch, but he wasn't taking his hands off Ivy.

"Good dog," he said gruffly, resting his chin on Ivy's head. "She knew there was trouble before I did."

"Thank goodness for both of you." Ivy shuddered against him.

He became aware of the cool air, their wet clothes, the dank smell of sodden wood. Smoke and ash spiraled to the sky, and he tightened his hold on Ivy, ignoring the sharp jab of pain in his left arm.

He wasn't letting her out of his sight tonight. Maybe not tomorrow, either.

They cleaned up what they could, and Ivy grabbed a chemise from her wardrobe as well as a dress. Then they shut the door to her bedroom.

Though the air was still laced with the odor of burned wood, the smell faded somewhat on the opposite side of the house. Ivy draped the garments over the handle of the pump on the other side of the house in hopes that most of the smell would dissipate. She then helped him tack quilts across the entrance into the guest hallway in order to close off that part of the house.

Building a fire in the fireplace, he filled the kettle and hung it to heat along with a brick. He hauled more water to the bathing tub and washbasin set up in a small closet across the hall from the guest rooms. He kept a close eye on the flame under the kettle. The water was barely warm when he dumped it into the tub and added a heated brick.

Ivy looked worn to a frazzle. He didn't know how much longer she'd last. The bathwater would be tepid, but she said she didn't care. All she wanted was to wash away the acrid stench of smoke.

While she bathed, Gideon brought the pup's crate into the far guest room. Thunder padded behind him, sniffing the floor, around the bed and bureau before curling up in her box.

After Ivy finished in the tub, Gideon used her water to wash. He then tugged on the dry trousers he'd retrieved from his saddlebags in the barn. The pants, too, carried a smoky odor, but it was the best he could do. And on this side of the house, he and Ivy were as far from the charred remains as he could get them.

Barefoot and bare-chested, he stood in the doorway of the bedroom where she was already asleep. Only now did his pulse slow to a normal rate. He'd never been so damn scared in his entire life. If something had happened to her—

He cut off the thought. She was fine, which was a miracle. And he was fine. And they were together. He had determined what damage he could in the darkness. They would know more in the daylight, but first thing tomorrow, they were going to town to talk to the sheriff.

Gideon would try to convince Ivy to stay in Paladin until he found the low-down snake who'd done this and stopped him. From now on, 100 percent of his efforts would be spent tracking down this bastard.

His wounded arm ached to the bone, but he dismissed the discomfort. He walked over and sat on the edge of the bed, reaching out to stroke Ivy's hair, still slightly damp from her towel-drying.

She slept on her side facing him, huddled on the mattress as if protecting herself from something. He needed to be closer to her.

Stretching out on top of the covers, he gathered her to him. She pressed close, her body relaxing. His chest hurt, and it had nothing to do with smoke or danger. The fullness in his heart was all about this slip of a woman.

The fire might have cast a haze over the night, but it had brought things into sharp focus for Gideon. He loved her.

It wasn't some need to "rescue" her, as he'd felt with Eleanor, or because half of the farm was now his. It was about Ivy and only Ivy.

He didn't want to ever let her go. He wanted her to be his wife in every way. Though he still had to let her decide if she wished to make a real go of their marriage, he knew exactly what he desired. Her. For the rest of his life.

He brushed a light kiss against her forehead and felt her stir against him.

"Gideon?"

"Hmm?"

"This is real? We're both okay?"

"We're both okay," he said softly.

She tilted her head back so she could see him. Moonlight skimmed over her petal-smooth skin, the arch of her dainty eyebrows and thick dark lashes.

"I'll move if you want. Not out of the room, but off of the bed. I just needed to feel for myself that you were all right."

"I don't want you to move." She touched his face, something new and soft in her eyes. Need. Invitation?

Was he reading that right? Somehow, he didn't know how, they were kissing. Hard and urgent at first, as if she needed the same reassurance he did that they were all right. Then her mouth softened under his. The kisses became slower, longer. Hot and sweet and giving.

The sound that came from deep in her throat set off something fierce and demanding inside him. He pulled her tight into him, hungry to feel the fullness of her breasts, the warmth of her body through the light fabric of her chemise.

She stroked his neck, her fingers a butterfly touch against his scar, and he didn't even mind. He lifted his head, grazing his thumb over her cheekbone. "Are you sore anywhere?"

"Only a little." The words were raspy, probably from smoke.

He rubbed a hand up and down her back. "Do you need anything?"

She snuggled into him, making him wish he could feel her without clothes or the sheet between them. He wanted her to touch him all over, even his scars.

"Where's Thunder?" she asked.

"Asleep in her crate over there in the corner."

"Thank you for the bathwater."

"You're welcome." Gideon kept his voice low, conscious of the hush in the room.

The quiet outside was occasionally broken by the chirp of crickets or the hoot of an owl. The night folded around them, cradling them in a world of their own.

Sliding a palm under her hair, he caressed her nape. "Are you warm enough?"

"Yes." She flattened a hand on his chest, flexing her fingers in the hair there. One finger traced a scar on his sternum.

He wanted her like hell afire, but now wasn't the time. Not after the scare they'd just had.

"You'll let me know if you need anything? Whatever you want."

She was silent for a long moment then raised herself so she could whisper in his ear, "I want you."

He started to say she didn't need to worry. He wasn't going anywhere. But she skimmed her hand down his belly, slightly below the waistband on his trousers.

His heart kicked hard. "*This* is what you want?"

"Yes."

"You're sure?"

"Yes." She kissed him again, sending a surge of heat through him.

He wanted to strip her naked and slide into her right now. Possess her. But the other night had been too fast. This time, he intended to go as long as he could.

The scrape of her nails across his abdomen drove a hard-edged want through him. He got out of bed and shucked his trousers.

Her gaze glided slowly, slowly down his body, and the need on her face kicked off an urgency inside him. Before his knees gave, he climbed back in beside her, under the covers this time.

She sat up, reaching to pull off her chemise.

"No. Let me do it," he said.

She gave him a shy smile and dropped her hands to her sides. He burned to get her clothes off right now. Touch every silky inch of her body with his hands, then his mouth. Kiss her until neither one of them could breathe. Where to start?

She made the decision for him, leaning forward to nuzzle his neck then nip his earlobe. Her soap didn't quite mask the faint smell of smoke, but he'd never smelled anything so sweet.

He reached for the ribbon on her shift, glad she wasn't wearing a nightgown like she'd had on earlier with a million buttons down the front that he likely would've clumsily torn off.

The garment loosened, and he dragged it over her shoulders and down her arms, nudging down the loose fabric until it pooled at her waist. Now that she was bared to him, his breath jammed in his throat.

Her nipples were tight and dusky in the pale light. He cupped her full breasts, his thumbs rubbing over her nipples. The sight of his rough hands on her delicate skin sent his blood streaking through him in a white-hot rush.

She pressed hard against his erection, and he lowered his head, curling his tongue around her taut flesh. His name spilled out of her in a broken moan.

Hell, he couldn't take much of that. Easing her down on her back, he swept her chemise off completely. For a long moment, he just stared at her. Silvery light coasted over her shoulders, the flat of her belly and the jut of her hip bones.

She lifted herself against him and set her teeth on his neck, sending all his blood south. He clenched his muscles, searching for control as his mouth returned to hers.

Threading his hands into her thick raven hair, he brushed his lips across her cheek, her jaw, a spot just below her ear that had her shifting restlessly against him. Gideon moved his lips to the hollow of her throat; he could feel her pulse racing beneath his tongue.

She slid her arms around his shoulders, making a ragged sound that frayed his restraint. "Gideon, I want to be close to you," she whispered. "I'm ready."

"I'm not."

She reached down and curled her fingers around him. "I think you are."

He stroked her hair. "The other night was too fast."

"I don't know if I can last much longer."

He smiled. "Let's see how far we get."

She pulled his head down to hers and kissed him hard and long. He swept a hand up her slender thigh, delving a finger inside her silky heat. Her body clenched him then went soft. Well, they hadn't gotten very far. He couldn't wait any longer.

He levered himself between her legs, nudging her thighs wider with one of his. Pushing slowly inside, he closed his eyes in pure pleasure. When he began to move, she kept her gaze fixed to his. The desire, the softness in her face speared clear to his heart. She wouldn't have asked for this if she wasn't willing to make their marriage real and permanent.

For the first time in his life, he felt like he belonged

somewhere. To *someone*. Every lash of the whip, every violent bruise and minute spent in the dark hole of prison had led him here. To her.

He slid his arms under her, holding her as close as possible, losing himself in the midnight depths of her eyes. Meeting every stroke of his body with her own, she clasped him tight to her.

She'd said they shouldn't sleep together again since she didn't want to stay married, and he'd honored that. But he had asked her to think about staying married and now she had answered him, taking him into her bed, her body. She'd said yes.

Chapter Thirteen

The next day was a blur. After rounding up the horses, Ivy and Gideon drove into town, where they reported the fire and Gideon's gunshot wound to the sheriff. Once home, they discovered half the town there, already well on the way to clearing away the debris. The men had then helped Gideon reframe and rebuild Ivy's bedroom while the women washed everything in the house from clothes and curtains to floors and walls.

Conrad was there, too. Gideon said he would check the stage driver's footprints at some point, and waiting to find out if he managed to do so nagged Ivy like a headache the rest of the day.

By the time everyone left at dark, the farm had been put to rights as best it could be. She leaned against a porch column, the pup at her feet as they waited for Gideon. Tonight was clear with no smoky haze or gray clouds blocking the moon, though there was still a faint pungent odor.

Gideon walked up the steps, bending to give the pup a scratch behind the ears. His hair curled damply against his nape. The blue work shirt he wore was streaked with grime and soot. He smelled of wood and a hint of smoke.

Bracing his back against the opposite column, he scrubbed at his face with a wet bandanna. Fatigue creased his features, and she knew he had to be as tired as she was.

She opened the front door, motioning him inside. "Did you have any luck with Conrad's footprints?"

"I managed to check them." As he crossed the threshold, he shook his head, clearly frustrated. "They weren't a match to what we found in the woods."

"Oh, forevermore!" Ivy blew out a breath, both disappointed and exasperated. "That leaves the mayor as our best suspect."

"And he's out of town."

"I hope it isn't for much longer. I'm ready for this to be over."

"So am I," Gideon said in a gritty voice.

They fell into bed exhausted.

At midmorning on Monday, she was in the root cellar making sure that no food in here had been ruined. All the fruit, pickles and beans she'd canned were fine. Underground and set away from her bedroom, the cellar hadn't suffered any damage. There was only the occasional whiff of smoke.

She came up the cellar stairs, intending to gather the remaining sheets, blankets and clothes that had been left on the line to dry overnight, but the *clop-clop* of an approaching horse had her changing direction.

She went to the front window, stopping cold when she saw the mayor in his buggy. What was he doing here?

Gideon was in the back pasture searching for the

two remaining cows that hadn't returned after the fire scare. The pup, playing with an old rag Ivy had knotted into a ball, dropped the toy and followed Ivy out the door then down the porch steps.

Leo braked his buggy at the horse trough along the fence. "Mrs. Black."

"Hello, Leo."

He remained seated as usual. "Conrad told me there was a fire out here the other night."

Did you set it? she wondered. "Yes, but as you can see, we're fine."

"It was only your bedroom?" His gaze shifted to the side of the house.

"Gideon and I managed to put it out before it did more damage. Yesterday, a big group from town came out to help clean up and rebuild the room."

"I see."

If he would get out of the buggy, she could get a look at his footprints. "Why don't you come in? I have fresh coffee."

The mayor shook his head. "I don't want to put you to any trouble."

"It's no trouble at all." Ivy wished Gideon were here.

Thunder guarded the gate, watching the mayor closely.

Leo's gaze scanned the yard, the corral and barn. "Where's your husband?"

"He's just out back." Though she didn't feel as if she were in immediate danger, the hair on her arms prickled. "Would you like to speak with him?"

"No." The tall red-haired man levered himself out of the buggy, leaning on his cane as he looked around.

Ivy held her breath, hoping he would take a few

steps toward her and leave an impression of his boots in the dirt.

The mayor sauntered over, and Ivy struggled to keep her face blank.

"I understand you now have a contract with Territorial Stage."

"Yes."

"Good thinking to strike an agreement with them directly."

Despite his words, the man didn't sound pleased about it.

He stepped up to the gate. Thunder growled. "You certainly have had a run of bad luck."

Hmph, Ivy thought, but didn't respond.

"After everything that's happened, I wouldn't blame you if you moved on. Have you thought about selling this place?"

Her spine went to steel. "No."

"Would you consider it?"

"I don't think so."

"Progress, Mrs. Black."

"You're talking about the railroad." Ivy walked toward him, intending to get a look at his footprints if she could. "Mr. Nichols said the Katy had no firm plans to run tracks through here."

"Maybe not, but the man has visited here twice. There has to be a reason."

She tried to sneak a look at the imprint just behind him, but she only got a glimpse. Not enough of a view to compare to the ones Gideon had found in the woods.

Jumper tapped his walking stick against his shoe, earning a bark from the dog. Holding the cane by its carved head, Leo pointed it at her. "I think the railroad's serious about coming through here, and when they do, how long do you think you can hang on to this place?"

"As long as I want."

"Don't be naive." Brown eyes hard, he turned toward the gate as if he might come through. "The Katy will plow over this place just like it has farms in other communities. Plus there will be no need for stage stops."

"I'll make do," she said tightly.

He came back toward her. "I'd pay you very well for this place."

"I'm not selling."

"That's shortsighted," he snapped. "I thought you a better businesswoman than that."

After Gideon's injury and the fire, she had no patience for the mayor's snide remarks. "Good day, Leo."

His gaze flickered to a spot behind her, and Gideon walked up beside her.

"Mayor." His voice was flat and unwelcoming.

The other man's greeting was every bit as warm.

Ivy still couldn't get a good look at Jumper's footprints, but he had left more than one set. She just hoped they were distinctive enough to identify.

Using his walking stick, he indicated the corral and barn. "All the trouble you've had out here could give this place a bad name."

Ivy drew in a sharp breath. "Are you the one who lied about my operation to Hal Davis and his son?"

His silence confirmed her suspicions.

"Why would you try to ruin my business, Leo?"

Unhurriedly going back to his buggy, he climbed in on the same side he'd gotten out.

Gideon's face was unreadable as he stared at the man. Jumper set his cane on the seat beside him then picked up the reins. "Hope you don't have any more dogs or horses killed out here. That certainly won't help your business, either."

Ivy wanted to smack him.

Gideon strode to the gate, and the mayor wheeled his buggy around.

Blood boiling, she watched him drive away. Not down the old road toward town, but past her woods and across the wide-open pastureland beyond.

It hit her then, what Leo had said.

"Did you hear him?" She hurried over to Gideon and clutched his arm. "That he hoped no more dogs or horses were killed out here."

"The man's a jackass, Ivy. He's angry that you won't sell and probably angry that the stage line gave you a contract."

"No, that's not it." Her voice shook. She didn't know if it was from anger or exhilaration that Jumper had given himself away. "I never told him about Tug being killed. I only told him about the horse."

"Maybe Conrad—"

She shook her head. "You, the Farrells and I are the only ones who know about Tug. Neither Josh nor Meg would have said anything to him."

Satisfaction lit his eyes. He turned her gently toward the gate and pointed to the ground. "Here's actual proof. These footprints match the ones we found in the woods."

"Wonderful!"

He started for the barn.

Ivy hurried behind him. "What are you doing?"

"I'm going after the bastard."

"I'm coming, too."

He looked as if he would argue, but he didn't. Grabbing up her skirts, she angled toward the house.

"C'mon!" Gideon called.

"I'm getting my gun."

He jogged across the yard. "I'll take care of the horses and the pup."

She wished she could change into her britches, but she wasn't wasting time on that. And he hadn't used precious minutes to saddle their mounts, which was fine with Ivy.

He waited outside the corral and helped her onto the horse's bare back. She pushed down her skirts as he vaulted onto his gelding. Together, they barreled past the pen.

Gideon and Ivy kneed their horses into a gallop, tearing past the woods and heading into open pasture. Jumper's buggy was quite a distance away, his horse trotting at a brisk pace.

Grass flashed beneath Gideon, spots of flowers visible from the corner of his eye. The wind was mild, the sun a deep yellow in a clear blue sky.

They were gaining on the mayor when Gideon saw him lean out of the buggy. He must have seen they were in pursuit because the vehicle lurched forward and the horse began a flat-out run.

Suddenly, Gideon realized Ivy was no longer beside him. He spun his mount around. She was more than a hundred yards away, standing beside her horse.

He urged his gelding forward.

"No!" she yelled, waving him on. "Keep going! Don't let him get away!"

Gideon wasn't leaving her there. He kneed his horse into motion.

"My mare's lame! Go after Leo! He's getting away!"

Glancing over his shoulder, Gideon saw she was right.

"Go!" she urged again. "I'll catch up!"

It went against everything inside him. Still, she had her gun if she needed it. And there was no telling where Jumper was headed. It sure wasn't town.

Gideon turned the horse sharply and gave the animal its head. They pounded across the lush alfalfa. The distance between him and the buggy began to narrow.

Jumper's horse couldn't keep up the speed while pulling a buggy. Gideon soon passed them and pulled his gun, slowing his gelding in front of the man.

He aimed the weapon at the mayor. "Stop!"

The man's gaze darted around, but he seemed to realize that no matter where he went, Gideon's horse would overtake him.

Sawing on the reins, he slowed his animal, and the buggy rolled to a stop.

"What's the meaning of this, Mr. Black?"

Gideon gave him a flat look. Seeing that both of Leo's hands were on the reins, he motioned toward the buggy. "Do you have a gun in there?"

Gideon dismounted, gesturing with his revolver at the mayor. "Step out. Hands where I can see them."

Raising his hands in the air, the mayor slid from the buggy, bringing his walking stick with him.

Gideon eased over to the vehicle and felt under the seat. "Ah. This what you used to shoot me?"

He pulled out a Peacemaker. Popping out the cylinder, he emptied the bullets then tossed the gun into the grass.

He moved in front of Jumper. "So, you're the one who's been behind everything that's happened at Ivy's farm."

The man didn't respond.

"I matched your footprints to a set I found in the woods."

Leo stiffened, gripping his cane with both hands.

"Why sabotage everything?"

"I was trying to scare her off."

"Scare her?" He thought his jaw might break clean in two. Anger drove through Gideon like a spike. "You could've killed her with that trap you set!"

For that alone, he wanted to squeeze the life out of the bastard. "And that fire wasn't no attempt to frighten her. You was goin' for murder. What could possibly justify that?" Viciousness welled up from some place deep inside that Gideon had never known existed. Gun leveled, he advanced on the cur.

Jumper retreated a step. "Do you know how much that land will be worth to the railroad? Not just in dollars, but control."

The Kiamichi River that ran through Ivy's property was another source of readily available water that wouldn't have to support Paladin the way Little River did.

"That ain't no call for murder."

"The two of you were in the way. If she'd just left, but no. She went and got married. I had to get rid of both of you."

Gideon knew he should turn the man over to the law, but killing him sounded better. He thumbed down the hammer on his pistol.

Suddenly, Leo yanked hard on the carved head of his walking stick.

What the hell? By the time Gideon registered that the man had pulled a knife out of the cane's shaft, he barely had time to react. The mayor slashed at his gun hand. The revolver flew into the air, and a razor-edged pain shot up his arm.

The gash went from the back of his hand up past his wrist. Blood welled up, soaking his shirtsleeve and slicking his palm.

Jumper lunged and Gideon leaped back, barely escaping a rip to his belly.

The knife was large, the blade wide and long enough to have killed the horse and Ivy's dog.

"You killed your own horse?" Gideon didn't understand anyone who put down a good animal. "Why the hell did you kill Ivy's dog?"

"It found me."

He noticed that the lowlife didn't claim the animal had attacked him.

The man rushed at Gideon, jabbing and chopping. He dodged, air whistling as the knife sliced past his cheek.

He circled the other man. In the split second it took Jumper to angle his body toward Gideon, he charged, ramming his head and shoulders into the bastard's gut.

He tackled Jumper to the ground, his hand slippery with blood, his gunshot arm throbbing in agony. Ignoring the pain, he slammed a fist into the mayor's face and tried to wrest the knife away, but couldn't.

With his injuries, it was all Gideon could do to escape a vicious hack to the face.

The two of them rolled, dirt and grass flying. By sheer grit, Gideon managed to wrestle Jumper to his back. The coppery smell of blood reached him. His blood. Sweat burned his eyes as he struggled to keep the knife from plunging into his throat.

The mayor grunted, heaving his body with enough force to reverse their positions. The bastard was a lot stronger than he looked. Malicious satisfaction glinted in his eyes.

Jumper put all his weight behind the assault, driving the blade toward Gideon's left eye. Locking both arms straight out, Gideon managed to hold the knife at bay, but the blood loss was starting to affect him.

His head swam; his lacerated arm burned red-hot. Gathering all his might, he managed to jostle Jumper off balance, but the man quickly recovered and bore down using both hands. The blade inched closer. Sunlight winked off the edge of the knife, blinding Gideon for a second.

From the corner of his eye, he thought he saw a flash of pink. Ivy? He wasn't dying on her if he could help it. With a surge of energy, he shoved at the mayor, but he was pinned. Jumper barely budged.

Suddenly a gunshot rang out from somewhere behind Gideon. A hole appeared between the mayor's eyes. Blood trickled out and the man collapsed, his weight smothering. Gideon pushed the mayor's body off and rolled to his knees.

Ivy ran toward him, pink skirts gathered in one hand, her gun in the other.

In seconds, she was on her knees in front of him. "Gideon!"

"I'm okay."

"You're cut!" She tore off her apron and rolled it into

a strip, using it as a tourniquet to bind his wound. Blood quickly soaked the cloth.

A lightness filled his chest, just like the day he'd walked out of Leavenworth.

His wife's gaze went to the dead man, and the rage on her face shifted to shock when she saw the knife. "Is that his?"

"Yeah. He kept it in the shaft of his cane. The carved head was actually the base of the knife."

"That's what he used to kill Tug. And his own horse."

Gideon nodded, getting slowly to his feet. When he wobbled, she grabbed him around the waist and clasped him tight.

"We don't have time for that," he joked weakly.

"Oh, you."

He smiled down at her, wishing he could hold her, but both of his arms felt like soggy rope. Truth be told, he was about spent. "Let's get Jumper to town. I'll tell you everything on the way."

"Thank goodness you're alive." She touched his face with a trembling hand. "I was afraid I might be too late. These blasted skirts slowed me down."

"You got here in the nick of time." It had been a little too close for his liking. He glanced over at the spot where she'd stopped to take the shot. "And that was some damn good shooting. I'm glad your brother didn't exaggerate about that."

"I'll unhitch Jumper's buggy, and we'll get his body on his horse. We'll both have to ride your gelding." She started toward the carriage.

"Ivy?"

"Yes?"

"Thanks for saving my life," he said gruffly. "In

more ways than one. I don't know what I did to deserve a wife like you, but I'm real glad I have you."

"How much blood have you lost? Do you know what you're saying?"

"I ain't joshin'."

"I know," she said softly. "And you're very welcome."

Maybe he had lost more blood than he realized because her response didn't sound exactly right.

Though Gideon wanted to go straight to the jail and turn over the body, Ivy insisted the doctor be their first stop. Since his hand and forearm hurt like the devil, he didn't argue.

Minutes later, he was on an exam table in Roe Manning's clinic. He gave a silent sigh of relief. Jumper was dead, and Ivy was safe.

The doctor unwound the blood-soaked tourniquet and dropped it into the trash, then cleaned the wound. "That's deep enough for stitches, but it could've been worse. The blade missed your bone and your tendons. Barely."

Reaching to the table behind him, he picked up a brown bottle. "The laudanum will make the stitching bearable."

"I don't want any of that."

"But—" Ivy started.

Gideon looked at Roe. "Just do what you need to."

"It's going to hurt like hell," the other man said.

"I know." But he didn't want to be fuzzy-headed while they were in town or when they answered questions about the mayor.

Picking up a needle, Manning threaded it and dipped

both into a bottle marked Carbolic Acid, then began to stitch the wound.

Biting back a roar of pain, Gideon gripped the edge of the table with his other hand. Hurt layered through his whole body. His arm quivered.

Josh Farrell strode into the clinic. "Saw y'all ride in with a body and just checked. It's Jumper!"

"Yes." Looking concerned, Ivy's gaze went from Gideon's face to the hand being sutured.

Josh took her by the shoulders, giving her the once-over. "Are you all right?"

"Yes. It's Gideon who's hurt."

"Who shot Leo?"

"Ivy." Gideon turned his head toward the sheriff. "It was a hell of a shot, too."

"He was about to kill Gideon."

Josh glanced over at the wound. "Where's the knife?"

"In the bastard's cane," Gideon rasped, trying to focus on something besides the searing agony running up his arm.

At the lawman's frown, Ivy nodded. "It's true. He carried it in the shaft of his walking stick. The head was really the handle of the knife."

Josh and Roe looked stunned.

The doctor shook his head. "He was hiding a knife in that stick?"

"Yes," Ivy and Gideon said together.

Gideon felt each stinging prick of the needle as it wove in and out of his flesh like a fiery awl. "Jumper's buggy is still in the field west of the woods in front of the farm."

"I'll send Coy to fetch it," the sheriff said.

The needle slid through his skin again and again.

Gideon grunted. How much longer? "The mayor confessed to everything after I told him I'd matched his prints to those we found in the woods."

"He confessed to what?" Roe tied off the last stitch. "Will someone tell me what's going on?"

"I will in a bit," Josh promised. He looked at Gideon and Ivy. "I'll take care of the body then come back to talk to both of you some more."

"All right," Ivy said.

She walked over to stand beside Gideon as the physician bandaged his hand and wrist. The man also redressed the gunshot wound, which had been healing nicely until his struggle with the mayor.

While they waited for Farrell, Ivy and Gideon caught Roe up on what had happened.

The sheriff finally returned, and Gideon reined in his impatience to get home. He wanted to change out of this bloody shirt. Be with his wife.

Josh held up a leather pouch. "I found plenty of stuff in Jumper's office."

"Like what?" Ivy moved over to stand beside her dark-haired friend.

Pulling out a sheaf of papers, he passed them to Ivy, who brought them over to Gideon.

"More drawings of Ivy's house," Josh said. "Several of them showed railroad tracks. There was also one that replaced Ivy's barn with a depot."

She gasped, outrage plain on her beautiful features. "That despicable, low-down cuss!"

"A letter from Porter Nichols about the possibility of a railroad was in one of the desk drawers. It was dated late September of last year."

Ivy shared a look with Gideon. That was about the

time she began receiving the sketches and poems that had gradually become slightly ominous.

After getting accounts of the morning from both Gideon and Ivy, Josh sent them home. It was late afternoon by the time they arrived at the farm. The pup was absurdly glad to see them, running in circles and barking, licking their feet, their hands, wherever she could.

Gideon checked on the horses and fed the dog, which took longer than usual because he could only use one hand. While he was busy, Ivy bathed.

When he came inside the house, she wore a light blue dress with darker blue trim on the round neckline and elbow-length sleeves.

Using only one arm, it took Gideon a bit to get his shirt off and a clean one on. Ivy had biscuits and ham waiting when he returned from the washbasin in the guest bathing room.

They ate in silence, although he couldn't keep his eyes off his wife. He wanted to get his hands on her, too. She was quiet. Now that he thought about it, she hadn't said a lot since they'd left town.

He felt a twinge of concern. "You sure you're okay?"

"Yes." Her smile was warm, but something in her eyes heightened his disquiet. "And I'm glad you will be."

Roe had sent some laudanum home with them, but Gideon didn't want anything to cloud his mind. His wife was finally safe. For good. He wanted to see her eyes without the shadows that had been there since he had arrived.

"The river water is still cold so I soaked your mare's fetlock and wrapped it. We need to watch her and keep her on stall rest. If we take it easy, I think she'll heal pretty soon."

"Thank you." Ivy rose, fetching the coffeepot. As she started to refill his cup, he noticed that her hands weren't quite steady.

"I don't need any more, thanks. Why don't you get off your feet?"

She hesitantly set the pot on a folded cloth on the table and began to ease down into her chair.

Gideon curled his good hand around her waist and pulled her into his lap. "This okay?" he asked against her hair, drawing in her fresh scent.

She nodded, although her spine stayed stiff. "It's hard to believe the trouble is really over."

"It'll be nice not having to look over our shoulders all the time." He brushed a kiss against her soft cheek.

She lightly touched his sutured hand. "Are you in pain?"

"Some." Not enough to let go of her. "Not a lot."

She'd left her hair down after her bath. He stroked a hand down the inky thickness then moved the heavy mass aside and nuzzled a spot beneath her ear.

Her head went to the side, but she didn't relax against him. His lips glided down her elegant neck and over her collarbone.

Lifting his head so he could see her, he grazed a thumb along the velvety line of her jaw. She opened her eyes, the black depths clouded with some emotion he didn't recognize.

It felt like his chest cracked open. "I love you."

He'd never said those words to anyone in his life, not even Eleanor.

A flicker of guilt streaked across Ivy's features. She sat up, placing a palm lightly over his heart. "We can't do this."

"I'm stronger than I look." He grinned. "I may have only one good hand, but everything else works."

"I mean…I don't think we should do this."

"Roe didn't say we couldn't."

She shook her head and slid off his lap.

He reached for her, but the expression on her face had him pulling back. "What's wrong?"

"I can't do this. I'm so sorry."

"It's fine, honey. We have the rest of our lives."

A tear spilled down her cheek. "I don't mean…*that*."

"Then what?" He settled a palm on her hip so she couldn't move farther away.

She bowed her head, staring down at the floor for a moment before she looked at him. The shadows were back in her eyes. "I can't stay married."

Chapter Fourteen

Gideon stood, too. His voice was quiet, his massive body still. Hurt and confusion came off him like a wave. "I thought we were past this."

They had both been completely immersed in all the problems befalling her farm, and later his gunshot wound then the fire. Now that everything was over, she couldn't quiet the doubts. They swirled up like a tornado—swift and crippling and impossible to outrun.

And deep inside was a fixed black stain of distrust that she couldn't get rid of, no matter how hard she tried.

"I told you why I had doubts."

"I thought we'd reached an understanding." He shoved a hand through his hair, grimacing when he raised his gunshot arm. "The other night after the fire, when we were together, I thought you were saying you'd changed your mind. That we were staying married."

"I needed you." She winced. She knew that sounded as if she had used him, and that hadn't been the case at all. "I know this isn't fair to you."

"Or you, either." He took a step toward her then stopped. "Tell me what I should do."

"There's nothing."

"I don't understand." Frustration sharpened his voice.

Her heart squeezed painfully tight. "I don't know if I can explain."

His blue gaze fixed intently on her. "Try."

The words were a plea, not a demand. She choked back a sob. "There's something wrong with me."

"Ivy—"

"Let me." She'd never put this into words before, wasn't sure she could. Hesitantly, she said, "A part of me is always wondering. Waiting."

"For the worst."

"Yes. It has nothing to do with you. Nothing."

"Did I rush you?"

"No."

He seemed to search for words. "Is this because I told you how I feel? I spooked you."

She couldn't bear that he was trying to take responsibility for this. "It's nothing you did or said. It's only me. I'm not sure I can ever be a real wife to you."

"If you're talking about sleeping together—"

"I'm not." The bewildered expression on his face spiked her guilt even higher. She tried a different approach. "You committed yourself completely to me."

"Yes."

"That's something I can't do." She swallowed hard. "I don't know if I can ever really trust you. Trust any man."

"How do you know you won't be able to? Don't you even want to try?"

She did. And for a while, it would work. But this distrust was a part of her forever, a dark, shriveled piece of herself that she couldn't seem to carve out. "You deserve so much more."

"*You* are more." He hesitated then said, "Everything I've ever wanted."

A tear rolled down her cheek, then another.

He came to her and slowly, carefully put his arms around her. "Please don't cry."

Sometimes she hated herself. For not seeing Tom the way she should have, for not forgiving him. For not forgiving herself.

If she did agree to try with Gideon, how long would he wait for something she might never be able to give? She couldn't make him pay a price that should have been paid only by Tom.

Gideon pulled back to look at her. The struggle to understand was plain on his face. Desperate. "So, you want to divorce?"

It broke her heart. "It's the best thing for you."

"It isn't." He stepped away, distancing himself finally.

He could see she was tearing herself up over this. "We don't have to decide anything right now, do we?"

"What do you mean?"

"The danger is over. I'll move back to the barn."

Her lashes were spiky and wet. "Do you believe I'll change my mind?"

"I'd like to think so," he said quietly. "But at the moment, I'm thinking more along the lines of just taking things slower. I don't want you to feel like I expect anything from you."

"That's just it! As my husband, you should expect things, and I shouldn't have a problem giving them!"

Gideon felt as if he were being split in two. The distress on her face, the earnestness told him she was being honest and putting him first. Problem was, he didn't want that from her. He wanted *her.*

More than anything, he wished he could tell her he understood, but he didn't. "You're making yourself sick over this. Let's just try it, okay?"

It took considerable effort not to let her see how badly he wanted her to agree.

She wiped her eyes. "All right."

"All right." Relief shot through him, but he didn't understand why, because they hadn't solved a damn thing. "I'll move on out to the barn."

"At least stay in one of the guest rooms."

He shook his head.

"Are you sure you want to do this?" She bit her lip. "Why should you have to live with this hanging over you?"

He wasn't sure he could, but he didn't know what else to do. He wasn't ready to walk away from her. Not yet. Maybe not ever. "You agree to try this?"

She nodded.

With a hollow feeling in his chest, he gathered his clothes from the guest room they had shared and grabbed his bedroll. The torment in Ivy's eyes ripped at his gut. This racking sense of helplessness had him wanting to slam his fist into a wall.

Thunder tagged along with him to the barn, but when Gideon lay down on his bunk, she went to the barn door and sat. She stared at the house, whining, not understanding why the three of them weren't together. He knew how she felt.

After another minute of the dog's whimpering, he snapped his fingers and she came to him, finally curling up beneath his bed and going to sleep.

But Gideon didn't sleep. Didn't close his eyes once. Everything that had happened between him and Ivy looped through his mind.

There were the dangerous things like the bear trap or when she'd been assaulted in the barn. But his memories veered toward the night on the porch when she'd come out to talk because she'd had a late reaction to nearly being injured or killed by that vicious trap. When she had confessed what had happened with Tom. When Gideon had laid himself bare by telling her about Eleanor and the stupidest decision he'd ever made.

The way Ivy had given herself to him, both before and after the fire.

By the time dawn broke, he was miserable. He couldn't help his wife. She had to change. He couldn't do it for her, and he couldn't make her do it. He'd never felt so hog-tied in his life.

Now he realized he couldn't see her every day, go to the barn at night while she went to the bedroom, keep his distance from her. He wanted marriage and she didn't. It was as simple, as gut-wrenching as that.

He had to go. If he stayed, it would only make things more difficult for both of them.

After packing his few belongings, he went up to the house. He stood in the doorway, watching her through the screen. Thunder sat at his feet, subdued as if she sensed something bad was about to happen.

Ivy stood over the stove. She was pretty and fresh in a golden-pink dress that looked like one of the colors streaking the early-morning sky. He watched her graceful movements as she checked the biscuits, mixed bits of ham in with the scrambled eggs because he liked them that way, not her.

The sun traced her curves, making her braid gleam like hot silk. He took in everything he could. The sensitive spot behind her ear, the gentle swirl of her skirts as she moved. The way her hair curled around her face when she stood over the heat of the stove.

Every image he could corral went into his mind, greedily trapped for the coming days when he had gone weeks, years without seeing her. Touching her. He would remember it all. And that's all he would have— memories.

Maybe he should go in and eat, tell her of his decision gently, but that would only prolong the agony for both of them.

"It's not going to work," he said baldly from the doorway. He cursed himself. He certainly could've given her the news less abruptly.

She whirled. Her eyes were puffy, red from crying. He wondered if she'd gotten any sleep.

"Ivy, I can't stay." The torment in her eyes grabbed him right in the heart, yet he forced himself to continue. "I want you as my wife, but I'm not going to pressure you to do that. My being here will only make you feel you owe me something. Something you may not want or be able to give."

He wanted to tell her she was the only woman he would ever love, but that might make her feel as if he expected the same words from her. So he left it unsaid.

Was he making this harder for her? For both of them? He didn't mean to, but dammit, it *was* hard. Walking away, giving her what she had asked for was as hard as trying to shovel sunshine.

She looked pale. "What about the farm?"

He frowned.

"It's half yours."

"I'll deed it back to you."

"No! I want you to have it."

The words felt torn out of him. "It doesn't make sense for me to keep it since I won't be here."

"But it belongs to you now."

Even though he knew she might feel pressured by his next words, that she would take this as him drawing a line in the sand, he said it anyway. "If I don't have you, I don't want it."

Her eyes widened. There was no mistaking the sorrow in her eyes, the regret. For an instant, just a heartbeat, he thought she might change her mind and tell him she believed they could make it work. But the moment passed. Then another.

His heart sank. The urge for one last kiss was overwhelming, but if he took it, he knew he wouldn't be able to leave.

"You'll hear from me about the farm." He turned to go down the steps.

"Wait."

His heart stopped and he closed his eyes, every cell in his body straining for her next words.

"Thunder should go with you."

Gideon felt like he'd taken a ten-pound hammer to the chest. "She's becoming a good watchdog, and you need one."

"She's more attached to you."

He glanced down. The pup stood between him and the door, clearly uncertain about whether she should follow him or go to Ivy.

"Please, Gideon." Her voice broke. "She belongs with you."

So do you. But he didn't say the words. He snapped his fingers and the dog padded alongside him to the barn, looking back every few steps.

He'd thought the worst day of his life had been the day he'd been chained and dragged from a wagon into Leavenworth. He'd been wrong.

Gideon had done exactly what she had asked. He had really gone. It was the right thing. Ivy just hadn't expected to feel as if her skin were being peeled off.

Silence hung heavy around her. Even the chickens weren't squawking. Breakfast went cold. Finally, she made herself wrap up the biscuits and she threw the eggs out the back door for any animal that wanted them. Thunder wouldn't be taking the scraps anymore.

Dazed, Ivy went about her chores, finally closing the door to the room she had shared with Gideon because she couldn't bring herself to strip the sheets yet. She checked her horse, and like Gideon had done, she drew a bucket of cold water from the river to soak the mare's fetlock before wrapping it again.

He wouldn't really walk away from the farm, not when he'd wanted his own place for so long. He might not stay for her, on her terms, but Ivy didn't believe he would really relinquish his claim.

She was gathering eggs when she heard a horse gallop up to the house. Pulse stuttering, she placed the eggs in a basket with trembling hands. She'd known it! He couldn't leave behind something he had worked half his life to have.

Smoothing down her apron, she hurried up the side of the house and around to the front. The horse there wasn't Gideon's black gelding. It was a dun mare. Coy Farrell's mare.

Her heart dropped to her knees even as she berated herself.

Gideon wasn't coming back.

She pasted a smile on her face and went to meet the young man. "Hi, Coy."

"Miss Ivy." He palmed off his hat.

"What can I do for you?"

"I brought something for you." He met her at the fence and gave her a folded piece of paper.

A heavy, official-looking document. Dread began to pound inside her. With shaking hands, she unfolded the page. It was a claim deed, reassigning Gideon's half of the farm to her.

"Mr. Black wanted me to make sure you got this. He said it's official."

The sight of his signature next to Titus Rowland's affirmed that. A knot lodged in her chest. Fighting tears, she tried to thank Coy, but the words simply wouldn't come.

She pasted on a smile. "There are biscuits left from breakfast if you'd like some."

"That sounds good."

"Let me get them." She started up the walk to the porch.

"Miss Ivy, should I just bed down in the barn?"

She turned. "Why would you do that?"

"Mr. Black wants me to help you around the farm."

The news made her throat ache. She couldn't decide if she was grateful or resentful. He was gone, so why was he taking care of her?

"I can't afford to pay you long-term, Coy."

"There's no need. Mr. Black already took care of it. I'm supposed to stay until you find someone permanent. After that, my wage goes to the new farmhand. Or two if you need. He said he wouldn't leave you in a bind."

Ivy wanted to scream, to be indignant, but she couldn't muster up the emotion. Until the moment she'd seen the deed, she hadn't really believed he would go. But he had. He'd given up his claim and left because she'd asked.

No, she harshly corrected, he'd gone because she had practically forced him.

Ivy watched as her young farmhand went to the barn. When Gideon had arrived, he'd been just as wary, just as guarded as she was. Because of Eleanor.

After that woman's horrible betrayal, it was surprising that he would ever open up to another woman. But he had. He had made a conscious choice to trust Ivy anyway. And he'd fallen in love with her, despite her glaring faults.

If he was willing to take the chance, she should be, too.

Instead, she'd run him off and maybe ruined everything between them. No other man had ever made her look so honestly at herself. Had ever known her the way Gideon did. And he had wanted her anyway. Could she bare her soul to him the way he'd done for her? Take a chance on him the way he had taken a chance on her?

She knew it was the only way she could have him.

It took her a week to get everything settled. A week

in which she doubted herself plenty. And him, too, if she were honest. But she was going after him. She only hoped it wasn't too late.

Ivy's stomach was in knots the entire two-day ride, and the tension didn't ease when she rode onto Diamond J land just after noon on Wednesday.

It had been nine days since she'd seen her husband. Her nerves were raw with a mix of dread and anticipation. She wondered if he was working close by. Or in the pasture herding pregnant cows up to the pen.

She reined up outside the barn and dismounted, hit with nostalgia as she looked around. The sturdy corrals, the well-kept yard around the house, the weathered gray barn all looked the same. Familiar. And just outside the kitchen was the massive oak tree where she and Smith had hung a swing as children. They'd spent hours out there.

She wished she had time to wash up, but she wanted to find Gideon as quickly as possible. Removing her hat, she hung it on the saddle horn, then smoothed her hair as best she could. Her own mare wasn't fit to ride yet, so she'd brought another from her stock.

Just as she started to walk toward the house to say hello to her parents and find out where her husband was, she heard people talking in the barn.

Her brother's voice. And his wife's.

Hands clammy, Ivy wiped them down the front of her trousers. A mottled ball of fur streaked toward her, and before she had time to react, Thunder jumped at her then pawed at her feet, begging for a scratch. The dog wiggled like a worm on a hook, her tail thumping, her body vibrating with excitement.

Ivy wished Gideon would greet her with even a speck of this much enthusiasm.

Smiling, she approached the barn's wide-open double doors as the pup ran around her in circles.

"You know why," came a deep masculine voice.

Gideon. Ivy froze.

"If I stay, I'll never get over her."

Her heart leaped. Maybe she hadn't ruined everything. The memory of the first time she'd met him flooded back. It had been in this barn, the night of her mother's Christmas party. She'd thought he was a trespasser and held him at gunpoint until Smith set her straight.

That party had also served to welcome Smith home. For two long years, they'd believed he was dead, and then last Christmas, he'd appeared. He'd been in prison, convicted of a crime he didn't commit, and that was where he'd met Gideon.

"You don't have to go," her brother said to his friend.

Gideon was leaving?

"Once I get settled, I'll send word."

Ivy's heart dropped to her knees. He was moving on.

"I wish you'd stay a little longer," Smith coaxed. "Just because my sister doesn't know what she has in you doesn't mean I don't."

"Smith's right," Caroline said. "You're a good friend to both of us, Gideon."

Ivy knew Smith considered her husband as close as a brother.

"Can't we change your mind?" Ivy's sister-in-law pleaded.

"It's best this way," he said quietly.

If her brother couldn't convince the man to stay, was there any way Ivy could?

She had to try.

She stepped into the doorway, her eyes slowly adjusting to the dimmer light of the barn. Smith and Caroline were facing away from her. Just beyond them, Gideon tied his bedroll behind his saddle then angled back toward her brother. His gaze locked on her, and he froze.

Her heart kicked hard. She was too far away to read whether it was welcome or bitterness in his eyes. When his face closed against her, she had her answer.

Just seeing him filled a hole inside her. Dressed in a white shirt that stretched across his broad shoulders and faded denims that sleeked down his muscular legs, she thought she could happily look at him forever.

Smith and Caroline followed Gideon's gaze, surprise widening their eyes when they saw her.

Her brother reached her first, grabbing her in a bear hug then moving out of the way so his blonde wife could hug her, too.

He was hardly limping. The surgery to reset the several broken bones he'd suffered in prison had been successful.

After a look back at Gideon, Smith lowered his voice. "I hope you're here for the reason I think you are."

"I am." She swallowed past the lump in her throat. "Am I too late?"

Sympathy flickered in his dark eyes. "You've got some convincin' to do."

She nodded. He bussed her on the cheek and Caroline did, too. Smith scooped up Thunder on his way out.

As her family left, Ivy walked inside, stopping yards

away from Gideon. His remoteness was palpable, pushing at her like heat from a fire.

Eyes narrowed, his gaze flicked over her. Picking up his gelding's reins, he walked toward her. Her nerves jumped. He was indeed packed to leave, she saw.

Uncertainty dried her mouth. He had every right to ignore her, rant at her. "Hi," she said softly when he reached her.

His jaw was anvil-hard, his voice flat. "Is there something you need me to sign?"

When she looked blankly at him, he clarified, "For the divorce."

"No." Grief pricked at her. "No, nothing like that."

"When you do, Smith will know how to get it to me." He moved past her.

"Don't go yet. I want to talk to you."

His shoulders went rigid. "I can't think of one reason why. Everything's been said."

Not that I love you and want to be with you! She walked around to stand in front of him. "Can't you give me just a few minutes?"

"I heard it all the first time," he said with a sense of finality that had panic fluttering.

"No, you didn't."

"I really need to get going. Can't lose much more daylight."

She couldn't blame him for wanting to hightail it away from her. "There are things I need to say."

"If this is about half of the farm, you can forget it."

"It's not."

He finally looked at her, and the bleakness in his eyes rattled her. "I'm not much of a mind to listen."

Leading his horse, he stepped around her and headed for the open doors.

She couldn't let him leave. She rushed around to block his path. Pure reflex had her pulling her gun from her trouser pocket.

"Well, this is familiar," he drawled.

Pushing back his hat, he made to go past her.

She leveled her weapon at him.

He practically rolled his eyes. "Woman, put that gun away. We both know you aren't going to shoot me."

No, she wouldn't, but she didn't know any other way to get him to stop. "You're going to listen to what I have to say."

There was a dark, dangerous look on his face, but she didn't waver. Just kept her gun aimed at him.

"Please," she added softly.

There was hurt in his eyes. And anger. And something she thought, hoped, was longing.

Where to start? "I'm sorry. For so many things, but especially for sending you away. For not trying. For not believing."

A muscle flexed in his jaw. He said nothing.

"You were right about everything you said." She shifted toward him, and he stepped back. She felt it like a slap. Who knew how much time he would give her? "After what Eleanor did to you, I realized you're taking a chance on me. All you asked was that I take a chance on you, too. And I want to."

"I'm not partial to the idea of having a wife who's waiting for a chance to escape our marriage."

She couldn't blame him for thinking that. How could she get through to him? "When you deeded the farm back to me, I couldn't believe it. I really thought you would stay for the land. You'd wanted it for so long."

His mouth tightened.

"You gave up everything you'd ever desired because I couldn't admit what you mean to me." She took a deep breath, moving closer. Close enough to draw in his familiar masculine scent. "That I want you to be my husband."

"For how long?" he asked fiercely.

"What do you mean?"

"I mean, are you going to change your mind again?"

"No." There was still wariness in his eyes, doubt. How could she convince him? "I sold the farm."

His jaw dropped. "What!"

"To Hal Davis."

There was the merest spark of joy in his eyes. For the first time since arriving, she felt hope.

His expression dumbfounded, he shook his head. "Why would you do that?"

She repeated what he'd said to her the day he left. "If I don't have you, I don't want it."

He studied her for so long that she felt each second like a sting to her skin. She wanted to touch him, but she kept her hands to herself.

Tension knotted her shoulders. "That's why it took me so long to get here. My things are coming later."

"Where are you planning to live?"

"With you."

His eyes flared hotly, yet she still sensed a reserve in him. "Why do you want to stay married?"

She looked blankly at him.

"Why?" he demanded impatiently, finally dropping

the reins and coming to her. "Because that's what I want?"

"No." Her lips curved as realization spread through her. "I want to stay married because I love you and I want to spend my life with you."

A muscle twitched in his jaw. As his gaze searched hers, he said gruffly, "Prove it."

"How?" She went to him, wanting to put her arms around him. Feel his arms around her. "I'll do whatever you want."

"Marry me. For real, this time."

Her chest was about to burst. Warmed by the smile in his eyes, she laid a hand on his chest. "We are married for real."

"I want a ceremony in front of people. In front of your family so everybody knows."

"All right. Yes!"

"Good!" Smith hollered from outside. Caroline's soft laugh followed. Thunder barked.

Ivy wanted Gideon to kiss her *now*. She threw herself at him, but he stopped her with a hand on her shoulder.

With his other hand, now unbandaged and the stitches gone, he plucked the pistol away from her and carefully set it on the ground. "You don't have to hold me at gunpoint anymore. I'm doing exactly what you want."

"Then kiss me, husband."

His mouth covered hers, his hands coming up to gently frame her face. When he lifted his head, she gripped his shirt with both hands, her knees weak.

He kissed her again, chuckling.

She slid her arms around his neck. "What's funny?"

"You're going to listen to what I have to say," he imitated in a low voice. "Please."

He grinned and pulled her tight into him. "It's not much of a threat when you say please."

"I was willing to do or say whatever I had to in order to get you to listen."

Moving his lips to her ear, he murmured, "I can't say no to you when you're wearin' those britches."

Her heart actually hurt with joy. How had she ever thought she could send him away? "Tell me again," she whispered.

His blue eyes darkened. "I love you."

"I'm going to need to hear that at least once a day."

"I wouldn't mind hearing it a time or two myself, Mrs. Black."

"I love you. I love you. I love you."

And she meant it with every part of herself.

* * * * *

REQUEST YOUR FREE BOOKS!

 HARLEQUIN® HISTORICAL:
Where love is timeless

2 FREE NOVELS PLUS 2 **FREE GIFTS!**

YES! Please send me 2 FREE Harlequin® Historical novels and my 2 FREE gifts (gifts are worth about $10). After receiving them, if I don't wish to receive any more books, I can return the shipping statement marked "cancel." If I don't cancel, I will receive 6 brand-new novels every month and be billed just $5.44 per book in the U.S. or $5.74 per book in Canada. That's a savings of at least 16% off the cover price! It's quite a bargain! Shipping and handling is just 50¢ per book in the U.S. and 75¢ per book in Canada.* I understand that accepting the 2 free books and gifts places me under no obligation to buy anything. I can always return a shipment and cancel at any time. Even if I never buy another book, the two free books and gifts are mine to keep forever.

246/349 HDN F4ZY

Name _____ (PLEASE PRINT) _____

Address _____ Apt. #

City _____ State/Prov. _____ Zip/Postal Code

Signature (if under 18, a parent or guardian must sign)

Mail to the **Harlequin® Reader Service:**
IN U.S.A.: P.O. Box 1867, Buffalo, NY 14240-1867
IN CANADA: P.O. Box 609, Fort Erie, Ontario L2A 5X3

Want to try two free books from another line?
Call 1-800-873-8635 or visit www.ReaderService.com.

* Terms and prices subject to change without notice. Prices do not include applicable taxes. Sales tax applicable in N.Y. Canadian residents will be charged applicable taxes. Offer not valid in Quebec. This offer is limited to one order per household. Not valid for current subscribers to Harlequin Historical books. All orders subject to credit approval. Credit or debit balances in a customer's account(s) may be offset by any other outstanding balance owed by or to the customer. Please allow 4 to 6 weeks for delivery. Offer available while quantities last.

Your Privacy—The Harlequin® Reader Service is committed to protecting your privacy. Our Privacy Policy is available online at www.ReaderService.com or upon request from the Harlequin Reader Service.

We make a portion of our mailing list available to reputable third parties that offer products we believe may interest you. If you prefer that we not exchange your name with third parties, or if you wish to clarify or modify your communication preferences, please visit us at www.ReaderService.com/consumerschoice or write to us at Harlequin Reader Service Preference Service, P.O. Box 9062, Buffalo, NY 14269. Include your complete name and address.

HHI3R

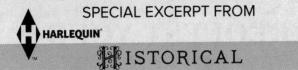
*Next month, get swept away by Rhys Denham and
Lady Thea as they embark on a journey of adventure,
passion and discovery…*

Rhys sighed and moved his mouth gently against the head
of the woman in his arms. This was the way to wake up.
Warm, rocking gently, arms full of soft, curvaceous femi-
ninity.

She smelled of roses, whoever she was. He must try to
recall her name in a minute; it was ungentlemanly to forget
in the morning. Not that he could recall the night before
either, but he supposed it must have been good. His body
was certainly awake and interested.

When he pulled her more tightly against him she snuggled back with an erotic little wriggle that inflamed him to
aching point.

"Mmm." Rhys nuzzled the silky-fine hair and let his right
hand stray lightly across her body. They were both dressed,
after a fashion, although their bare feet had obviously made
friends in the night. Perhaps she had pulled on her gown
again afterward for warmth, because under the fine wool
he could feel uncorseted curves and the sweet weight of an
unfettered breast. As his thumb moved across the nipple it
hardened, and he smiled.

His companion stirred, stretched, her feet sliding down
against his. She yawned and he came completely awake. He
was in the chaise, on the ship, heading for France, and in his
arms, pressed against him, her breast cupped in his hand,
was Lady Althea Curtiss.

Rhys bit back the word that sprang to his lips and went very still. Was she awake? Had she realized? Probably not or she'd be screaming the place down or, given that this was Thea, applying that sharp elbow where it would do most harm. He let his hand fall away from her breast, lifted the other from her hip and arched his midsection as far back as he could. If he tried to slide his arm from under her she would probably wake.

Damn it. *Thea,* the innocent, respectable friend whom he had already shocked with that embrace.

Rhys thought about Almack's, tripe and onions, Latin verbs, tailors' accounts. It didn't work. His brain, apparently having lost all its blood in a mad southward dash, was disobediently musing on just where Thea had acquired those curves from and when she had begun to smell of roses and how that mousy mane of hair could be so silky.

"Rhys?" His name was muffled in a yawn.

Don't miss
UNLACING LADY THEA by Louise Allen
available from Harlequin® Historical April 2014.

HARLEQUIN®

HISTORICAL

Where love is timeless

COMING IN APRIL 2014
Welcome to Wyoming
by Kate Bridges

Seeking justice for his murdered colleagues, Detective Simon Garr
has gone undercover as infamous jewel thief Jarrod Ledbetter.
All is going to plan, until he finds out that Jarrod's mail-order
bride is on her way to Wyoming! Simon can't afford to jeopardize
his cover, and he's left with only one option—he must marry
the woman!

When his poor bride Natasha O'Sullivan arrives she doesn't have
a clue what she is walking into—but Simon finds there is more to
her than first meets the eye. Because Natasha has brought along
secrets of her own....

Mail-Order Weddings
From blushing bride to Wild West wife!

Available wherever books and ebooks are sold.

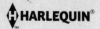

HISTORICAL

Where love is timeless

COMING IN APRIL 2014

London's Most Wanted Rake
by Bronwyn Scott

Rumor has it that Channing Deveril, founder of
The League of Discreet Gentlemen, is tired of warming women's
beds. But when he encounters the alluring Alina Marliss, the
stage is set for his most ambitious assignment yet....

Alina is accustomed to teetering on the edge of scandal, so
Channing's skillful seduction is a complication she definitely
doesn't need! She might crave his expert touch, but she has no
intention of losing her head—much less her heart—over
London's most notorious rake!

Rakes Who Make Husbands Jealous
Only London's best lovers need apply!

Available wherever books and ebooks are sold.

HISTORICAL

Where love is timeless

The Wedding Ring Quest
by Carla Kelly

Penniless Mary Rennie knows she's lucky to have a home in Edinburgh, but she does crave more excitement in her life. So when her cousin's ring is lost in one of several fruitcakes heading around the country as gifts, Mary seizes the chance for adventure.

When widowed captain Ross Rennie and his son meet Mary in a coaching inn, they take her under their wing. After years of battling Napoleon, Ross's soul is war-weary, but Mary's warmth and humor touch him deep inside. Soon, he's in the most heart-stopping situation of his life—considering a wedding-ring quest of his own!

Coming in April 2014

Available wherever books and ebooks are sold.

Love the Harlequin book you just read?

Your opinion matters.

Review this book on your favorite book site, review site, blog or your own social media properties and share your opinion with other readers!

Be sure to connect with us at:
Harlequin.com/Newsletters
Facebook.com/HarlequinBooks
Twitter.com/HarlequinBooks